Sir Arthur Quiller-Couch ('Q'
loved of Cornishmen. He was
doctor and grandson of Dr. J
mother was a Devonian. He was educated at Newton Abbot and Clifton. In 1882 he went to Oxford to study Classics at Trinity College. Having taken his degree he lectured at Oxford for a year and published his first novel, *Dead Man's Rock* (1887).

Q's father had died in 1886, leaving substantial debts. He decided to accept a job with his London publisher, Cassell, and to try and make a living as a writer. *The Astonishing History of Troy Town* (1888) and *The Splendid Spur* (1889) were followed by short stories, poems, and much journalism. In 1889 he was married and before long his father's creditors were sent packing. But in 1892 he was advised to leave London for health reasons. He and his wife decided to settle in Fowey. It was to be their much-loved home for the rest of Q's life.

In 1898 he was invited to edit *The Oxford Book of English Verse*, a work with which his name will for ever be associated. But he continued to write historical novels, among them *The Ship of Stars* (1899), *Hetty Wesley* (1903), and *Major Vigoureux* (1907). He worked prodigiously for the Liberal Party in Cornwall and for the newly-formed County Education Committee. In 1910 he was knighted for political services and in 1912, to the astonishment of those who had thought of him hitherto as a romantic novelist, Q was appointed King Edward VII Professor of English Literature at Cambridge University. He proved a successful and very popular teacher and he worked hard to establish the School of English at Cambridge.

Q had courageously opposed the Boer War but in 1914 he helped to raise a Pioneer Battalion for the Duke of Cornwall's Light Infantry. His only son, Bevil, fought throughout the First World War only to die of pneumonia just after the Armistice. Q was devastated but continued his lecturing at Cambridge and produced a steady flow of books, although by 1920 he had virtually finished with fiction. In Fowey and throughout Cornwall he had become a beloved local institution. He died at his house, The Haven, in May, 1944, as American troops were preparing to embark from Fowey for the Normandy beaches.

THE CORNISH LIBRARY

NUMBER TEN

The Ship of Stars

SIR ARTHUR QUILLER-COUCH

Q

Foreword by
A. L. ROWSE

ANTHONY MOTT LTD

LONDON

Published by Anthony Mott Limited 1983
50 Stile Hall Gardens, London W4 3BU

First published 1899 by
Cassell & Company Ltd

ISBN 0 907746 12 8

Printed in Great Britain by
Richard Clay (The Chaucer Press) Ltd
Bungay, Suffolk

To THE RIGHT HON.
LEONARD HENRY COURTNEY, M.P.

My Dear Mr. Courtney,

It is with a peculiar pleasure and, I dare to hope, with some appropriateness that I dedicate to you this story of the West Country, which claims you with pride. To be sure, the places here written of will be found in no map of your own or any neighbouring constituency. A visitor may discover Nannizabuloe, but only to wonder what has become of the lighthouse, or seek along the sand-hills without hitting on Tredinnis. Yet much of the tale is true in a fashion, even to fact. One or two things which happen to Sir Harry Vyell did actually happen to a better man, who lived and hunted foxes not a hundred miles from the "model borough" of Liskeard, and are told of him in my friend Mr. W. F. Collier's memoir of Harry Terrell, a bygone Dartmoor hero: and a true account of what followed the wreck of the *Samaritan* will be found in a chapter of Remembrances by that true poet and large-hearted man, Robert Stephen Hawker.

But a novel ought to be true to more than fact :and if this one come near its aim, no one will need to be told why I dedicate it to you. If it do not (and I wish the chance could be despised!), its author will yet hold that among the names of living Englishmen he could have chosen none fitter to be inscribed above a story which in the telling has insensibly come to rest upon the two texts, "Lord, make men as towers!" and "All towers carry a light." Although for you Heaven has seen fit to darken the light, believe me it shines outwards over the waters and is a help to men: a guiding light tended by brave hands. We pray, sir—we who sail in little boats—for long life to the tower and the unfaltering lamp.

A. T. Q. C.

St. John's Eve,
1899.

FOREWORD

Quiller-Couch is the first of Cornish writers and *The Ship of Stars* is one of the best and truest novels ever to come out of Cornwall. When a well known writer leaves the scene of his labours his work goes into an eclipse for a time – as happened with R. L. Stevenson and John Buchan, with both of whom Q had some affinity. In his day Q was both popular and highly regarded critically – justly so – and it is high time that the public should have the chance, and the pleasure, of appreciating his work again.

The Ship of Stars is a beautiful book, and it has the further interest that it is – though Q flinched from writing directly about himself – in part autobiographical. Though his name is closely attached to Fowey, which he gave a place to in literature, this book begins, as Q did, in Bodmin with the bright comings and goings of a Victorian county town. And the boy who grows to man's estate, through some tribulation of heart and testing of character, is recognizably Q.

Q began with more sheer literary gift than most writers, and Taffy's head is full of dreams and stories, with an innate bent for story-telling, trained too in the classics, to get to Oxford with a scholarship – and Q was always a good classical scholar.

The tale is very true to Victorian life in Cornwall. It has everything in it: the old-time tyrant of an uncouth squire, who wrecks the interior of an ancient church – and in the way nature has of imitating art, this is what happened in our time, as told in another book in this series, Bernard Walke's *Twenty Years at St. Hilary*. Q knew all about the sea coast and the sea, the stories of sea-farers and sailors were in his blood – the wreck, the struggle with sea and tides and shifting sands on our North Coast, are from the life – so too his own struggle to get a safe harbour built on that iron coast, for he was as public-spirited as he was liberal-minded.

The book is full of Cornish folklore, and Q could not go wrong in Cornish dialect – as Hardy naturally did, as a Dorset man, in *A Pair of Blue Eyes*, with which *The Ship of Stars* has something in common.

Q was a better stylist than Hardy and – though his novels do not plumb the depths of Hardy's sense of tragedy – this story has the touch of both the tragic and heroic about it. The tale itself is one of tender sentiment, without sentimentality, and with Q's gallantry about women, the essential nobleness of his nature, which gives us something refreshing and different – though not less true – from too much in contemporary life and writing.

A. L. ROWSE

CONTENTS.

THE SHIP OF STARS.

CHAPTER I.

THE BOY IN THE GATE-HOUSE.

UNTIL his ninth year the boy about whom this story is written lived in a house which looked upon the square of a county town. The house had once formed part of a large religious building, and the boy's bedroom had a high groined roof, and on the capstone an angel carved, with outspread wings. Every night the boy wound up his prayers with this verse which his grandmother had taught him :

> " Matthew, Mark, Luke, and John,
> Bless the bed that I lie on.
> Four corners to my bed,
> Four angels round my head ;
> One to watch, one to pray,
> Two to bear my soul away."

Then he would look up to the angel and say : " Only Luke is with me." His head was full of queer texts and beliefs. He supposed the three other angels to be always waiting in the next room, ready to bear away the soul of his grandmother (who was bedridden), and that he had Luke for an angel because he was called Theophilus, after the friend for whom St. Luke had written his Gospel and the Acts of the Holy Apostles. His name in full was Theophilus John Raymond, but people called him Taffy.

Of his parents' circumstances he knew very little, except that they were poor, and that his father was a clergyman attached to the parish church. As a matter of fact, the Reverend Samuel Raymond was senior curate there, with a stipend of ninety-five pounds a year. Born at Tewkesbury, the son of a miller, he had won his way to a servitorship at Christ Church, Oxford ; and somehow, in the course of one Long Vacation, had found money for travelling expenses to join a reading party under the Junior Censor. The party spent six summer weeks at a farmhouse near Honiton, in Devon. The farm belonged to an invalid widow named Venning, who let it be managed by her daughter Humility and two paid labourers, while she herself sat by the window in her kitchen parlour, busied incessantly with lace-work of that beautiful kind for which Honiton is famous.

He was an unassuming youth ; and although in those days servitors were no longer called upon to black the boots of richer undergraduates, the widow and her daughter soon divined that he was lowlier than the others, and his position an awkward one, and were kind to him in small ways, and grew to like him. Next year, at their invitation, he travelled down to Honiton alone, with a box of books ; and, at twenty-two, having taken his degree, he paid them a third visit, and asked Humility to be his wife. At twenty-four, soon after his admission to deacon's orders, they were married. The widow sold the small farm, with its stock, and followed to live with them in the friary gate-house; this having been part of Humility's bargain with her lover, if the word can be used of a pact between two hearts so fond.

About ten years had gone since these things happened, and their child Taffy was now past his eighth birthday.

It seemed to him that, so far back as he could remember, his mother and grandmother had been making lace continually. At night, when his mother took the candle away with her and left him alone in the dark, he was not afraid; for, by closing his eyes, he could always see the two women quite plainly; and always he saw them at work, each with a pillow on her lap, and the lace upon it growing, growing, until the pins and bobbins wove a pattern that was a dream, and he slept. He could not tell what became of all the lace, though he had a collar of it which he wore to church on Sundays, and his mother had once shown him a parcel of it, wrapped in tissue-paper, and told him it was his christening robe.

His father was always reading, except on Sundays, when he preached sermons. In his thoughts nine times out of ten Taffy associated his father with a great pile of books; but the tenth time with something totally different. One summer—it was in his sixth year—they had all gone on a holiday to Tewkesbury, his father's old home; and he recalled quite clearly the close of a warm afternoon which he and his mother had spent there in a green meadow beyond the abbey church. She had brought out a basket and cushion, and sat sewing, while Taffy played about and watched the haymakers at their work. Behind them, within the great church, the organ was sounding; but by-and-by it stopped, and a door opened in the abbey wall, and his father came across the meadow toward them with his surplice on his arm. And then Humility unpacked the basket and produced a kettle, a spirit-lamp, and a host of things good to eat. The boy thought the whole adventure splendid. When tea was done, he sprang up with one of those absurd notions which come into children's heads:

"Now let's feed the poultry," he cried, and flung his last scrap of bun three feet in air toward the gilt weather-cock on the abbey tower. While they laughed, "Father, how tall is the tower?" he demanded.

"A hundred and thirty-two feet, my boy, from ground to battlements."

"What are battlements?"

He was told.

"But people don't fight here," he objected.

Then his father told of a battle fought in the very meadow in which they were sitting; of soldiers at bay with their backs to the abbey wall; of crowds that ran screaming into the church; of others chased down Mill Street and drowned; of others killed by the Town Cross; and how—people said in the upper room of a house still standing in the High Street—a boy prince had been stabbed.

Humility laid a hand on his arm.

"He'll be dreaming of all this. Tell him it was a long time ago, and that these things don't happen now."

But her husband was looking up at the tower.

"See it now with the light upon it!" he went on. "And it has seen it all. Eight hundred years of heaven's storms and man's madness, and still four-square and as beautiful now as when the old masons took down their scaffolding. When I was a boy——"

He broke off suddenly. "Lord, make men as towers," he added quietly after a while, and nobody spoke for many minutes.

To Taffy this had seemed a very queer saying; about as queer as that other one about "men as trees walking." Somehow—he could not say why—he had never asked any questions about it. But many times he had perched himself on a flat tomb-stone under the church tower at home, and tilted his head back and stared up at the courses and pinnacles, wondering what his father could have meant, and how a man could possibly be like a tower. It ended in this—that whenever he dreamed about his father, these two towers, or a tower which was more or less a combination of both, would get mixed up with the dream as well.

The gate-house contained a sitting-room and three bedrooms (one hardly bigger than a box-cupboard); but a building adjoined it which had been the old Franciscans' refectory, though now it was divided by common planking into two floors, the lower serving for a feoffee office, while the upper was supposed to be a muniment-room, in charge of the feoffees' clerk. The clerk used it for drying his garden-seeds and onions, and spread his hoarding apples to ripen on the floor. So when Taffy grew to need a room of his own, and his father's books to cumber the very stairs of the gate-house, the money which Humility and her mother made by their lace-work, and which arrived always by post, came very handy for the rent which the clerk asked for his upper chamber.

Carpenters appeared and partitioned it off into two rooms, communicating with the gate-house by a narrow doorway pierced in the wall. All this, whilst it was doing, interested Taffy mightily ; and he announced his intention of being a carpenter one of these days.

" I hope," said Humility, " you will look higher, and be a preacher of God's Word, like your father."

His father frowned at this and said : " Jesus Christ was both."

Taffy compromised : " Perhaps I'll make pulpits."

This was how he came to have a bedroom with a vaulted roof and a window that reached down below the floor.

CHAPTER II.

MUSIC IN THE TOWN SQUARE.

THIS window looked upon the Town Square, and across it to the Mayoralty. The square had once been the Franciscans' burial-ground, and was really no square at all, but a semicircle. The townspeople called it Mount Folly. The chord of the arc was formed by a large Assize Hall, with a broad flight of granite steps, and a cannon planted on either side of the steps. The children used to climb about these cannons, and Taffy had picked out his first letters from the words *Sevastopol* and *Russian Trophy*, painted in white on their lead-coloured carriages.

Below the Assize Hall an open gravelled space sloped gently down to a line of iron railings and another flight of granite steps leading into the main street. The street curved uphill around the base of this open ground, and came level with it just in front of the Mayoralty, a tall stuccoed building where the public balls were given, and the judges had their lodgings in assize time, and the Colonel his quarters during the militia training.

Fine shows passed under Taffy's window. Twice a year came the judges, with the sheriff in uniform and his chaplain, and his coach, and his coachman and lackeys in powder and plush and silk stockings, white or flesh-coloured ; and the barristers with their wigs, and the javelin men and silver trumpets. Every spring, too, the Royal Rangers Militia came up for training. Suddenly one morning, in the height of the bird-nesting season, the street would swarm with countrymen tramping up to the barracks on the hill, and back, with bundles of clothes and unblackened boots dangling. For the next six weeks the town would be full of bugle calls, and brazen music, and companies marching and parading in suits of invisible green, and clanking officers in black, with little round forage caps, and silver badges on their side-belts ; and, towards evening, with men lounging and smoking, or washing themselves in public before the doors of their billets.

Usually too, Whitsun Fair fell at the height of the militia training ; and then for two days booths and caravans, sweet-standings and shooting-galleries lined the main street, and Taffy went out with a shilling in his pocket to enjoy himself. But the bigger shows—the menagerie, the marionettes, and the travelling Theatre Royal—were pitched on Mount Folly, just under his window. Sometimes the theatre would stay a week or two after the fair was over, until even the boy grew tired of the naphtha-lamps and the voices of the tragedians, and the cornet wheezing under canvas, and began to long for the time when they would leave the square open for the boys to come and play at prisoners' bars in the dusk.

One evening, a fortnight before Whitsun Fair, he had taken his book to the open window, and sat there with it. Every night he had to learn a text which he repeated next morning to his mother. Already, across the square, the Mayoralty house was brightly lit, and the bandsmen had begun to arrange their stands and music before it; for the Colonel was receiving company. Every now and then a carriage arrived, and set down its guests.

After a while Taffy looked up and saw two persons crossing the square—an old man and a little girl. He recognised them, having seen them together in church the day before, when his father had preached the sermon. The old man wore a rusty silk hat, cocked a little to one side, a high stock collar, black cutaway coat, breeches and gaiters of grey cord. He stooped as he walked, with his hands behind him and his walking-stick dangling like a tail—a very positive old fellow, to look at. The girl's face Taffy could not see; it was hidden by the brim of her Leghorn hat.

The pair passed close under the window. Taffy heard a knock at the door below, and ran to the head of the stairs. Down in the passage his mother was talking to the old man, who turned to the girl and told her to wait outside.

"But let her come in and sit down," urged Humility.

"No, ma'am; I know my mind. I want one hour with your husband."

Taffy heard the door shut, and went back to his window-seat.

The little girl had climbed the cannon opposite, and sat there dangling her feet and eyeing the house.

"Boy," said she, "what a funny window-seat you've got! I can see your legs under it."

"That's because the window reaches down to the floor, and the bench is fixed across by the transom here."

"What's your name?"

"Theophilus; but they call me Taffy."

"Why?"

"Father says it's an imperfect example of Grimm's Law."

"Oh! Then, I suppose you're quite the gentleman? My name's Honoria."

"Is that your father downstairs?"

"Bless the boy! What age do you take me for? He's my grandfather. He's asking your father about his soul. He wants to be saved, and says if he's not saved before next Lady-day, he'll know the reason why. What are you doing up there?"

"Reading."

"Reading what?"

"The Bible."

"But, I say, can you really?"

"You listen." Taffy rested the big Bible on the window-frame; it just had room to lie open between the two mullions—"*Now when they had gone throughout Phrygia and Galatia, and were forbidden of the Holy Ghost to preach the word in Asia, after they were come to Mysia they assayed to go into Bithynia; but the Spirit suffered them not. And they, passing by Mysia, came down to Troas. And a vision appeared to Paul in the night. . . .*"

"I don't wonder at it. Did you ever have the whooping-cough?"

"Not yet."

"I've had it all the winter. That's why I'm not allowed in to play with you. Listen!"

She coughed twice, and wound up with a terrific whoop.

"Now, if you'd only put on your nightshirt and preach, I'd be the congregation and interrupt you with coughing."

"Very well," said Taffy, "let's do it."

"No; you didn't suggest it. I hate boys who have to be told."

Taffy was huffed, and pretended to return to his book. By-and-by she called up to him:

"Tell me, what's written on this gun of yours?"

"Sevastopol—that's a Russian town. The English took it by storm."

"What! the soldiers over there?"

"No, they're only bandsmen; and they're too young. But I expect the Colonel was there. He's upstairs in the Mayoralty, dining. He's quite an old man, but I've heard father say he was as brave as a lion when the fighting happened."

The girl climbed off the gun.

"I'm going to have a look at him," she said; and turning her back on Taffy, she sauntered off across the square, just as the band struck up the first note of the overture from *Semiramide.* A waltz of Strauss followed, and then came a cornet solo by the bandmaster, and a medley of old English tunes. To all of these Taffy listened. It had fallen too dark to read, and the boy was always sensitive to music. Often when he played alone broken phrases and scraps of remembered tunes came into his head and repeated themselves over and over. Then he would drop his game and wander about restlessly, trying to fix and complete the melody ; and somehow in the process the melody always became a story, or so like a story that he never knew the difference. Sometimes his uneasiness lasted for days together. But when the story came complete at last—and this always sprang on him quite suddenly—he wanted to caper and fling his arms about and sing aloud ; and did so, if nobody happened to be looking.

The bandmaster, too, had music, and a reputation for imparting it. Famous regimental bands contained pupils of his ; and his old pupils, when they met, usually told each other stories of his atrocious temper. But he kept his temper to-night, for his youngsters were playing well, and the small crowd standing quiet.

The English melodies had scarcely closed with "Come, lasses and lads," when across in Mayoralty a blind was drawn, and a window thrown open, and Taffy saw the warm room within, and the officers and ladies standing with glasses in their hands. The Colonel was giving the one toast of the evening :

" Ladies and gentlemen—The Queen ! "

The adjutant leaned out and lifted his hand for signal, and the band crashed out with the National Anthem. Then there was silence for a minute. The window remained open. Taffy still caught glimpses of jewels and uniforms, and white necks bending, and men leaning back in their chairs, with their mess-jackets open, and the candle-light flashing on their shirt-fronts. Below, in the dark street, the bandmaster trimmed the lamp by his music-stand.

In the rays of it he drew out a handkerchief and polished the keys of his cornet; then passed the cornet over to his left hand, took up his baton, and nodded.

What music was that, stealing, rippling, across the square? The bandmaster knew nothing of the tale of Tannhäuser, but was wishing that he had violins at his beck, instead of stupid flutes and reeds. And Taffy had never heard so much as the name of Tannhäuser. Of the meaning of the music he knew nothing—nothing beyond its wonder and terror. But afterward he made a tale of it to himself.

In the tale it seemed that a vine shot up and climbed on the shadows of the warm night; and the shadows climbed with it and made a trellis for it right across the sky. The vine thrust through the trellis faster and faster, dividing, throwing out little curls and tendrils; then leaves and millions of leaves, each leaf unfolding about a drop of dew, which trickled and fell and tinkled like a bird's song.

The beauty and scent of the vine distressed him. He wanted to cry out, for it was hiding the sky. Then he heard the tramp of feet in the distance, and knew that they threatened the vine, and with that he wanted to save it. But the feet came nearer and nearer, tramping terribly.

He could not bear it. He ran to the stairs, stole down them, opened the front door cautiously, and slipped outside. He was half-way across the square before it occurred to him that the band had ceased to play. Then he wondered why he had come, but he did not go back. He found Honoria standing a little apart from the crowd, with her hands clasped behind her, gazing up at the window of the banqueting-room.

She did not see him at once.

"Stand on the steps, here," he whispered, "then you can see him. That's the Colonel—the man at the end of the table, with the big, grey moustache."

He touched her arm. She sprang away and stamped her foot.

"Keep off with you! Who *told* you?—Oh! you bad boy!"

"Nobody. I thought you hated boys who wait to be told."

"And now you'll get the whooping-cough, and goodness knows what will happen to you, and you needn't think I'll be sorry!"

"Who wants you to be sorry! As for you," Taffy went on sturdily, "I think your grandfather might have more sense than to keep you waiting out here in the cold, and giving your cough to the whole town!"

"Ha! you do, do you?"

It was not the girl who said this. Taffy swung round, and saw an old man staring down on him. There was just light enough to reveal that he had very formidable grey eyes. But Taffy's blood was up.

"Yes, I do," he said, and wondered at himself.

"Ha! Does your father whip you sometimes?"

"No, sir."

"I should if you were my boy. I believe in it. Come, Honoria!"

The child threw a glance at Taffy as she was led away. He could not be sure whether she took his side or her grandfather's.

That night he had a very queer dream.

His grandmother had lost her lace-pillow, and after searching for some time, he found it lying out in the square. But the pins and bobbins were darting to and fro on their own account, at an incredible rate, and the lace as they made it turned into a singing beanstalk, and rose and threw out branches all over the sky. Very soon he found himself climbing among those branches, up and up until he came to a Palace, which was really the Assize Hall, with a flight of steps before it and a cannon on either side of the steps. Within sat a giant, asleep, with his head on the table and his face hidden; but his neck bulged at the back just like the bandmaster's during a cornet solo. A harp stood on the table. Taffy caught this up, and was stealing downstairs with it, but at the third stair the harp—which had Honoria's head and face—began to cough, and wound up with a *whoop!* This woke the giant—he turned out to be Honoria's grandfather—who came roaring after him. Glancing down below as he ran, Taffy saw his mother and the bandmaster far below with axes, hacking at the foot of the beanstalk. He tried to call out and prevent them, but they kept smiting. And the worst of it was, that down below, too, his father was climbing into a pulpit, quite as if nothing was happening. The pulpit grew and became a tower, and his father kept calling, "Be a tower! Be a tower, like me!"

But Taffy couldn't for the life of him see how to manage it. The beanstalk began to totter; he felt himself falling, and leapt for the tower. . . .

And awoke in his bed shuddering, and, for the

first time in his life, afraid of the dark. He would have called for his mother, but just then down by the turret clock in Fore Street the buglers began to sound the "Last Post," and he hugged himself and felt that the world he knew was still about him, companionable and kind.

Twice the buglers repeated their call, in more distant streets, each time more faintly; and the last flying notes carried him into sleep again.

CHAPTER III.

PASSENGERS BY JOBY'S VAN.

At breakfast next morning he saw by his parents' faces that something unusual had happened. Nothing was said to him about it, whatever it might be. But once or twice after this, coming into the parlour suddenly, he found his father and mother talking low and earnestly together; and now and then they would go up to his grandmother's room and talk.

In some way he divined that there was a question of leaving home. But the summer passed and these private talks became fewer. Toward August, however, they began again; and by-and-by his mother told him. They were going to a parish on the North Coast, right away across the Duchy, where his father had been presented to a living. The place had an odd name—Nannizabuloe.

"And it is lonely," said Humility, "the most of it sea-sand, so far as I can hear."

It was by the sea, then. How would they get there?

"Oh, Joby's van will take us most of the way."

Of all the vans which came and went in the Fore Street, none could compare for romance with Joby's. People called it the Wreck Ashore; but its real name, "Vital Spark, J. Job, Proprietor," was painted on its orange-coloured sides in letters of vivid blue, a blue not often seen except on ship's boats. It disappeared every Tuesday and Saturday over the hill and into a mysterious country, from which it emerged on Mondays and Fridays with a fine flavour of the sea renewed upon it and upon Joby. No other driver wore a blue guernsey, or rings in his ears, as Joby did. No other van had the same mode of progressing down the street in a series of short tacks, or brought such a crust of brine on its panes, or such a mixture of mud and fine sand on its wheels, or mingled scraps of dry sea-weed with the straw on its floor.

"Will there be ships?" Taffy asked.

"I dare say we shall see a few, out in the distance. It's a poor, outlandish place. It hasn't even a proper church."

"If there's no church, father can get into a boat and preach; just like the Sea of Galilee, you know."

"Your father is too good a man to mimic the Scriptures in any such way. There is a church, I believe, though it's a tumble-down one. Nobody has preached in it for years. But Squire Moyle may do something now. He's a rich man."

"Is that the old gentleman who came to ask father about his soul?"

"Yes; he says no preaching ever did him so much good as your father's. That's why he came and offered the living."

"But he can't go to heaven if he's rich."

"I don't know, Taffy, wherever you pick up such wicked thoughts."

"Why, it's in the Bible!"

Humility would not argue about it; but she told her husband that night what the child had said.

"My dear," he answered, "the boy must think of these things."

"But he ought not to be talking disrespectfully," contended she.

One Tuesday, towards the end of September, Taffy saw his father off by Joby's van; and the Friday after, walked down with his mother to meet him on his return. Almost at once the household began to pack. The packing went on for a week, in the midst of which his father departed again, a waggon-load of books and furniture having been sent forward on the road that same morning. Then followed a day or two during which Taffy and his mother took their meals at the window-seat, sitting on corded boxes; and an evening when he went out to the cannon in the square, and around the little back garden, saying good-bye to the fixtures and the few odds and ends which were to be left behind—the tool-shed (Crusoe's hut, Cave of Adullam, and Treasury of the Forty Thieves), the stunted sycamore-tree which he had climbed at different times as Zacchæus, Ali Baba, and Man Friday with the bear behind him; the clothes' prop, which, on the strength of its forked tail, had so often played Dragon to his St. George. When he returned to the empty house, he found his mother in the passage. She had been for a walk alone. The candle was lit, and he saw she had been crying. This told him where she had been; for, although he remembered nothing about it, he knew he had once possessed a small sister, who lived with him less than two months. He had, as a rule, very definite notions of death and the grave; but he never thought of her as dead and buried, partly because his mother would never allow him to go with her to the cemetery, and partly because of a picture in a certain book of his, called *Child's Play*. It represented a little girl wading across a pool among water-lilies. She wore a white nightdress, kilted above her knees, and a dark cloak, which dragged behind in the water. She let it trail, while she held up a hand to cover one of her eyes. Above her were trees and an owl, and a star shining under the topmost branch; and on the opposite page this verse:

"I have a little sister,
They call her Peep-peep,
She wades through the waters,
Deep, deep, deep;
She climbs up the mountains,
High, high, high;
This poor little creature
She has but one eye."

For years Taffy believed that this was his little sister, one-eyed, and always wandering; and that his mother went out in the dusk to persuade her to return; but she never would.

When he woke next morning his mother was in the room; and while he washed and dressed she folded his bed-clothes and carried them down to a waggon which stood by the door, with horses already harnessed. It drove away soon after. He found breakfast laid on the window-seat. A neighbour had lent the crockery, and Taffy was greatly taken with the pattern on the cups and saucers. He wanted to run round again and repeat his good-byes to the house, but there was no time. By-and-by the door opened, and two men, neighbours of theirs, entered with an invalid's litter; and, Humility directing, brought down old Mrs. Venning. She wore the corner of a Paisley shawl over her white cap, and carried a nosegay of flowers in place of her lace-pillow; but otherwise looked much as usual.

"Quite the traveller, you see!" she cried gaily to Taffy.

Then the woman who had lent the breakfast-ware came running to say that Joby was getting impatient. Humility handed the door-key to her, and so the little procession passed out and down across Mount Folly.

Joby had drawn his van up close to the granite steps. They were the only passengers, it seemed. The invalid was hoisted in and laid with her couch across the seats, so that her shoulders rested against one side of the van and her feet against the other. Humility climbed in after her; but Taffy, to his joy, was given a seat outside the box.

"C'k!"—they were off.

As they crawled up the street a few townspeople paused on the pavement and waved farewells. At the top of the town they overtook three sailor-boys, with bundles, who climbed up and perched themselves a-top of the van, on the luggage.

On they went again. There were two horses—a roan and a grey. Taffy had never before looked down on the back of a horse, and Joby's horses astonished him; they were so broad behind, and so narrow at the shoulders. He wanted to ask if the shape were at all common, but felt shy. He stole a glance at the silver ring in Joby's left ear, and blushed when Joby turned and caught him.

"Here, catch hold!" said Joby handing him the whip. "Only you mustn't use it too fierce."

"Thank you."

"I suppose you'll be a scholar, like your father? Can 'ee spell?"

"Yes."

"Cipher?"

"Yes."

"That's more than I can. I counts upon my fingers. When they be used up, I begins upon my buttons. I ha'n't got no buttons—visible that is—'pon my week-a-day clothes; so I keeps the long sums for Sundays, and adds 'em up and down my weskit during sermon. Don't tell any person."

"I won't."

"That's right. I don't want it known. Ever see a gipsy?"

"Oh, yes—often."

"Next time you see one you'll know why he wears so many buttons. You've a lot to learn."

The van zigzagged down one hill and up another, and halted at a turnpike. An old woman in a pink sun-bonnet bustled out and handed Joby a pink ticket. A little way beyond they passed the angle of a mining district, with four or five engine-houses high up like castles on the hillside, and rows of stamps clattering and working up and down like ogres' teeth. Next they came to a church town, with a green and a heap of linen spread to dry (for it was Tuesday), and a flock of geese that ran and hissed after the van, until Joby took the whip and, leaning out, looped the gander by the neck and pulled him along in the dust. The sailor-boys shouted with laughter and struck up a song about a fox and a goose, which lasted all the way up a long hill and brought them to a second turnpike, on the edge of the moors. Here lived an old woman in a blue sun-bonnet; and she handed Joby a yellow-ticket.

"But why does she wear a blue bonnet and give yellow tickets?" Taffy asked, as they drove on.

Joby considered for a minute. "Ah, you're one to take notice, I see. That's right, keep your eyes skinned when you travel."

Taffy had to think this out. The country was changing now. They had left stubble fields and hedges behind, and before them the granite road stretched like a white ribbon, with moors on either hand, dotted with peat-ricks and reedy pools and cropping ponies, and rimmed in the distance with clay-works glistening in the sunny weather.

"What sort of place is Nannizabuloe?"

"I don't go on there. I drop you at Indian Queens."

"But what sort of place is it?"

"Well, I'll tell you what folks say of it:

"'All sea and san's,
Out of the world and into St. Ann's.'

That's what they say, and if I'm wrong you may call me a liar."

"And Squire Moyle?" Taffy persevered. "What kind of man is he?"

Joby turned and eyed him severely. "Look here, sonny. I got my living to get."

This silenced Taffy for a long while, but he picked up his courage again by degrees. There was a small window at his back, and he twisted himself round, and nodded to his mother and grandmother inside the van. He could not hear what they answered, for the sailor-boys were singing at the top of their voices:

"I will sing you One, O!
What is your One, O?
Number One sits all alone, and ever more shall be-e so."

"They're home 'pon leave," said Joby. The song went on and reached Number Seven:

"I will sing you Seven, O!
What is your Seven, O?
Seven be seven stars in the ship a-sailing round in
Heaven, O!"

One of the boys leaned from the roof and twitched Taffy by the hair. "Hullo, nipper! Did you ever see a ship of stars?" He grinned and pulled open his sailor's jumper and singlet; and there, on his naked breast, Taffy saw a ship tattooed, with three masts, and a half-circle of stars above it, and below it the initials W. P.

"D'ee think my mother'll know me again?" asked the boy, and the other two began to laugh.

"Yes, I think so," said Taffy gravely; which made them laugh more than ever.

"But why is he painted like that?" he asked Joby, as they took up their song again.

"Ah, you'll larn over to St. Ann's, being one to notice things." The nearer he came to it, the more mysterious this new home of Taffy's seemed to grow. By-and-by Humility let down the window and handed out a pasty. Joby searched under his seat and found a pasty, twice the size of Taffy's, in a nose-bag. They ate as they went, holding up their pasties from time to time and comparing progress. Late in the afternoon they came to hedges again, and at length to an inn; and in front of it Taffy spied his father waiting with a farm-cart. While Joby baited his horses, the sailor-boys helped to lift out the invalid and trans-ship the luggage; after which they climbed on the roof again, and were jogged away northward in the dusk, waving their caps and singing.

The most remarkable thing about the inn was its signboard. This bore on either side the picture of an Indian queen and two blackamoor children, all with striped parasols, walking together across a desert. The queen on one side wore a scarlet turban and a blue robe; but the queen on the other side wore a blue turban and a scarlet robe. Taffy dodged from side to side, comparing them, and had not made up his mind which he liked best when Humility called him indoors to tea.

They had ham and eggs with their tea, which they took in a great hurry; and then his grandmother was lifted into the cart and laid on a bed of clean straw beside the boxes, and he and his mother clambered up in front. So they started again, his father walking at the horse's head.

They took the road toward the sunset. As the dusk

fell closer around, Mr. Raymond lit a horn lantern and carried it before them. The rays of it danced and wheeled upon the hedges and gorse bushes. Taffy began to feel sleepy, though it was long before his usual bedtime. The air seemed to weigh his eyelids down. Or was it a sound lulling him? He looked up suddenly. His mother's arm was about him. Stars flashed above, and a glimmer fell on her gentle face—a dew of light, as it were. Her dark eyes appeared darker than usual as she leaned and drew her shawl over his shoulder.

Ahead, the rays of the lantern kept up their dance, but they flared now and again upon stone hedges built in zigzag layers, and upon unknown feathery bushes, intensely green and glistening like metal.

The cart jolted and the lantern swung to a soundless tune that filled the night. When Taffy listened it ceased; when he ceased listening, it began again.

The lantern stopped its dance and stood still over a ford of black water. The cart splashed into it and became a ship, heaving and lurching over a soft, irregular floor that returned no sound. But suddenly the ship became a cart again, and stood still before a house with a narrow garden-path and a light streaming along it from an open door.

His father lifted him down; his mother took his hand. They seemed to wade together up that stream of light. Then came a staircase and room with a bed in it, which, oddly enough, turned out to be his own. He stared at the pink roses on the curtains. Yes; certainly it was his own bed. And satisfied of this, he nestled down in the pillows and slept, to the long cadence of the sea.

CHAPTER IV.

THE RUNNING SANDS.

HE awoke to find the sun shining in at his window. At first he wondered what had happened. The window seemed to be in the ceiling, and the ceiling sloped down to the walls, and all the furniture had gone astray into wrong positions. Then he remembered, jumped out of bed, and drew the blind.

He saw a blue line of sea, so clearly drawn that the horizon might have been a string stretched from the corner eaves to the snow-white light-house standing on the farthest spit of land; blue sea and yellow sand curving round it, with a white edge of breakers; inshore, the sand rising to a cliff ridged with grassy hummocks; farther inshore, the hummocks united and rolling away up to inland downs, but broken here and there on their way with scars of sand; over all, white gulls wheeling. He could hear the nearest ones mewing as they sailed over the house.

Taffy had seen the sea once before, at Dawlish, on the journey to Tewkesbury; and again on the way home. But here it was bluer altogether, and the sands were yellower. Only he felt disappointed that no ship was in sight, nor any dwelling nearer than the light-house and the two or three white cottages behind it. He dressed in a hurry and said his prayers, repeating at the close, as he had been taught to do, the first and last verses of the Morning Hymn:

> " Awake, my soul, and with the sun
> Thy daily stage of duty run;
> Shake off dull sloth, and joyful rise
> To pay thy morning sacrifice.
>
> " Praise God, from whom all blessings flow;
> Praise Him, all creatures here below;
> Praise Him above, ye heavenly host,
> Praise Father, Son, and Holy Ghost."

He ran downstairs. In this queer house the stairs led right down into the kitchen. The front door, too, opened into the kitchen, which was really a slate-paved hall, with a long table set between the doorway and the big open hearth. The floor was always strewn with sand; there was no trouble about this, for the wind blew plenty under the door.

Taffy found the table laid, and his mother busily slicing bread for his bread and milk. He begged for a hot cake from the hearth, and ran out of doors to eat it. Humility lifted the latch for him, for the cake was so hot that he had to pass it from hand to hand.

Outside, the wind came upon him with a clap on the shoulder, quite as if it had been a comrade waiting.

Taffy ran down the path and out upon the sandy hummocks, setting his face to the wind and the roar of the sea, keeping his head low, and still shifting the cake from hand to hand. By-and-by he fumbled and dropped it ; stooped to pick it up, but saw something which made him kneel and peer into the ground.

The whole of the sand was moving ; not by fits and starts, but constantly ; the tiny particles running over each other and drifting in and out of the rushes, like little creatures in a dream. While he looked, they piled an embankment against the edge of his cake. He picked it up, ran forward a few yards, and peered again. Yes, here too ; here and yonder, and over every inch of that long shore.

He ate his cake and climbed to the beach, and ran along it, watching the sandhoppers that skipped from under his boots at every step, and were lost on the instant. The beach here was moist and firm. He pulled off his boots and stockings, and ran on, conning his footprints and the driblets of sand split ahead from his bare toes. By-and-by he came to the edge of the surf. The strand here was glassy wet, and each curving wave sent a shadow flying over it, and came after the shadow, thundering and hissing, and chased it up the shore, and fell back, leaving for a second or two an edge of delicate froth which reminded the boy of his mother's lace-work.

He began a sort of game with the waves, choosing one station after another, and challenging them to catch him there. If the edge of froth failed to reach his toes, he won. But once or twice the water caught him fairly, and ran rippling over his instep and about his ankles.

He was deep in this game when he heard a horn blown somewhere high on the towans behind him.

He turned. No one was in sight. The house lay behind the sand-banks, the first ridge hiding even its chimney-smoke. He gazed along the beach, where the perpetual haze of spray seemed to have removed the light-house to a vast distance. A sense of desolation came over him with a rush, and with something between a gasp and a sob he turned his back to the sea and ran, his boots dangling from his shoulders by their knotted laces.

He pounded up the first slope and looked for the cottage. No sign of it! An insane fancy seized him. These silent moving sands were after *him.*

He was panting along in real distress when he heard the baying of dogs, and at the same instant from the top of a hummock caught sight of a figure outlined against the sky, and barely a quarter of a mile away; the figure of a girl on horseback—a small girl on a very tall horse.

Just as Taffy recognised her, she turned her horse, walked him down into the hollow beyond, and disappeared. Taffy ran towards the spot, gained the ridge where she had been standing, and looked down.

In a hollow about twenty feet deep and perhaps a hundred wide were gathered a dozen riders, with five or six couples of hounds and two or three dirty terriers. Two of the men had dismounted. One of these, stripped to his shirt and breeches, was leaning on a long-handled spade and laughing. The other—a fellow in a shabby scarlet coat—held up what Taffy guessed to be a fox, though it seemed a very small one. It was bleeding. The hounds yapped and leapt at it, and fell back a-top of each other snarling, while the Whip grinned and kept them at bay. A knife lay between his wide-planted feet, and a visgy * close behind him on a heap of disturbed sand.

The boy came on them from the eastward, and his shadow fell across the hollow.

"Hullo!" said one of the riders, looking up. It was Squire Moyle himself. "Here's the new Passon's boy!"

All the riders looked up. The Whip looked up too, and turned to the old Squire with a wider grin than before.

"Shall I christen en, maister?"

The Squire nodded. Before Taffy knew what it meant, the man was climbing toward him with a grin, clutching the rush bents with one hand, and holding out the blood-dabbled mask with the other. The child turned to run, but a hand clutched his ankle. He saw the man's open mouth and yellow teeth; and, choking with disgust and terror, slung his boots at them with all his small force. At the same instant he was jerked off his feet, the edge of the bank crumbled and broke, and the two went rolling down the sandy slope in a heap. He heard shouts of laughter, caught a glimpse of blue sky, felt a grip of fingers on his throat, and smelt the verminous odour of the dead cub, as the Whip thrust the bloody mess against his face and neck. Then the grip relaxed, and—it seemed to him, amid dead silence—Taffy sprang to his feet, spitting sand and fury.

"You—you devils!" He caught up the visgy and stood, daring all to come on. "You devils!"

* Mattock.

He tottered forward with the visgy lifted—it was all he could manage—at Squire Moyle. The old man let out an oath, and the curve of his whip-thong took the boy across the eyes and blinded him for a moment, but did not stop him. The grey horse swerved, and half-wheeled, exposing his flank. In another moment there would have been mischief; but the Whip, as he stood wiping his mouth, saw the danger and ran in. He struck the visgy out of the child's grasp, set his foot on it, and with an open-handed cuff sent him floundering into a sand-heap.

"Nice boy, that!" said somebody, and the whole company laughed as they walked their horses slowly out of the hollow.

They passed before Taffy in a blur of tears; and the last rider to go was the small girl Honoria on her tall sorrel. She moved up the broad shelving path, but reined up just within sight, turned her horse, and came slowly back to him.

"If I were you, I'd go home." She pointed in its direction.

Taffy brushed the back of his hand across his eyes. "Go away. I hate you—I hate you all!"

She eyed him while she smoothed the sorrel's mane with her riding-switch.

"They did it to me three years ago, when I was six. Grandfather called it 'entering' me."

Taffy kept his eyes sullenly on the ground. Finding that he would not answer, she turned her horse again and rode slowly after the others. Taffy heard the soft footfalls die away, and when he looked up she had vanished.

He picked up his boots and started in the direction to which she had pointed. Every now and then a sob shook him. By-and-by the chimneys of the house hove in sight among the ridges, and he ran toward it. But within a gunshot of the white garden-wall his breast swelled suddenly and he flung himself on the ground and let the big tears run. They made little pits in the moving sand ; and more sand drifted up and covered them.

" Taffy ! Taffy ! Whatever has become of the child ? "

His mother was standing by the gate in her print frock. He scrambled up and ran toward her. She cried out at the sight of him, but he hid his blood-smeared face against her skirts.

CHAPTER V.

TAFFY RINGS THE CHURCH BELL.

THEY were in the church—Squire Moyle, Mr. Raymond, and Taffy close behind. The two men were discussing the holes in the roof and other dilapidations.

"One, two, three," the Squire counted. "I'll send a couple of men with tarpaulin and rick-ropes. That'll tide us over next Sunday, unless it blows hard."

They passed up three steps under the belfry arch. Here a big bell rested on the flooring. Its rim was cracked, but not badly. A long ladder reached up into the gloom.

"What's the beam like?" the Squire called up to someone aloft.

"Sound as a bell," answered a voice.

"I said so. We'll have en hoisted by Sunday. I'll send a waggon over to Wheel Gooniver for a tackle and winch. Damme, up there! Don't keep sheddin' such a muck o' dust on your betters!"

"I can't help no other, Squire!" said the voice overhead; "such a cauch o' pilm an' twigs, an' birds' droppins'! If I sneeze I'm a lost man."

Taffy, staring up as well as he could for the falling

rubbish, could just spy a white smock above the beam, and a glint of daylight on the toe-scutes of two dangling boots.

" I'll dam soon make you help it. *Is* the beam sound ? "

" Ha'n't I told 'ee so ? " said the voice querulously.

" Then come down off the ladder, you son of a——."

" Gently, Squire ! " put in Mr. Raymond.

The Squire groaned. " There I go again—an' in the House of God itself ! Oh ! 'tis a case with me ! I've a heart o' stone—a heart o' stone." He turned and brushed his rusty hat with his coat-cuff. Suddenly he faced round again. " Here, Bill Udy," he said to the old labourer who had just come down the ladder, " catch hold of my hat an' carry en fore to porch. I keep forgettin' I'm in church, an' then on he goes."

The building stood half a mile from the sea, surrounded by the rolling towans and rabbit burrows, and a few lichen-spotted tombstones slanting inland. Early in the seventeenth century a London merchant had been shipwrecked on the coast below Nannizabuloe and cast ashore, the one saved out of thirty. He asked to be shown a church in which to give thanks for his preservation, and the people led him to a ruin bedded in the sands. It had lain since the days of Arundel's Rebellion. The Londoner vowed to build a new church there on the towans, where the songs of prayer and praise should mingle with the voice of the waves which God had baffled for him. The people warned him of the sand ; but he would not listen to reason. He built his church —a squat Perpendicular building of two aisles, the wider divided into nave and chancel merely by a granite step in the flooring; he saw it consecrated, and returned to his home and died. And the church steadily decayed. He had mixed his mortar with sea-sand. The stonework oozed brine, the plaster fell piece-meal; the blown sand penetrated like water; the foundations sank a foot on the south side, and the whole structure took a list to leeward. The living passed into the hands of the Dean and Chapter of Exeter, and from them, in 1730, to the Moyles. Mr. Raymond's predecessor was a kinsman of theirs by marriage, a pluralist, who lived and died at the other end of the Duchy. He had sent curates from time to time; the last of whom was dead, three years since, of solitude and drink. But he never came himself, Squire Moyle having threatened to set the dogs on him if ever he set foot in Nannizabuloe; for there had been some dispute over a dowry. The result was that nobody went to church, though a parson from the next parish held an occasional service. The people were Wesleyan Methodists or Bryanites. Each sect had its own chapel in the fishing village of Innis, on the western side of the parish; and the Bryanites a second one, at the cross-roads behind the downs, for the miners and warreners and scattered farmfolk.

Ding—ding—ding—ding—ding.

It was Sunday morning, and Taffy was sounding the bell, by a thin rope tied to its clapper.

The heavy bell-rope would be ready next week;

but Humility must first contrive a woollen binding for it, to prevent its chafing the ringer's hands.

Out on the towans the rabbits heard the sound, and ran scampering. Others, farther away, paused in their feeding, and listened with cocked ears.

Ding—ding—ding.

Mr. Raymond stood in the belfry at the boy's elbow. He wore his surplice, and held his prayer-book, with a finger between the pages. Glancing down toward the nave, he saw Humility sitting in the big vicarage pew—no other soul in church.

He took the cord from Taffy, " Run to the door, and see if anyone is coming."

Taffy ran, and after a minute came back.

" There's Squire Moyle coming along the path, and the little girl with him, and some servants behind—five or six of them. Bill Udy's one."

" Nobody else ? "

" I expect the people don't hear the bell," said Taffy. " They live too far away."

" God hears. Yes, and God sees the lamp is lit."

" What lamp ? " Taffy looked up at his father's face, wondering.

" All towers carry a lamp of some kind. For what else are they built ? "

It was exactly the tone in which he had spoken that afternoon at Tewkesbury about men being like towers. Both these sentences puzzled the boy ; and yet Taffy never felt so near to understanding him as he had then, and did again now. He was shy of his father. He did not know that his father was just as shy of him. He began to ring with all his soul—*ding—ding-ding, ding-ding*.

The old Squire entered the church, paused, and blew his nose violently, and taking Honoria by the hand, marched her up to the end of the south aisle. The door of the great pew was shut upon them, and they disappeared. Before Honoria vanished Taffy caught a glimpse of a grey felt hat with pink ribbons.

The servants scattered and found seats in the body of the church. He went on ringing, but no one else came. After a minute or two Mr. Raymond signed to him to stop and go to his mother, which he did, blushing at the noise of his shoes on the slate pavement. Mr. Raymond followed, walked slowly past, and entered the reading-desk.

"When the wicked man turneth away from his wickedness that he hath committed, and doeth that which is lawful and right, he shall save his soul alive. . . ."

Taffy looked towards the Squire's pew. The bald top of the Squire's head was just visible above the ledge. He looked up at his mother, but her eyes were fastened on her prayer-book. He felt—he could not help it—that they were all gathered to save this old man's soul, and that everybody knew it and secretly thought it a hopeless case. The notion dogged him all through the service, and for many Sundays after. Always that bald head above the ledge, and his father and the congregation trying to call down salvation on it. He wondered what Honoria thought, boxed up with it and able to see its face.

Mr. Raymond mounted an upper pulpit to preach his sermon. He chose his text from Saint Matthew, Chapter vii., verses 26 and 27:

"*And every one that heareth these sayings of mine*

and doeth them not, shall be likened unto a foolish man which built his house upon the sand ;

" And the rain descended, and the floods came, and the winds blew, and beat upon that house ; and it fell ; and great was the fall of it."

Taffy never followed his father's sermons closely. He would listen to a sentence or two, now and again, and then let his wits wander.

" You think this church is built upon the sands. The rain has come, the winds have blown and beaten on it ; the foundations have sunk and it leans to leeward. . . . By the blessing of God we will shore it up, and upon a foundation of rock. Upon what rock, you ask ? . . . Upon that rock which is the everlasting foundation of the Church spiritual. . . . Hear what comfortable words our Lord spake to Peter. . . . Our foundation must be faith, which is God's continuing Presence on earth, and which we shall recognise hereafter as God Himself. . . . . Faith is the substance of things hoped for, the evidence of things not seen. . . . In other words, it is the rock we search for. . . . Draw near it, and you will know yourself in God's very shadow—the shadow of a great rock in a weary land. . . . As with this building, so with you, O man, cowering from wrath, as these walls are cowering. . . ."

The benediction was pronounced, the pew-door opened, and the old man marched down the aisle, looking neither to right nor to left, with his jaw set like a closed gin. Honoria followed. She had not so much as a glance for Taffy ; but in passing she gazed frankly at Humility, whom she had not seen before.

Humility was rather ostentatiously cheerful at dinner that day ; a sure sign that at heart she was disappointed. She had looked for a bigger congregation. Mrs. Venning, who had been carried downstairs for the meal, saw this and asked few questions. Both the women stole glances at Mr. Raymond when they thought he was not observing them. He at least pretended to observe nothing, but chatted away cheerfully.

"Taffy," he said, after dinner, "I want you to run up to Tredinnis with a note from me. Maybe I will follow later, but I must go to the village first."

CHAPTER VI.

A COCK-FIGHT.

A FOOTPATH led Taffy past the church, and out at length upon a high road, in face of two tall granite pillars with an iron gate between. The gate was surmounted with a big iron lantern, and the lantern with a crest—two snakes' heads intertwined. The gate was shut, but the fence had been broken down on either side, and the gap, through which Taffy passed, was scored with wheel-ruts. He followed these down an ill-kept road bordered with furze-whins, tamarisks, and clumps of bannel broom. By-and-by he came to a ragged plantation of stone pines, backed by a hedge of rhododendrons, behind which the hounds were baying in their kennels. It put him in mind of the "Pilgrim's Progress." He heard the stable clock strike three, and caught a glimpse, over the shrubberies, of its cupola and gilt weather-cock. And then a turn of the road brought him under the gloomy northern face of the house, with its broad carriage sweep and sunless portico. Half the windows on this side had been blocked up and painted black, with white streaks down and across to represent framework.

He pulled at an iron bell-chain which dangled by the great door. The bell clanged far within and a dozen dogs took up the note, yelping in full peal. He heard footsteps coming; the door was opened, and the dogs poured out upon him—spaniels, terriers, lurchers, greyhounds, and a big Gordon setter—barking at him, leaping against him, sniffing his calves. Taffy kept them at bay as best he could and waved his letter at a wall-eyed man in a dirty yellow waistcoat, who looked down from the doorstep but did not offer to call them off.

"Any answer?" asked the wall-eyed man.

Taffy could not say. The man took the letter and went to inquire, leaving him alone with the dogs.

It seemed an age before he reappeared, having in the interval slipped a dirty livery coat over his yellow waistcoat. "The Squire says you're to come in." Taffy and the dogs poured together into a high, stone-flagged hall; then through a larger hall and a long dark corridor. The footman's coat, for want of a loop, had been hitched on a peg by its collar, and stuck out behind his neck in the most ludicrous manner; but he shuffled ahead so fast that Taffy, tripping and stumbling among the dogs, had barely time to observe this before a door was flung open and he stood blinking in a large room full of sunlight.

"Hallo! Here's the parson's bantam!"

The room had four high, bare windows through which the afternoon sunshine streamed on the carpet. The carpet had a pattern of pink peonies on a delicate buff ground, and was shamefully dirty. And the vast apartment, with its white paint and gilding and Italian sketches in water-colour and statuettes under glass, might have been a lady's drawing-room. But paint and gilding were tarnished; the chintz chair-covers soiled and torn; the pictures hung askew; and a smell of dog filled the air.

Squire Moyle sat huddled in a deep chair beside the fire-place, facing the middle of the room, where a handsome, high-complexioned gentleman, somewhat past middle age, lounged on a settee and dangled a gold-mounted riding crop. A handsome boy knelt at the back of the settee and leaned over the handsome gentleman's shoulder. On the floor, between the two men, lay a canvas bag; and something moved inside it. At the end of the room, by the farthest window, Honoria knelt over a big portfolio. She wore the grey frock and pink sash which Taffy had seen in church that morning, and she tossed her dark hair back from her eyes as she looked up.

The Squire crumpled up the letter in his hand.

"Put the bag away," he said to the handsome gentleman. "'Tis Sunday, I tell 'ee, and Parson will be here in an hour. This is young six-foot I was telling about." He turned to Taffy—

"Boy, go and shake hands with Sir Harry Vyell."

Taffy did as he was bidden. "This is my son George," said Sir Harry; and Taffy shook hands with him, too, and liked his face.

"Put the bag away, Harry," said the Squire.

"Just to comfort 'ee, now!"

"I tell 'ee I won't look at en."

Sir Harry untied the neck of the bag, and drew out a smaller one; untied this, and out strutted a game-cock.

The old Squire eyed it. "H'm, he don't seem flourishing."

"Don't abuse a bird that's come twelve miles in a bag on purpose to cheer you up. He's a match for anything you can bring."

"Tuts, man, he's dull—no colour nor condition. Get along with 'ee; I wouldn' ask a bird of mine to break the Sabbath for a wastrel like that."

Sir Harry drew out a shagreen-covered case and opened it. Within, on a lining of pale blue velvet, lay two small sharp instruments of steel, very highly polished. He lifted one, felt its point, replaced it, set down the case on the carpet, and fell to toying with the ears of the Gordon setter, which had come sniffing out of curiosity.

"You're a very obstinate man," said Squire Moyle. After a long pause he added, "I suppose you're wanting odds?"

"Evens will do," said Sir Harry.

The old man turned and rang the bell.

"Tell Jim to fetch in the red cock," he shouted to the wall-eyed footman—who must have been waiting in the corridor, so promptly he appeared.

"And Jim won't be long about it either," whispered Honoria. She had come forward quietly, and stood at Taffy's elbow.

Sir Harry shook a finger at her and laid it on his lips. But the old Squire did not hear. He sat glum, pulling a whisker and keeping a sour eye on the bird, which was strutting about in rather foolish bewilderment at the pink peonies on the carpet.

"I'm giving you every chance," he grumbled at length.

"Oh, as for that," Sir Harry replied, equably,

"have it out in the yard, if you please, on your own dunghill."

"No. Indoors is bad enough."

Jim appeared just then, and turned out to be Taffy's old enemy, the Whip, bearing the Squire's game-cock in a basket. He took it out; a very handsome bird, with a hackle in which gold purple and the richest browns shone and were blended.

Sir Harry had picked up his bird and was heeling it with the long steel spurs; a very delicate process, to judge by the time occupied and the pucker on his good-tempered brow.

"Ready?" he asked at length.

Jim, who had been heeling the Squire's bird, nodded and the pair were set down. They ruffled and flew at each other without an instant's hesitation. The visitor, which five minutes before had been staring at the carpet so foolishly, was prompt enough now. For a moment they paused, beak to beak, eye to eye, furious, with necks outstretched and hackles stiff with the rage of battle. They began to rise and fall like two feathers tossing in the air, very quietly. But for the soft whir of wings there was no sound in the room. Taffy could scarcely believe they were fighting in earnest. For a moment they seemed to touch—to touch and no more, and for a moment only—but in that moment the stroke was given. The home champion fluttered down, stood on his legs for a moment, as if nothing had happened, then toppled over and lay twitching, as his conqueror strutted over him and lifted his throat to crow.

Squire Moyle rose, clutching the corner of his

chair. His mouth opened and shut, but no words came. Sir Harry caught up his bird, whipped off his spurs, and thrust him back into the bag. The old man dropped back, letting his chin sink on his high stock-collar.

" It serves me right. Who shall deliver me from the wrath to come ? "

" Oh ! as for that——" Sir Harry finished tying the neck of the bag, and lazily fell to fingering the setter's ear.

The old man was muttering to himself. Taffy looked at the dead bird, then at Honoria. She was gazing at it too, with untroubled eyes.

" But I *will* be saved ! I tell you, Harry, I *will !* Take those birds away. Honoria, hand me my Bible. It's all here "—he tapped the heavy book —" miracles, redemption, justification by faith—I *will* have faith. I *will* believe, every damned word of it ! "

Sir Harry broke in with a peal of laughter. Taffy had never heard a laugh so musical.

The old man was adjusting his spectacles ; but he took them off and laid them down, his hands shaking with rage.

" You came here to taunt me "—his voice shook as his hand—" me, an old man, with no son to my house. You think, because I'm seeking higher things, there's no fight left in us or in the parish. I tell you what ; make that boy of yours strip and stand up, and I'll back the Parson's youngster for doubles or quits. Off with your coat, my son, and stand up to him ! "

Taffy turned round in a daze. He did not understand. His eyes met Honoria's, and they were fastened on him curiously. He was white in the face; the sight of the murdered game-cock had sickened him.

"He doesn't look flourishing." Sir Harry mimicked the Squire's recent manner.

Taffy turned with the look of a hunted animal. He did not want to fight. He hated this house and its inhabitants. The other boy was stripping off his jacket with a good-humoured smile.

"I—I don't want——" Taffy began fumbling with a button. "Please——"

"Off with your coat, boy! You were game enough t'other day. If you lick en, I'll put a new roof on your father's church."

Taffy was still fumbling with his jacket-button when a bell sounded, clanging through the house.

"The parson!"

Squire Moyle clutched at his Bible like a child who has been caught playing in school. Sir Harry stepped to the window and flung up the sash. "Out you tumble, youngsters—you too, Miss, if you like. Pick up your coat, George—cut and run to the stables; I'll be round in a minute—quick, out you go!"

The children scrambled over the sill and dropped on to the stone terrace. As his father closed the sash behind him, George Vyell laughed out. Then Taffy began to laugh; he laughed all the way as they ran. When they reached the stables he was swaying with laughter. There was a hepping-stock by the stable-wall, and he flung himself on to the slate steps. He could not stop laughing. The two others stared at him. They thought he had gone mad.

" Here comes Dad ! " cried George Vyell.

This sobered Taffy. He sat up and brushed his eyes. Sir Harry whistled for Jim, and told him to saddle the horses.

George and Honoria stood by the stable-door and watched the saddling. The horses were led out ; Sir Harry's, a tall grey, George's, a roan cob.

" Look here ! " Sir Harry said to Jim ; " you take my bird, and comfort your master with him. I don't want him any more."

The two rode out of the yard and away up the avenue. Honoria planted herself in front of Taffy.

" Would you have fought just now ? " she asked.

" I—I don't know. That's my father calling."

" But, would you have fought ? "

" I must go to him." He would not look her in the face.

" Tell me."

" Don't bother ! I don't know."

He ran out of the yard.

CHAPTER VII.

GEORGE.

IT appeared that Honoria and Taffy were to do lessons together, and Mr. Raymond was to teach them. This had been the meaning of his visit to Tredinnis House. They began the very next day in the library at Tredinnis—a deserted room carpeted with badgers' skins, and lined with undusted books—works on farriery, veterinary surgery, and sporting subjects, long rows of the *Annual Register*, the *Arminian Magazine*.

Taffy began by counting the badgers' skins. There were eighteen, and the moths had got into them, so that the draught under the door puffed little drifts of hair over the polished boards. Then he settled down to the first Latin declension—*Musa*, a muse ; vocative, *Musa*, O muse ! ; genitive, *Musæ*, of a muse. Honoria began upon the A B C.

Mr. Raymond brought a pile of his own books, and worked at them, scribbling notes in the margin or on long slips of paper, while the children learnt. A servant came in with a message from Squire Moyle, and he left them for a while.

" I call this nonsense," said Honoria. " How am I to get these silly letters into my head ? "

Taffy was glad of the chance to show off. " Oh,

that's easy. You make up a tale about them. See here. A is the end of a house; it's just like one with a beam across. B is a cat with his tail curled under him—watch me drawing it. C is an old woman stooping; and D is another cat, only his back is more rounded. Once upon a time, there lived in a cottage an old woman who went about with two cats, one on each side of her—that's how you go on."

"But I can't go on. You must do it for me."

"Well, each of these cats had a comb, and was combed every Saturday night. One was a good cat, and kept his comb properly—like E, you see. But the other had broken a tooth out of his—that's F——"

"I expect he was a fulmart," said Honoria.

Taffy agreed. He didn't know what a fulmart was, but he was not going to confess it. So he went on hurriedly, and Honoria thought him a wonder. They came to W.

"So they got into a ship (I'll show you how to make one out of paper, exactly like W), and sailed up into the sky, for the ship was a Ship of Stars—you make X's for stars; but that's a witch-ship; so it stuck fast in Y, which is a cleft ash-stick, and then came a stroke of lightning, Z, and burnt them all up!" He stopped, out of breath.

"I don't understand the ending at all," said Honoria. "What is a Ship of Stars?"

"Haven't you ever seen one?"

"No."

"I have. There's a story about it——"

"Tell me about it."

"I'll tell you lots of stories afterwards; about

the Frog-king and Aladdin and Man Friday and The Girl who trod on a Loaf."

"And the Ship of Stars?"

"N—no." Taffy felt himself blushing. "That's one of the stories that won't come—and they're the loveliest of all," he added, in a burst of confidence.

Honoria thought for a moment, but did not understand in the least. All she said was, "what funny words you use!" She went back to her alphabet—A, house; B, cat. It came more easily now.

After lessons she made him tell her a story; and Taffy, who wished to be amusing, told her about the "Valiant Tailor who killed Seven at a Blow." To his disgust, it scarcely made her smile. But after this she was always asking for stories, and always listened solemnly, with her dark eyes fixed on his face. She never seemed to admire him at all for his gift, but treated it with a kind of indulgent wonder, as if he were some queer animal with uncommon tricks. This dashed Taffy a bit, for he liked to be thought a fine fellow. But he went on telling his stories, and sometimes invented new ones for her. George Vyell was much more appreciative. Sir Harry had heard of the lessons, and wrote to beg that his son might join the class. So George rode over three times a week to learn Latin, which he did with uncommon slowness. But he thought Taffy's stories stunning, and admired him without a shade of envy. The two boys liked each other; and when they were alone Taffy stood an inch or two higher in self-conceit than when Honoria happened to be by. But he took more pains with his stories if she was listening. As for her lessons, Honoria got through them by honest plodding. She never quite saw the use of them, but she liked Mr. Raymond. She learnt more steadily than either of the boys.

One day George rode over with two pairs of boxing-gloves dangling from his saddle. After lessons he and Taffy had a try with them, in a clearing behind the shrubberies where the gardener had heaped his sweepings of dry leaves to rot down for manure.

"But, look here," said George, after the first round; "you'll never learn if you hit so wild as that. You must keep your head up, and watch my eyes and feint."

Taffy couldn't help it. As soon as ever he struck out, he forgot that it was not real fighting. And he felt ashamed to look George straight in the face, for his own eyes were full of tears of excitement. At the end of the bout, when George said, "Now we must shake hands; it's the proper thing to do," he looked bewildered for a moment. It made George laugh in his easy way, and then Taffy laughed too.

After this they had a bout almost every day; and he was soon able to hold his own and treat it as sport. But somehow he always felt a passion behind it, whispering to him to put some nastiness into his blows, especially when Honoria came to look on. And yet he liked George far better than he liked Honoria. Indeed, he adored George, and the Monday, Wednesday, and Friday mornings when George appeared were the bright spots in his week. Lessons were over at twelve o'clock; by one o'clock Taffy had to be home for dinner. Loneliness filled the afternoons, but the child peopled them with extravagant fancies. He and George were crusaders sworn to defend the Holy Sepulchre, and bound by an oath of brotherhood, though George was a Red Cross Knight and he a plain squire; and after the most surprising adventures Taffy received the barbed and poisoned arrow intended for his master, and died most impressively, with George and Honoria, and Richard Cœur de Lion, and most of the characters from "Ivanhoe," sobbing round his bed. There was a Blondel variant too, with George imprisoned in a high tower; and a monstrous conglomerate tale in which most of the heroes of history and romance played second fiddle to George, whose pre-eminence, though occasionally challenged by Achilles, Sir Lancelot, or the Black Prince, was regularly vindicated by Taffy's timely help.

This tale, with endless variations, actually lasted him for two good years. The scene of it never lay among the towans, but round about his old home or the well-remembered meadow at Tewkesbury. That was his plain of Troy, his Field of Cressy, his lists of Ashby de la Zouche. The high road at the back of the towans crossed a stream, by a ford and a footbridge; and the travelling postman, if he had any letters for the Parsonage, would stop by the footbridge and blow a horn. He little guessed what challenges it sounded to the small boy who came running for the post.

The postman came by, as a rule, at two o'clock or thereabouts. One afternoon in early spring Mr. Raymond happened to be starting for a walk when the horn was blown, and he and Taffy went to meet the post together. There were three or four letters which the Vicar opened; and one for Humility, which he put in his pocket. In the midst of his reading, he looked up, smiled over his spectacles, and said:

"Oxford has won the boat-race."

Taffy had been deep in the Fifth Æneid for some weeks, and boat-racing ran much in his mind.

"Who is Oxford?" he asked.

Mr. Raymond took off his spectacles and wiped them. It came on him suddenly that this child, whom he loved, was shut out from many of his dearest thoughts.

"Oxford is a city," he answered; and added, "the most beautiful city in the world."

"Shall I ever go there?" Taffy asked.

Mr. Raymond walked off without seeming to hear the question. But that evening after supper he told the most wonderful tales of Oxford, while Taffy listened and hoped his mother would forget his bed-time; and Humility listened too, bending over her *guipure*. The love with which he looked back to Oxford was the second passion of Samuel Raymond's life; and Humility was proud of it, not jealous at all. He forgot all the struggle, all the slights, all the grip of poverty. To him those years had become an heroic age, and men Homeric men. And so he made them appear to Taffy, to whom it was wonderful that his father should have moved among such giants.

"And shall I go there too?"

Humility glanced up quickly, and met her husband's eyes.

"Some day, please God!" she said. Mr. Raymond stared at the embers of wreck-wood on the hearth.

From that night Oxford became the main scene of Taffy's imaginings; a wholly fictitious Oxford, pieced together of odds and ends from picture-books, and peopled with all the old heroes. And so, with contests on the models of the Fifth Æneid, the story went forward gallantly for many months.

But the afternoons were long; and at times the interminable sand-hills and everlasting roar of the sea oppressed the child with a sense of loneliness beyond words. The rabbits and gulls would not make friends with him, and he ached for companionship. Of that ache was born his half-crazy adoration of George Vyell. There were hours when he lay in some nook of the towans, peering into the ground, seeing pictures in the sand—pictures of men and regiments and battles, shifting with the restless drift; until, unable to bear it, he flung out his hands to efface them, and hid his face in the sand, sobbing, "George! George!"

At night he would creep out of bed to watch the lighthouse winking away in the north-east. George lived somewhere beyond. And again it would be "George! George!"

And when the happy mornings came, and George with them, Taffy was as shy as a lover. So George never guessed. It might have surprised that very careless young gentleman, when he looked up from his verbs which govern the dative, and caught Taffy's eye, could he have seen himself in his halo there.

CHAPTER VIII.

THE SQUIRE'S SOUL.

Two years passed, and a third winter. The church was now well on its way to restoration. The roof had been repaired, the defective timbers removed and sound ones inserted, the south wall strengthened with three buttresses, the foundations on that side examined and shored up. The old Squire did not halt here. Furniture arrived for the interior; a handsome altar cloth, a small gilt cross, a dozen hanging lamps, an oaken lectern, cushions, hymn-books, a big new Bible with purple book-markers. He promised to take out the east window—which was just a patchwork of common glass, like a cucumber frame—and replace it with sound mullions and stained glass, in memory of his only daughter, Honoria's mother. She had run away from Tredinnis House, and married a penniless captain; and Honoria's surname was Callastair, though nobody uttered it in the old man's hearing. Husband and wife had died in India, of cholera, within three years of their marriage; and the old man had sent for the child. Having relented so far, he went on to do it thoroughly, in his own fashion. He neglected Honoria; but she might have anything she wanted for the asking. It seemed, though, that she wanted very little.

He allowed Mr. Raymond to choose the design for this window. He only stipulated that the subject should be Jonah and the whale. "There's no story 'll compare with it for trying a man's faith."

When the window came, and was erected, he complained that it left out most of the whale, of which the jaws and one wicked little red eye were all that appeared. "It looks half-hearted. Why didn't they swim en all in? 'Tis neck or nothin' wi' that story; but they've made it neck *and* nothin'. An' after colouring en violet too!"

In return, the Vicar had hunted up some county histories and heraldic works in the library at Tredinnis, and was now busy re-emblazoning with his own hand the devices carved on the Moyle pew.

Little by little, too, the congregation had grown. The people came shyly at first. They mistrusted the Established Church. But they treated the Vicar with politeness when he visited them. And seeing him so awkward, and how with all his book-learning he listened to their opinions and blushed when he offered any small service, they grew to like him, being shy themselves. They pitied him too, knowing the old Squire better than he did. So from Sunday to Sunday Taffy, pulling at his rope in the belfry, counted the new-comers, and Humility talked about them on the way home and at dinner. They were fisher folk for the most part; the men in blue guernseys and corduroy trousers, and some with curled black beards and rings in their ears; the women, in gayer colours than you see in an up-country church; a southern-seeming race, with southern-sounding names—Santo, Jose, Hugo, Bennet, Cara. They belonged—so Mr. Raymond often told himself—to the class which Christ called His Apostles. Sometimes, scanning an olive-coloured face, he would be minded of the Sea of Gennesareth; and, a minute later, the sight of the grey coast-line with its whirled spray would chill the fancy.

The congregation always lingered outside the porch after service; and then one would say to another: "Wall, there's more in the man than you'd think. See you up to the meetin' this evenin' I s'pose? So long!"

But having come once, they came again. And the family at the Parsonage were full of hope, though Taffy longed sometimes for a play-fellow, and sometimes for he knew not what, and Humility bent over her lace pillow and thought of green lanes and of Beer Village and women at work by sunshiny doorways; and wondered if their faces had changed.

"O, that I were where I would be!
  Then would I be where I am not;
But where I am, there I must be,
  And where I would be, I cannot."

She never told a soul of her home thoughts. Her husband never guessed them. But Taffy (without knowing why), whenever this verse from his old playbook came into his head, connected it with his mother.

But the old Squire was getting impatient. He took quite a feudal view of the saving of his soul, and would have dragged the whole parish to church by main force, had it been possible.

Late one afternoon, Taffy was lying in one of his favourite nooks in the lee of the towans, when he heard voices and looked up. And there sat the old gentleman gazing down on him from horseback, with Bill Udy at his side. The Squire was in hunting dress.

"What be doin' down there?" he asked. "Praying?"

"No, sir."

"I wish you would. I wish you'd pray for me. I've heerd that a child'll do good sometimes when grown folk can't. I doubt your father isn't goin' to do the good I looked for from en. He don't believe in sudden conversion. Here, Bill, take the mare and lead her home."

He dismounted, and seated himself with a groan on the edge of the sand-pit.

"Look here; I've got convictions of sin, but I can't get no forrader. What's to be done?"

"I don't know, sir," Taffy stammered, with his eyes on the Squire's spurs.

"You can pray for me, I suppose?"

"Yes, sir."

"Well, do it. Do it to-night. I've got convictions, boy; but my heart's like a stone. I've had a wisht day of it. If the weather holds back, we'll kill a May fox this year. But where's the comfort? All the time to-day 'twas '*Lippety-lop, no peace for the wicked! Lippety-lop, no peace for the wicked!*' I couldn't stand it; I came away. You'll do it, won't 'ee?"

"Yes, sir."

"Is your father at home? I'll call an' speak to en. He does me good; but he can't melt what I carry here."

He tapped his breast and rising without another word strode off across the sand-hills with his head down and his hands clasped beneath his coat-tails, which flapped in the wind as he went.

Taffy ran and overtook Bill Udy and the mare.

"He's in a wisht poor state, id'n a'?" said Bill Udy, who was parish clerk. "Bless 'ee, tidn' no manner of use. His father before en was took in just the same way. Turned religious late in life. What d' 'ee think he did? Got his men together one Sunday mornin', marched them up to Meetin' house, up to Four Turnin's; slipped his ridin' crop through the haps o' the door, an' 'Now my Billies,' says he, through the key-hole, 'not a man or woman of 'ee leaves the place till you've said that Amazin' Creed. Come along,' he says, '"*Whosoever will be saved,*" an' the sooner 'tis over, the sooner you gets home to dinner.' A fine talk there was! Squire, he's just such another. Funny things he've a-done. Married a poor soul from Roseland way—a Miss Trevanion—quite a bettermost lady. When Miss Susannah was born—that's Miss Honoria's mother—she went to be churched. What must he do, to show his annoyance that 'twasn't a boy, but drive a she-ass into church? Very stiff behaviour. He drove the beast right fore an' into the big pew. The Moyles, you see, 've got a mule for their shield of arms. He've had his own way too much; that's of it.

"One day he dropped into church just before sarmon-time. There was a rabbit squattin' outside 'pon his father's tombstone. Squire crep' up an' clapped his Sunday hat 'pon top of en. Took en into church. One o' the curate chaps was preachin'—a timorous little fellah. By-'n'-by Squire slips out his rabbit. 'Wirroo, boys! Coorse en, coorse en—we'll have en for dinner!' Aw, a pretty dido! The curate fellah ran out to door an' the rabbit after en. Folks did say the rabbit was the old Squire's soul, an' that he'd turned black inside the young Squire's hat. Very stiff behaviour.

"He've had his own way too much; that's what it is. When he was pricked for sheriff, he hired a ramshackle po'shay, painted a mule 'pon the panel, an' stuffed the footmen's stockings with bran till it looked a case of dropsy. He was annoyed at bein' put to the expense. The judge lost his temper at bein' met in such a way, an' pitched into en in open court, specially about the mule. He didn't know 'twas the Squire's shield of arms. Squire stood it for some time; but at last he ups an' says, 'If you was an old woman of *mine,* I'd dress 'ee different; an' if you was an old woman of mine an' kep' scolding like that, I'd have 'ee in the duckin'-stool for your sauce!' He almost went to gaol for that. But they put it on the ground the judge had insulted his shield of arms, an' so he got off.

"Well, wish-'ee-well! Don't you trouble about *he.* He've had his own way too much, but he won't get it this time."

That night Taffy dreamt that he met Squire Moyle walking along the shore; but the sand clogged him, and his spurs sank in it and his riding-boots. When he was ankle deep he began to call out, "Pray for me!" Then Taffy saw a black rabbit running on the firm sand to the breakers; and the Squire cried "Pray for me! I must catch en! 'Tis my father's soul running off!" and put his hand into his breast and drew out a stone and flung it. But the stone, as soon as it touched the sand, turned into another rabbit, and the pair ran off together along the shore. The old man tried to follow, but the sand held him; and the tide was rising. . . .

CHAPTER IX.

ENTER THE KING'S POSTMAN.

A FAINT south wind murmured beneath the eaves. It died away, and for an hour there was peace on the towans. Then the sands began to trickle again, and the rushes to whisper and bend away from the sea, toward the high moors over which the gulls had flown yesterday and disappeared. By-and-by a spit or two of rain came flying out of the black north-west. The drops fell in the path of the sand, but the sand drove over and covered them, racing faster and faster.

Day rose, and Taffy awoke. The house walls were shaking. With each blow the wind ran up a scale of notes and ended with a howl. He looked out. Sea and sky had melted into one; only now and then white surf line heaved into sight, and melted back into grey. After breakfast he and his father started to battle their way to Tredinnis House, while Humility barricaded the door behind them. Taffy wore a suit of oilers, of which he was mightily proud.

They made their way under the lee of the towans to escape the stinging sand. Within Tredinnis Gates they found a couple of pine-trees blown down across the road, and scrambled over their trunks.

Before lessons, Taffy boasted a lot of his journey to Honoria, and almost forgot to be sorry that George did not appear, though it was Wednesday.

They had no trouble in reaching home. The gale hurled them along. Taffy, leaning his back against it, could scarcely feel his feet touching ground. Humility unfastened the door, looking white and anxious. Before they could close it again, the wind swept a big dish off the dresser with a crash.

Taffy slept soundly that night. He did not hear a knocking which sounded on the house-door, soon after eleven o'clock. The man who knocked came from Tresedder, one of the moor farms. "Oh, sir! did 'ee see the rockets go up over Innis? There'll be dead men down 'pon the Island rocks."

Taffy slept on. When he came downstairs next morning there was a stranger in the kitchen—a little old man, huddled in a blanket before the great fireplace, where a line of clothes hung drying. Humility was stooping to wedge a sand-bag under the door. She looked up at Taffy with a wan little smile.

"There has been a wreck," she said.

"Glory be!" exclaimed the stranger from the fire-place.

Taffy glanced at him, but could see little more than the back of a bald head above the blankets.

"Where's the ship?" he asked.

"Gone," answered the Vicar, coming at that moment from the inner room where his books were. "She must have broken up in less than ten minutes after she struck the Island—parted and gone down in six fathoms of water."

"And the men? Was father there?" It bewildered Taffy that all this should have happened while he was sleeping.

"There was no time to fix the rocket apparatus. She was late in making her distress signals. But I doubt if anything could have been done. She went down too quickly."

"But——" Taffy's gaze wandered to the bald head.

"He was washed clean over the ridge where she struck, and swept into Innis Pool—one big wave carried him into safety—one man out of six."

"Hallelujah!" cried the rescued man facing round in his chair. "Might ha' been scat like an egg-shell, and here I be shoutin' praises!" Taffy saw that he was a clean-shaven little fellow, with puckered cheeks and two wisps of grey hair curling forward from his ears.

Mr. Raymond frowned. "I am sure," said he, "you ought not to be talking so much."

"I will sing and give praise, sir, beggin' you pardon, with the best member that I have. Who is weak, and I am not weak? Who is offended and I burn not? Hallelujah! A-men!"

He took his basin of bread and milk from Humility's hand, and ate by the fire. She had wrung his clothes through fresh water, and as soon as they were thoroughly dry he retired upstairs to change. He came back to his seat by the fire.

"Now, I be like 'Possel Paul," he said, rubbing his hands, and stretching them out to the blaze. "After his shipwreck, you know, when the folks 'pon the island showed en kindness. This is the Lord's doing, and it is marvellous in your eyes.

"'Not fearing nor doubting,
With Christ by my side,
I hopes to die shouting,
The Lord will provide!'"

Humility thought that for certain the shipwreck had turned his head.

"But where do you come from?" she asked.

"They call me Jacky Pascoe, ma'am; but I calls myself the King's Postman—

"'Jacky Pascoe is my name,
Wendron is my nation,
Nowhere is my dwelling-place,
For Christ is my salvation——'

"I was brought to a miner, over to Wheal Jewel, in Illogan Parish; but got conversion fifteen years since, an' now I go about praising the Name. I've been miner, cafender, cooper, mason, seaman, scissor-grinder, umbrella-mender, holli-bubber, all by turns. I sticks my hands in my pockets, an' waits on the Lord; an' what he tells me to do, I do. This day week I was up to Fowey, working on the tip.* There was a little schooner there, the *Garibaldi*, of Newport, discharging coal. The Lord said to me, 'Arise, go in that there schooner!' I sought out the skipper, and said, 'Where be bound for next?' 'Back to Newport,' says he. 'That'll suit me,' I says, an' persuaded en to take me. But the Lord knew where she were bound better'n the skipper; and here I be!"

It seemed to his hearers that this man took little thought of his drowned shipmates. Mr. Raymond looked up as he strapped his books together.

* Loading vessels from the jetties.

"You were not the only man in that schooner," he said, rather severely.

"Glory be! Who be I, to question the Lord's ways? One day I picked up a map, an' seed a place on it called 'Little Sins.' 'Little Sins wants great Deliverance,' says I, an' I started clane off an' walked to the place, though I'd never so much as heard of it till then. 'Twas harvest-time there, an' I danced into the field, shouting 'Glory, glory. The harvest is plenty, but the labourers be few!' The farmer was moved to give me a job 'pon the spot. I bided there two year, an' built them a chapel an' preached the Word in it. They offered me money to stop an' preach; and I laid it before the Lord. But He said, 'You're the King's Postman. Keep moving, keep on moving!' I've built two more chapels since then."

Late that afternoon three bodies were recovered from the sea—the captain, the mate, and a boy of about sixteen; and were buried in the churchyard next day, as soon as the inquest was over. Pascoe followed the coffins, and pointed the service at the grave-side with interjaculations of his own. "Glory be!" "A-men!" "Hallelujah!" "Great Redemption!" To the Vicar's surprise the small crowd after a minute began to follow the man's lead, until at length he could scarcely read for these interruptions.

At supper that night Pascoe sprang a question on the Vicar.

"Be you convarted?" he asked, looking up with his mouth full of bread and cheese.

"I hope so."

"Aw, you *hopes!* 'Tis a bad case with 'ee, then. When a man's convarted, he *knows*. Seemin' to me, you baint. You don't show enough of the bright side. Now, as I go along, my very toes keep ticking salvation. Down goes one foot, 'Glory be!' Down goes the other, 'A-men!' Aw! I must dance for joy!"

He got up and danced around the kitchen.

"I wish the man would go," Humility thought to herself.

His very next words answered her wish.

"I'll be leavin' to-morrow, friends. I've got a room down to the village, an' I've borreyed a razor. I'm goin' to tramp round the mines at the back here, an' shave the miners at a ha'penny a chin. That'll pay my way. There's a new preacher planned to the Bible Christians, down to Innis, an' I'm goin' to help he. My dears, don't 'ee tell me the Lord didn' know what He was about when He cast the *Garibaldi* ashore!"

He left the Parsonage next day. "Ma'am," he said to Humility on leaving, "I salute this here house. Peace be on this here house, for it is worthy. He that receiveth a prophet in the name of a prophet shall receive a prophet's reward."

Two mornings later, Taffy, looking out from his bedroom window soon after daybreak, saw the prophet trudging along the road. He had a clean white bag slung across his shoulder; it carried his soap and razors, no doubt. And every now and then he waved his walking-stick and skipped as he went.

CHAPTER X.

A HAPPY DAY.

A VOLLEY of sand darkened and shook the pane. Taffy, sponging himself in his tub and singing between his gasps, looked up hastily, then flung a big towel about him and ran to the window.

Honoria was standing below; and Comedy, her gray pony, with a creel and a couple of fishing rods strapped to his canvas girth.

"Wake up! I've come to take you fishing."

Mr. Raymond had started off at daybreak to walk to Truro on business; so there would be no lessons that morning, and Taffy had been looking forward to a lonely whole holiday.

"I've brought two pasties," said Honoria, "and a bottle of milk. We'll go over to George's country and catch trout. He is to meet us at Vellingey Bridge. We arranged it all yesterday, only I kept it for a surprise."

Taffy could have leapt for joy. "Go in and speak to mother," he said; "she's in the kitchen."

Honoria hitched Comedy's bridle over the gate, walked up the barren little garden, and knocked at the door. When Mrs. Raymond opened it she held out a hand politely.

"How do you do?" she said, "I have come to ask if Taffy may go fishing with me."

Except in church, and outside the porch for a formal word or two, Humility and Honoria had never met. This was Honoria's first visit to the Parsonage, and the sight of the clean kitchen and shining pots and pans filled her with wonder. Humility shook hands and made a silent note of the child's frock, which was torn and wanted brushing.

"He may go, and thank you. It's lonely for him here, very often."

"I suppose," said Honoria gravely, "I ought to have called before. I wish——" She was about to say that she wished Humility would come to Tredinnis. But her eyes wandered to the orderly dresser and the scalding-pans by the fireplace.

"I mean—if Taffy had a sister it would be different."

Humility bent to lift a kettle off the fire. When she faced round again, her eyes were smiling though her lip trembled a little.

"How bright you keep everything here!" said Honoria.

"There's plenty of sand to scour with; it's bad for the garden though."

"Don't you grow any flowers?"

"I planted a few pansies the first year; they came from my home up in Devonshire. But the sand covered them. It covers everything." She smiled, and asked suddenly, "May I kiss you?"

"Of course you may," said Honoria. But she blushed as Humility did it, and they both laughed shyly.

"Hullo!" cried Taffy from the foot of the stairs.

Honoria moved to the window. She heard the boy and his mother laughing and making pretence to quarrel, while he chose the brownest of the hot cakes from the wood-ashes. She stared out upon Humility's buried pansies. It was strange—a minute back she had felt quite happy.

Humility set them off, and watched them till they disappeared in the first dip of the towans; and then sat down in the empty kitchen and wept a little before carrying up her mother's breakfast.

Honoria rode in silence for the first mile; but Taffy sang and whistled by turns as he skipped alongside. The whole world flashed and glittered around the boy and girl; the white gulls fishing, the swallows chasing one another across the dunes, the lighthouse on the distant spit, the white-washed mine-chimneys on the ridge beside the shore. Away on the rises of the moor one hill-farm laughed to another in a steady flame of furze blossom—laughed with a tinkling of singing larks. And beyond the last rise lay the land of wonders, George's country. "Hark!" Honoria reined up. "Isn't that the cuckoo?" Taffy listened. Yes, somewhere among the hillocks seaward its note was dinning.

"Count!"

"Cuckoo, cherry-tree,
Be a good bird and tell to me
How many years before I die?"

"Ninety-six!" Taffy announced.

"Ninety-two," said Honoria, "but we won't quarrel about it. Happy month to you!"

"Eh?"

"It is the first of May. Come along; perhaps we shall meet the Mayers, though we're too late, I expect. Hullo! there's a miner—let's ask him."

The miner came upon them suddenly—footsteps make no sound among the towans; a young man in a suit stained orange-tawny, with a tallow candle stuck with a lump of clay in the brim of his hat, and a striped tulip stuck in another lump of clay at the back and nodding.

"Good-morning, miss. You've come a day behind the fair."

"Is the Maying over?" Honoria asked.

"Iss, fay. I've just been home to shift myself."

He walked along with them and told them all about it in the friendliest manner. It had been a grand Maying—all the boys and girls in the parish—with the hal-an-tow, of course—such dancing! Fine and tired some of the maids must be—he wouldn't give much for the work they'd do to-day. Two May mornings in one year would make a grass-captain mad, as the saying was. But there—'twas a poor spirit that never rejoiced.

"Which do you belong to?" Taffy nodded toward the mine-chimneys on the sky-line high on their left, which hid the sea, though it lay less than half a mile away and the roar of it was in their ears—just such a roar as the train makes when rushing through a tunnel.

"Bless you, I'm a tinner. I belong to Wheal Gooniver, up the valley. Wheal Vlo there, 'pon the cliff, he's lead. And the next to him, Wheal Penhale, he's iron. I came a bit out of my way with you for company."

Soon after parting from him they crossed the valley-stream (Taffy had to wade it), and here they happened on a dozen tall girls at work "spalling" the tin-ore, but not busy. The most of them leaned on their hammers or stood with hands on hips, their laughter drowning the *thud, thud* of the engine-house and the rattle of the stamps up the valley. And the cause of it all seemed to be a smaller girl who stood by with a basket in her arms.

"Here you be, Lizzie!" cried one. "Here's a young lady and gentleman coming with money in their pockets."

Lizzie turned. She was a child of fourteen, perhaps; brown skinned, with shy, wild eyes. Her stockings were torn, her ragged clothes decorated with limp bunches of bluebells, and her neck and wrists with twisted daisy chains. She skipped up to Honoria and held out a basket. Within it, in a bed of fern, lay a May-doll among a few birds' eggs—a poor wooden thing in a single garment of pink calico.

"Give me something for my doll, miss!" she begged.

"Aw, that's too tame," one of the girls called out, and pitched her voice to the true beggar's whine: "Spare a copper! My only child, dear kind lady, and its only father broke his tender neck in a blasting accident, and left me twelve to maintain!"

All the girls began laughing again. Honoria did not laugh. She was feeling in her pocket.

"What is your name?" she asked.

"Lizzie Pezzack. My father tends the lighthouse. Give me something for my doll, miss!"

Honoria held out a half-crown piece.

"Hand it to me."

The child did not understand. "Give me something——" she began again in her dull, level voice.

Honoria stamped her foot. "Give it to me!" She snatched up the doll and thrust it into the fishing creel, tossed the coin into Lizzie's basket, and taking Comedy by the bridle, moved up the path.

"She've adopted en!" They laughed and called out to Lizzie that she was in luck's way. But Taffy saw the child's face as she stared into the empty basket, and that it was perplexed and forlorn.

"Why did you do that?" he asked, as he caught up with Honoria. She did not answer.

And now they turned away from the sea, and struck a high road which took them between upland farms and across the ridge of cultivated land to a valley full of trees. A narrow path led inland up this valley. They had followed it under pale green shadows, in Indian file, the pony at Honoria's heels and Taffy behind, and stepped out into sunlight again upon a heathery moor where a trout stream chattered and sparkled. And there by a granite bridge they found George fishing, with three small trout shining on the turf beside him.

This was a day which Taffy remembered all his life, and yet most confusedly. Indeed there was little to remember it by—little to be told except that all the while the stream talked, the larks sang, and in the hollow of the hills three children were happy. George landed half a dozen trout before lunch-time; but Taffy caught none, partly because he knew nothing about fishing, partly because the chatter of the stream set him telling tales to himself and he forgot the rod in his hand. And Honoria, after hooking a tiny fish and throwing it back into the water, wandered off in search of larks' nests. She came slowly back when George blew a whistle announcing lunch.

"Hullo! What's this?" he asked, as he dived a hand into her creel. "Ugh! a doll! I say, Taffy, let's float her down the river. What humbug, Honoria!"

But she had snatched the doll and crammed it back roughly into the creel. A minute later, when they were not looking, she lifted the lid again and disposed the poor thing more gently.

"Why don't you talk, one of you?" George demanded, with his mouth full.

Taffy shook himself out of his waking dream—"I was wondering where it goes to," he said, and nodded toward the running water.

"It goes down to Langona," said George, "and that's just a creek full of sand, with a church right above it in a big grass meadow—the queerest small church you ever saw. But I've heard my father tell that hundreds of years back a big city stood there, with seven fine churches and quays, and deep water alongside and above, so that ships could sail right up to the ford. They came from all parts of the world for tin and lead, and the people down in the city had nothing to do but sit still and grow rich."

"Somebody must have worked," interrupted Honoria; "on the buildings and all that."

"The building was done by convicts. The story is that convicts were transported here from all over the kingdom."

"Did they live in the city?"

"No; they had a kind of camp across the creek. They dug out the harbour too, and kept it clear of sand. You can still see the marks of their pickaxes along the cliffs; I'll show them to you some day. My father knows all about it, because his great-great-great-great-grandfather (and a heap more 'greats,' I don't know how many) was the only one saved when the city was buried."

"Was he from the city, or one of the convicts?" asked Honoria, who had not forgiven George's assault upon her doll.

"He was a baby at the time, and couldn't remember," George answered, with fine composure. "They say he was found high up the creek, just where you cross it by the foot-bridge. The bridge is covered at high water; and if you try to cross below, especially when the tide is flowing, just you look out! Twice a day the sands become quick there. They've swallowed scores. I'll tell you another thing: there's a bird builds somewhere in the cliffs there—a crake, the people call it—and they say that whenever he goes crying about the sands, it means that a man will be drowned there."

"Rubbish! I don't believe in your city."

"Very well, then, I'll tell you something else. The fishermen have seen it—five or six of them. You know the kind of haze that gets up sometimes on hot days, when the sun's drawing water? They say that if you're a mile or two out and this happens between you and Langona Creek, you can see the city quite plain above the shore, with the seven churches and all."

"*I* can see it!" Taffy blurted this out almost without knowing that he spoke; and blushed furiously when George laughed. "I mean—I'm sure——" he began to explain.

"If you can see it," said Honoria, "you had better describe George's property for him." She yawned. "He can't tell the story himself—not one little bit."

"Right you are, miss," George agreed. "Fire away, Taffy."

Taffy thought for a minute, then, still with a red face, began. "It is all true, as George says. A fine city lies there, covered with the sands; and this was what happened. The King of Langona had a son, a handsome young Prince, who lived at home until he was eighteen, and then went on his travels. That was the custom, you know. The Prince took only his foster-brother, whose name was John, and they travelled for three years. On their way back, as they came to Langona Creek, they saw the convicts at work, and in one of the fields was a girl digging alone. She had a ring round her ankle, like the rest, with a chain and iron weight, but she was the most beautiful girl the Prince had ever seen. So he pulled up his horse and asked her who she was, and how she came to be wearing the chain. She told him she was no convict, but the daughter of a convict, and it was the law for the convict's children to wear these things. 'To-night,' said the Prince, 'you shall wear a ring of gold and be a Princess,' and he commanded John to file away the ring and take her upon his horse. They rode across the creak and came to the palace; and the Prince, after kissing his father and mother, said, 'I have brought you all kinds of presents from abroad; but best of all I have brought home a bride.' His parents, who wondered at her beauty, and never doubted but that she must be a king's daughter, were full of joy, and set the bells ringing in all the seven churches. So for a year everybody was happy, and at the end of that time a son was born."

"You're making it up," said Honoria. Taffy's *own* stories always puzzled her, with hints and echoes from other stories she half-remembered, but could seldom trace home. He had too cunning a gift.

George said, "Do be quiet! Of course he's making it up, but who wants to know *that?*"

"Two days afterward," Taffy went on, "the Prince was out hunting with his foster-brother. The Princess in her bed at home complained to her mother-in-law, 'Mother, my feet are cold. Bring me another rug to wrap them in.' The Queen did so, but as she covered the Princess's feet she saw the red mark left by the ankle ring, and knew that her son's wife was no true Princess, but a convict's daughter. And full of rage and shame she went away and mixed two cups. The first she gave to the Princess to drink; and when it had killed her (for it was poison) she dipped a finger into the dregs and rubbed it inside the child's lips, and very soon he was dead too. Then she sent for two ankle-chains and weights—one larger and one very small—and fitted them on the two bodies and had them flung into the creek. When the Prince came home he asked after his wife. 'She is sleeping,' said the Queen, 'and you must be thirsty with hunting?'

She held out the second cup, and the Prince drank and passed it to John, who drank also. Now in this cup was a drug which took away all memory. And at once the Prince forgot all about his wife and child; and John forgot too.

"For weeks after this the Prince complained that he felt unwell. He told the doctors that there was an empty place in his head, and they advised him to fill it by travelling. So he set out again, and John went with him as before. On their journey they stayed for a week with the King of Spain, and there the Prince fell in love with the King of Spain's daughter, and married her, and brought her home at the end of a year, during which she, too, had brought him a son.

"The night after their return, when the Prince and his second wife slept, John kept watch outside the door. About midnight he heard the noise of a chain dragging, but very softly, and up the stairs came a lady in white with a child in her arms. John knew his former mistress at once, and all his memory came back to him, but she put a finger to her lips and went past him into the bed-chamber. She went to the bed, laid a hand on her husband's pillow, and whispered:

"'Wife and babe below the river,
Twice will I come and then come never.'

Without another word she turned and went slowly past John and down the stairs."

"I know *that*, anyhow," Honoria interrupted. "That's 'East of the Sun and West of the Moon,' or else it's the Princess whose brother was changed into a Roebuck, or else——" But George flicked a pebble at her, and Taffy went on, warming more and more to the story :—

"In the morning, when the Prince woke, his second wife saw his pillow on the side farthest from her, and it was wet. 'Husband,' she said, 'you have been weeping to-night.' 'Well,' said he, 'that is queer, though, for I haven't wept since I was a boy. It's true, though, that I had a miserable dream.' But when he tried to remember it, he could not.

"The same thing happened on the second night, only the dead wife said :

"'Wife and babe below the river,
Once will I come and then come never.'

And again in the morning there was a mark on the pillow where her wet hand had rested. But the Prince in the morning could remember nothing. On the third night she came and said :

"'Wife and babe below the river,
Now I am gone and gone for ever,'

and went down the stairs with such a reproachful look at John that his heart melted and he ran after her. But at the outer door a flash of lightning met him, and such a storm broke over the palace and city as had never been before and never will be again.

"John heard screams, and the noise of doors banging and feet running throughout the palace ; he turned back and met the Prince, his master, coming downstairs with his child in his arms. The lightning stroke had killed his second wife where she lay. John followed him out into the streets, where the people were running to and fro, and through the whirling sand to the ford which crossed the creek a mile above the city. And there, as they stepped into the water, a woman rose before John, with a child in her arms, and said: 'Carry us.' The Prince, who was leading, did not see. John took them on his back, but they were heavy because of the iron chains and weights on their ankles, and the sands sank under him. Then, by-and-by, the first wife put her child into John's arms and said, 'Save him,' and slipped off his back into the water. 'What sound was that?' asked the Prince. 'That was my heart cracking,' said John. So they went on till the sand rose half-way to their knees. Then the Prince stopped and put his child into John's arms. 'Save him,' he said, and fell forward on his face; and John's heart cracked again. But he went forward in the darkness until the water rose to his waist, and the sand to his knees. He was close to the farther shore now, but could not reach it unless he dropped one of the children; and this he would not do. He bent forward, holding out one in each arm, and could just manage to push them up the bank and prop them there with his open hand; and while he bent, the tide rose and his heart cracked for the third time. Though he was dead, his stiff arms kept the children propped against the bank. But just at the turning of the tide the one with the ankle-weight slipped and was drowned. The other was found next morning by the inland people, high and dry. And some *do* say," Taffy wound up, "that his brother was not really drowned, but turned into a bird, and that, though no one has seen him, it is his voice that gives the '*crake,*' imitating the sound made by John's heart when it burst; but others say it comes from John himself, down there below the sands."

There was silence for a minute. Even Honoria had grown excited toward the end.

"But it was unfair!" she broke out. "It ought to have been the convict-child that was saved."

"If so, I shouldn't be here," said George; "and it's not very nice of you to say it."

"I don't care. It was unfair; and anyone but a boy"—with scorn—"would see it." She turned upon the staring Taffy—"I hate your tale; it was horrid."

She repeated it, that evening, as they turned their faces homeward across the heathery moor. Taffy had halted on the top of a hillock to wave good-night to George. For years he remembered the scene—the brown hollow of the hills; the clear evening sky, with the faint purple arch, which is the shadow of the world, climbing higher and higher upon it; and his own shadow stretching back with his heart toward George, who stood fronting the level rays and waved his glittering catch of fish.

"What was that you said?" he asked, when at length he tore himself away and caught up with Honoria.

"That was a horrid story you told. It spoiled my afternoon, and I'll trouble you not to tell any more of the sort."

CHAPTER XI.

LIZZIE REDEEMS HER DOLL AND HONORIA THROWS A STONE.

A BROAD terrace ran along the southern front of Tredinnis House. It had once been decorated with leaden statues, but of these only the pedestals remained.

Honoria, perched on the terraced wall, with her legs dangling, was making imaginary casts with a trout-rod, when she heard footsteps. A child came timidly round the angle of the big house—Lizzie Pezzack.

"Hullo! What do you want?"

"If you please, miss——"

"Well?"

"If you please, miss——"

"You've said that twice."

Lizzie held out a grubby palm with a half-crown in it: "I wants my doll back, if you please, miss."

"But you sold it."

"I didn't mean to. You took me so sudden."

"I gave you ever so much more than it was worth. Why, I don't believe it cost you three ha'pence!"

"Tuppence," said Lizzie.

"Then you don't know when you're well off. Go away."

"'Tisn't that, miss——"

"What is it, then?"

Lizzie broke into a flood of tears.

Honoria, the younger by a year or so, stood and eyed her scornfully; then turning on her heel marched into the house.

She was a just child. She went upstairs to her bedroom, unlocked her wardrobe, and took out the doll, which was clad in blue silk, and reposed in a dog-trough lined with the same material. Honoria had recklessly cut up two handkerchiefs (for underclothing) and her Sunday sash, and had made the garments in secret. They were prodigies of bad needlework. With the face of a Medea she stripped the poor thing, took it in her arms as if to kiss it, but checked herself sternly. She descended to the terrace with the doll in one hand and its original calico smock in the other.

"There, take your twopenny baby!"

Lizzie caught and strained it to her breast; covered its poor nakedness hurriedly, and hugged it again with passionate kisses.

"You silly! Did you come all this way by yourself?"

Lizzie nodded. "Father thinks I'm home, minding the house. He's off duty this evening, and he walked over here to the Bryanite Chapel, up to Four Turnings. There's going to be a big Prayer Meeting to-night. When his back was turned I slipped out after him, so as to keep him in sight across the towans."

" Why ?"

" I'm terrible timid. I can't bear to walk across the towans by myself. You can't see where you be —they're so much alike—and it makes a person feel lost. There's so many bones, too."

" Dead rabbits."

" Yes, and dead folks, I've heard father say."

" Well, you'll have to go back alone, any way."

Lizzie hugged the doll. " I don't mind so much now. I'll keep along by the sea and run, and only open my eyes now and then. Here's your money, miss."

She went off at a run. Honoria pocketed the half-crown and went back to her fly-fishing. But after a few casts she desisted, and took her rod to pieces slowly. The afternoon was hot and sultry. She sat down in the shadow of the balustrade and gazed at the long, blank façade of the house baking in the sun ; at the tall, uncurtained windows ; at the peacock stalking to and fro like a drowsy sentinel.

" You are a beast of a house," she said contemplatively ; " and I hate every stone of you ! "

She stood up and strolled toward the stables. The stable yard was empty but for the Gordon setter dozing by the pump-trough. Across from the kitchens came the sound of the servants' voices chattering. Honoria had never made friends with the servants.

She tilted her straw hat further over her eyes, and sauntered up the drive with her hands behind her ; through the great gates and out upon the towans. She had started with no particular purpose, and had none in her mind when she came in sight of the Parsonage, and of Humility seated in the doorway with her lace pillow across her knees.

It had been the custom among the women of Beer Village to work in their doorways on sunny afternoons, and Humility followed it.

She looked up smiling. "Taffy is down by the shore, I think."

"I didn't come to look for him. What beautiful work!"

"It comes in handy. Won't you step inside and let me make you a cup of tea?"

"No, I'll sit here and watch you." Humility pulled in her skirts, and Honoria found room on the doorstep beside her. "Please don't stop. It's wonderful. Now I know where Taffy gets his cleverness."

"You are quite wrong. This is only a knack. All his cleverness comes from his father."

"Oh, books! Of course, Mr. Raymond knows all about books. He's writing one, isn't he?"

Mrs. Raymond nodded.

"What about?"

"It's about St. Paul's Epistle to the Hebrews; in Greek, you know. He has been working at it for years."

"And he's indoors working at it now? What funny things men do!" She was silent for a while, watching Humility's bobbins. "But I suppose it doesn't matter just *what* they do. The great thing is to do it better than anyone else. Does Mr. Raymond think Taffy clever?"

"He never talks about it."

"But he *thinks* so. I know; because at lessons

when he says anything to Taffy it's quite different from the way he talks to George and me. He doesn't favour him, of course; he's much too fair. But there's a difference. It's as if he *expected* Taffy to understand. Did Mr. Raymond teach him all those stories he knows?"

"What stories?"

"Fairy tales, and that sort of thing."

"Good gracious me, no!"

"Then *you* must have. And you *are* clever, after all. Asking me to believe you're not, and making that beautiful lace all the while, under my very eyes!"

"I'm not a bit clever. Here's the pattern, you see, and there's the thread, and the rest is only practice. I couldn't make the pattern out of my head. Besides, I don't like clever women."

"A woman must try to be *something*." Honoria felt that this was vague, but wanted to argue.

"A woman wants to be loved," said Mrs. Raymond thoughtfully. "There's such a heap to be done about the house that she won't find time for much else. Besides, if she has children, she'll be planning for them."

"Isn't that rather slow?"

Humility wondered where the child had picked up the word. "Slow?" she echoed, with her eyes on the horizon beyond the dunes. "Most things are slow when you look forward to them."

"But these fairy-tales of yours?"

"I'll tell you about them. When my mother was a girl of sixteen she went into service as a nursemaid in a clergyman's family. Every evening the clergyman used to come into the nursery and tell the children a fairy-tale. That's how it started. My mother left service to marry a farmer —it was quite a grand match for her—and when I was a baby she told the stories to me. She has a wonderful memory still, and she tells them capitally. When I listen I believe every word of them ; I like them better than books, too, because they always end happily. But I can't repeat them a bit. As soon as I begin they fall to pieces, and the pieces get mixed up, and, worst of all, the life goes right out of them. But Taffy, he takes the pieces and puts them together, and the tale is better than ever: quite different, and new, too. That's the puzzle. It's not memory with him ; it's something else."

" But don't you ever make up a story of your own ? " Honoria insisted.

Now you might talk with Mrs. Raymond for ten minutes, perhaps, and think her a simpleton ; and then suddenly a cloud (as it were) parted, and you found yourself gazing into depths of clear and beautiful wisdom.

She turned on Honoria with a shy, adorable smile :

" Why, of course I do—about Taffy. Come in and let me show you his room and his books."

An hour later, when Taffy returned, he found Honoria seated at the table and his mother pouring tea. They said nothing about their visit to his room ; and though they had handled every one of his treasures, he never discovered it. But he did notice—or rather, he felt—that the two understood each other. They did ; and it was an understanding he would never be able to share, though he lived to be a hundred.

Mr. Raymond came out from his study and drank his tea in silence. Honoria observed that he blinked a good deal. He showed no surprise at her visit, and after a moment seemed unaware of her presence. At length he raised the cup to his lips, and finding it empty set it down and rose to go back to his work. Humility interfered and reminded him of a call to be paid at one of the upland farms. The children might go too, she suggested. It would be very little distance out of Honoria's way.

Mr. Raymond sighed, but went for his walking-stick; and they set out.

When they reached the farmhouse he left the children outside. The town-place was admirably suited for a game of "Follow-my-leader," which they played for twenty minutes with great seriousness, to the disgust of the roosting poultry. Then Taffy spied a niche, high up, where a slice had been cut out of a last year's haystack. He fetched a ladder. Up they climbed, drew the ladder after them, and played at being Outlaws in a Cave, until the dusk fell.

Still Mr. Raymond lingered indoors. "He thinks we have gone home," said Honoria. "Now the thing would be to creep down and steal one of the fowls, and bring it back and cook it."

"We can make believe to do it," Taffy suggested.

Honoria considered for a moment.. "I'll tell you what: there's a great Bryanite meeting to-night, down at the Chapel. I expect there'll be a devil hunt."

"What's that?"

"They turn out the lights and hunt for him in the dark."

" But he isn't *really* there ? "

" I don't know. Suppose we play at scouts and creep down the road ? If the Chapel is lit up we can spy in on them ; and then you can squeeze your nose on the glass and make a face, while I say ' Boo ! ' and they'll think the Old Gentleman is really come."

They stole down the ladder and out of the town-place. The Chapel stood three-quarters of a mile away, on a turfed wastrel where two high roads met and crossed.

Long before they reached it they heard clamorous voices and groans.

" I expect the devil hunt has begun," said Honoria. But when they came in sight of the building, its windows were brightly lit. The noise inside was terrific.

The two children approached it with all the precaution proper to scouts. Suddenly the clamour ceased and the evening fell so silent that Taffy heard the note of an owl away in the Tredinnis plantations to his left. This silence was daunting, but they crept on and soon were standing in the illuminated ring of furze whins which surrounded the Chapel.

" Can you reach up to look in ? "

Taffy could not ; so Honoria obligingly went on hands and knees, and he stood on her back.

" Can you see ? What's the matter ? "

Taffy gasped. " *He's* in there ! '

" What ?—the Old Gentleman ? "

" Yes ; no—your grandfather ! "

" What ? Let me get up. Here, you kneel——"

It was true. Under the rays of a paraffin lamp, in face of the kneeling congregation, sat Squire Moyle; his body stiffly upright on the bench, his jaws rigid, his eyes with horror in them fastened upon the very window through which Honoria peered—fastened, it seemed to her, upon her face. But, no; he saw nothing. The Bryanites were praying; Honoria saw their lips moving. Their eyes were all on the old man's face. In the straining silence his mouth opened—but only for a moment—while his tongue wetted his parched lips.

A man by the pulpit-stairs shuffled his feet. A sigh passed through the Chapel as he rose and relaxed the tension. It was Jacky Pascoe. He stepped up to the Squire, and, laying a hand on his shoulder, said, gently, persuasively, yet so clearly that Honoria could hear every word:

"Try, brother. Keep on trying. O, I've knowed cases—— You can never tell how near salvation is. One minute the heart's like a stone, and the next maybe 'tis melted and singing like fat in a pan. 'Tis working! 'tis working!"

The congregation broke out with cries: "Amen!" "Glory, glory!" The Squire's lips moved and he muttered something. But stony despair sat in his eyes.

"Ay, glory, glory! You've been a doubter, and you doubt no longer. Soon you'll be a shouter. Man, you'll dance like as David danced before the Ark! You'll feel it in your toes! Come along, friends, while he's resting a minute! Sing all together—oh, the blessed peace of it!——

"'I long to be there, His glory to share——'"

He pitched the note, and the congregation took up the second line with a rolling, gathering volume of song. It broke on the night like the footfall of a regiment at charge. Honoria scrambled off Taffy's back, and the two slipped away to the high road.

"Shall you tell your father?"

"I—I don't know."

She stooped and found a loose stone. "He shan't find salvation to-night," she said heroically.

As the stone crashed through the window the two children pelted off. They ran on the soft turf by the wayside, and only halted to listen when they reached Tredinnis's great gates. The sound of feet running far up the road set them off again, but now in opposite ways. Honoria sped down the avenue, and Taffy headed for the Parsonage, across the towans. Ordinarily this road at night would have been full of terrors for him; but now the fear at his heels kept him going, while his heart thumped on his ribs. He was just beginning to feel secure, when he blundered against a dark figure which seemed to rise straight out of the night.

"Hullo!"

Blessed voice! The wayfarer was his own father.

"Taffy! I thought you were home an hour ago. Where on earth have you been?"

"With Honoria." He was about to say more, but checked himself. "I left her at the top of the avenue," he explained.

CHAPTER XII.

TAFFY'S CHILDHOOD COMES TO AN END.

THE summer passed. There was a talk in the early part of it that the Bishop would be coming, next spring, to consecrate the restored church and hold a confirmation service. Taffy and Honoria were to be confirmed, and early in August Mr. Raymond began to set apart an hour each day for preparing them. In a week or two the boy's head was full of religion. He spent much of his time in the church, watching the carpenter at work upon the new seats; his mind ran on the story of Samuel, and he wished his mother had followed Hannah's example and dedicated him to God; he had a suspicion that God would be angry with her for not doing so.

He did not observe that, as the autumn crept on, a shadow gathered on Humility's face. One Sunday the old Squire did not come to church; and again on the next Wednesday, at the harvest festival, Honoria sat alone in the Tredinnis pew. The shadow was on his mother's face as he chatted about this on their way home to the Parsonage; but the boy did not perceive it. He loved his parents, but their lives lay outside his own, and their sayings and doings passed him like a vain show. He walked in the separate world of childhood, and it seemed an enormous world yet, though a few weeks were to bring him abruptly to the end of it.

But just before he came to the precipice he was given a glimpse of the real world—and of a world beyond that, far more splendid and romantic than any region of his dreams.

The children had no lessons during Christmas, or for three weeks after. On the last morning before the holidays George brought a letter for Mr. Raymond, who read it, considered for a while, and laid it among his papers.

" It's an invitation," George announced in a whisper. " I wonder if he'll let you come."

" Where ? " whispered Taffy.

" Up to Plymouth—to the Pantomime."

" What's that ? "

" Oh—clowns, and girls dressed up like boys, and policemen on slides, and that sort of thing."

Taffy sat bewildered. He vaguely remembered Plymouth as a mass of roofs seen from the train, as it drew up for a minute or two on a high bridge. Someone in the railway carriage had talked of an engine called *Brutus*, which (it appeared) had lately run away and crashed into the cloak-room at the end of the platform. He still thought of railway engines as big, blundering animals, with wills of their own, and of Plymouth as a town rendered insecure by their vagaries ; but the idea that its roofs covered girls dressed up like boys and policemen on slides was new to him, and pleasant on the whole, though daunting.

" Will you give my thanks to Sir Harry," said Mr.

Raymond, after lessons, "and tell him that Taffy may go."

So on New Year's Day Taffy found himself in Plymouth. It was an experience which he could never fit into his life except as a gaudy interlude ; for when he awoke and looked back upon it, he was no longer the boy who had climbed up beside Sir Harry and behind Sir Harry's restless pair of bays. The whirl began with that drive to the station ; began again in the train ; began again as they stepped out on the pavement at Plymouth, just as a company of scarlet-coated soldiers came down the roadway with a din of brazen music. The crowd, the shops, the vast hotel, completely dazed him, and he seriously accepted the waiter, in his black suit and big white shirt-front, as a contribution to the fun of the entertainment.

"We must dine early," Sir Harry announced at lunch ; "the Pantomime begins at seven."

"Isn't—isn't this the Pantomime ?" Taffy stammered.

George giggled. Sir Harry set down his glass of claret, stared at the boy, and broke into musical laughter. Taffy perceived he had made some ridiculous mistake and blushed furiously.

"God bless the child—the Pantomime's at the theatre !"

"Oh !" Taffy recalled the canvas booth and wheezy cornet of his early days with a chill of disappointment.

But with George at his side it was impossible to be anything but happy. After lunch they sallied out, and it would have been hard to choose the gayest of the three. Sir Harry's radiant good-temper seemed to gild the streets. He took the boys up to the Hoe and pointed out the war-ships; he whisked them into the Camera Obscura; thence to the Citadel, where they watched a squad of recruits at drill; thence to the Barbican, where the trawling-fleet lay packed like herring, and the shops were full of rope and oilskin suits and marine instruments, and dirty children rolled about the roadway between the legs of seabooted fishermen; and so up to the town again, where he lingered in the most obliging manner while the boys stared into the fishing-tackle shops and toy shops. On the way he led them up a narrow passage and into a curious room, where fifteen or twenty men were drinking, and talking at the top of their voices. The most of them seemed to know Sir Harry well and greeted him with an odd mixture of respect and familiarity. Their talk was full of mysterious names and expressions, and Taffy thought at first they must be Freemasons. "The Moor point-to-point was a walk-over for the Milkman; Lapidary was scratched, which left it a soft thing, unless Sir Harry fancied a fox-catcher like Nursery Governess, in which case Billy behind the bar would do as much business as he liked at six-to-one." After a while Taffy discovered they were talking about horses, and wondered why they should meet to discuss horses in a dingy room up a back yard. "Youngster of yours is growin', Surrarry," said a red-faced man. "Who's his stable companion?" Taffy was introduced, and to his embarrassment Sir Harry began to relate his ridiculous mistake at lunch. The men roared with laughter.

He made another, quite as ridiculous, at the pastry-cook's where Sir Harry ordered tea. "What'll you take with it? Call for what you like, only don't poison yourselves." Taffy referring his gaze from the buns and confections on the counter to the card in his hands, which was inscribed with words in unknown tongues, made a bold plunge and announced that he would take a "*marasheno*."

This tickled Sir Harry mightily. He ordered the waitress with a wink to "bring the young gentleman a *marasheno*"; and Taffy, who had expected something in the shape of a macaroon, was confronted with a tiny glass of a pale liquor, which, when tasted, in the most surprising manner put sunshine into his stomach and brought tears into his eyes. But under Sir Harry's quizzical gaze he swallowed it down bravely, and sat gasping and blinking.

It may have been that the maraschino induced a haze upon the rest of the afternoon. The gas-lamps were lit when they left the pastry-cook's and entered a haberdasher's where Taffy, without knowing why, was fitted with a pair of white kid gloves. Of dinner at the hotel he remembered nothing except that the candles on the tables had red shades, of which the silverware gave funny reflections; that the same waiter flitted about in the penumbra; and that Sir Harry, who was dressed like the waiter, said, "Wake up, young Marasheno! Do you take your coffee black?" "It's usually pale brown at home," answered Taffy; at which Sir Harry laughed again. "Black will suit you better to-night," he said, and poured out a small cupful, which Taffy drank and found exceedingly nasty. And a moment later he was wide awake, and the three were following a young woman along a passage which seemed to run in a complete circle. The young woman flung open a door; they entered a little room with a balcony in front; and the first glorious vision broke on the child with a blaze of light, a crash of music, and the murmur of hundreds of voices.

Faces, faces, faces!—faces mounting from the pit below him, up and up to the sky-blue ceiling, where painted goddesses danced and scattered pink roses around the enormous gasalier. Fauns piping on the great curtain, fiddles sawing in the orchestra beneath, ladies in gay silks and jewels leaning over the gilt balconies opposite—which were real, and which a vision only? He turned helplessly to George and Sir Harry. Yes, *they* were real. But what of Nannizabuloe, and the sand-hills, and the little parsonage to which that very morning he had turned to wave his handkerchief?

A bell rang, and the curtain rose upon a company of russet-brown elves dancing in a green wood. The play was *Jack the Giant-killer;* but Taffy, who knew the story in the book by heart, found the story on the stage almost meaningless. That mattered nothing; it was the world, the new and unimagined world, stretching deeper and still deeper as the scenes were lifted—a world in which solid walls crumbled, and forests melted, and loveliness broke through the ruins, unfolding like a rose; it was this that seized on the child's heart until he could have wept for its mere beauty. Often he had sought out the trout-pools on the moors behind the towans, and lying at full length had watched the fish moving between the stones and water-plants; and watching through a summer's afternoon had longed to change places with them and glide through their grottoes or anchor among the reed-stalks and let the ripple run over him. As long back as he could remember, all beautiful sights had awakened this ache, this longing—

> "O, that I were where I would be!
> Then would I be where I am not;
> For where I am I would not be,
> And where I would be, I cannot."

It seemed to him that these bright beings on the stage had broken through the barriers, had stepped beyond the flaming ramparts, and were happy. Their horseplay, at which George laughed so immoderately, called to Taffy to come and be happy, too; and when Jack the Giant-killer changed to Jack in the Beanstalk, and when in the Transformation Scene a real beanstalk grew and unfolded its leaves, and each leaf revealed a fairy seated, with the lime-light flashing on star and jewelled wand, the longing became unbearable. The scene passed in a minute. The clown and pantaloon came on, and presently Sir Harry saw Taffy's shoulders shaking, and set it down to laughter at the harlequinade. He could not see the child's face.

But, perhaps, the queerest event of the evening (when Taffy came to review his recollections) was this: He must have fallen into a stupor on leaving the theatre, for when he awoke he found himself on a couch in a gas-lit room, with George beside him, and Sir Harry was shaking him by the collar, and saying,

"God bless the children, I thought they were in bed hours ago!" A man—the same who had talked about racehorses that afternoon—was standing by the table, on which a quantity of cards lay scattered among the drinking-glasses; and he laughed at this, and his laugh sounded just like the rustling of paper. "It's all very well——" began Sir Harry, but checked himself and lit a candle, and led the two boys off shivering to bed.

The next morning, too, had its surprises. To begin with, Sir Harry announced at breakfast that he must go and buy a horse. He might be an hour or two over the business, and meanwhile the boys had better go out into the town and enjoy themselves. Perhaps a sovereign apiece might help them.

Taffy, who had never in his life possessed more than a shilling, was staring at the gold piece in his hand, when the door opened, and Sir Harry's horse-racing friend came in to breakfast and nodded "Good-morning."

"Pity you're leaving to-day," he said, as he took his seat at a table hard by them.

"My revenge must wait," Sir Harry answered.

It seemed a cold-blooded thing to be said so carelessly. Taffy wondered if Sir Harry's search for a horse had anything to do with this revenge, and the notion haunted him in the intervals of his morning's shopping.

But how to lay out his sovereign? That was the first question. George, who within ten minutes had settled his own problem by purchasing a doubtful fox-terrier of the Boots of the hotel, saw no difficulty. The Boots had another pup for sale—one of the same litter.

"But I want something for mother, and the others—and Honoria."

"Botheration! I'd forgotten Honoria, and now the money's gone! Never mind; she can have my pup."

"Oh!" said Taffy ruefully. "Then she won't think much of my present."

"Yes, she will. Suppose you buy a collar for him—you can get one for five shillings."

They found a saddler's and chose the dog-collar which came to four shillings; and for eighteenpence the shopman agreed to have "*Honoria from Taffy*," engraved on it within an hour. Humility's present was chosen with surprising ease—a large, framed photograph of the Bishop of Exeter; price, six shillings.

"I don't suppose," objected George, "your mother cares much for the Bishop of Exeter."

"Oh, yes, she does," said Taffy; "he's coming to confirm us next spring. Besides," he added, with one of those flashes of wisdom which surely he derived from her, "mother won't care what it is, so long as she's remembered. And it costs more than the collar."

This left him with eight-and-sixpence; and for three-and-sixpence he bought a work-box for his grandmother, with a view of Plymouth Hoe on the lid. But now came the crux. What should he get for his father?

"It must be a book," George suggested.

"But what kind of a book? He has so many."

"Something in Latin."

The bookseller's window was filled with yellow-backed novels and toy-books, which obviously would not do. So they marched in and demanded a book suitable for a clergyman who had a good many books already—"a middle-aged clergyman," George added.

"You can't go far wrong with this," suggested the bookseller, producing Crockford's "Clerical Directory" for the current year. But this was too expensive; "and," said Taffy, "I think he would rather have something in Latin." The bookseller rubbed his chin, went to his shelves, and took down a small *De Imitatione Christi*, bound in limp calf. "You can't go far wrong with this, either," he assured them. So Taffy paid down his money.

Just as the boys reached the hotel, Sir Harry drove up in a cab; and five minutes later they were all rattling off to the railway station. Taffy eyed the cab-horse curiously, never doubting it to be Sir Harry's new purchase; and was extremely surprised when the cabman whipped it up and trotted off—after receiving his money, too. But in the bustle there was no time to ask questions.

It was about three in the afternoon, and the sun already low in the south-west, when they came in sight of the cross-roads and Sir Harry pulled up his bays. And there, on the green by the sign-post, stood Mrs. Raymond. She caught Taffy in her arms and hugged him till he felt ashamed, and glanced around to see if the others were looking; but the phaeton was bowling away down the road.

"But why are *you* here, mother?"

Mrs. Raymond gazed a while after the carriage

before speaking. "Your father had to be at the church," she said.

"But there's no service——" He broke off "See what I've brought for you!" And he pulled out the portrait. "Do you know who it is?"

Humility thanked him and kissed him passionately. There was something odd with her this afternoon.

"Don't you like your present?"

"Darling, it is beautiful," she stooped and kissed him again, passionately.

"I've a present for father, too; a book. Why are you walking so fast?" In a little while he asked again, "Why are you walking so fast?"

"I—I thought you would be wanting your tea."

"Mayn't I take father his book first?"

She did not answer.

"But mayn't I?" he persisted.

They had reached the garden-gate. Humility seemed to hesitate. "Yes; go," she said at length; and he ran, with the *De Imitatione Christi* under his arm.

As he came within view of the church he saw a knot of men gathered about the door. They were pulling something out from the porch. He heard the noise of hammering, and Squire Moyle, at the back of the crowd, was shouting at the top of his voice:

"The church is yours, is it? I'll see about that! Pitch out the furnitcher, my billies—*that's* mine, anyway!"

Still the hammers sounded within the church.

"Don't believe in sudden convarsion, don't 'ee?

I reckon you will when you look round your church. Bishop coming to consecrate it, is he? Consecrate *my* furnitcher? I'll see you and your bishop to blazes first!"

A heap of shattered timber came flying through the porch.

"*Your* church, hey? *Your* church?"

The crowd fell back and Mr. Raymond stood in the doorway, between Bill Udy and Jim the Huntsman. Bill Udy held a brazen ewer and paten, and Jim a hammer; and Mr. Raymond had a hand on one shoulder of each.

For a moment there was silence. As Taffy came running through the lych-gate a man who had been sitting on a flat tombstone and watching, stood up and touched his arm. It was Jacky Pascoe, the Bryanite.

"Best go back," he said, "'tis a wisht poor job of it."

Taffy halted for a moment. The Squire's voice had risen to a sudden scream—he sputtered as he pointed at Mr. Raymond.

"There he is, naybours! Get behind the varmint, somebody, and stop his earth! Calls hisself a minister of God! Calls it *his* church!"

Mr. Raymond took his hands off the men's shoulders, and walked straight up to him. "Not *my* church," he said, aloud and distinctly. "God's church!"

He stretched out an arm. Taffy, running up, supposed it stretched out to strike. "Father!"

But Mr. Raymond's palm was open as he lifted it over the Squire's head. "God's church," he repeated. " In whose service, sir, I defy you. Go! or if you will, and have the courage, come and stand while I kneel amid the ruin you have done and pray God to judge between us."

He paused, with his eyes on the Squire's.

" You dare not, I see. Go, poor coward, and plan what mischief you will. Only now leave me in peace a little."

He took the boy's hand and they passed into the church together. No one followed. Hand in hand they stood before the dismantled chancel. Taffy heard the sound of shuffling feet on the walk outside, and looked up into Mr. Raymond's face.

" Father!"

" Kiss me, sonny."

The *De Imitatione Christi* slipped from Taffy's fingers and fell upon the chancel step.

So his childhood ended.

CHAPTER XIII.

THE BUILDERS.

THESE things happened on a Friday. After breakfast next morning Taffy went to fetch his books. He did so out of habit and without thinking; but his father stopped him.

"Put them away," he said. "Some day we'll go back to them, but not yet."

Instead of books Humility packed their dinner in the satchel. They reached the church and found the interior just as they had left it. Taffy was set to work to pick up and sweep together the scraps of broken glass which littered the chancel. His father examined the wreckage of the pews.

While the boy knelt at his task, his thoughts were running on the Pantomime. He had meant, last night, to recount all its wonders and the wonders of Plymouth; but somehow the words had not come. After displaying his presents he could find no more to say: and feeling his father's hand laid on his shoulder, had burst into tears and hidden his face in his mother's lap. He wanted to console them, and they were pitying *him*—why he could not say—but he knew it was so.

And now the Pantomime, Plymouth, everything,

seemed to have slipped away from him into a far past. Only his father and mother had drawn nearer and become more real. He tried to tell himself one of the old stories; but it fell into pieces like the fragments of coloured glass he was handling, and presently he began to think of the glass in his hands and let the story go.

"On Monday we'll set to work," said his father. "I dare say Joel"—this was the carpenter down at Innis village—"will lend me a few tools to start with. But the clearing up will take us all to-day."

They ate their dinner in the vestry. Taffy observed that his father said: "*We* will do this," or "*Our* best plan will be so-and-so," and spoke to him as to a grown man. On the whole, though the dusk found them still at work, this was a happy day.

"But aren't you going to lock the door?" he asked, as they were leaving.

"No," said Mr. Raymond. "We shall win, sonny; but not in that way."

On the morrow Taffy rang the bell for service as usual. To his astonishment Squire Moyle was among the first-comers. He led Honoria by the hand, entered the Tredinnis pew and shut the door with a slam. It was the only pew left unmutilated. The rest of the congregation—and curiosity made it larger than usual—had to stand; but a wife of one of the miners found a hassock and passed it to Humility, who thanked her for it with brimming eyes. Mr. Raymond said afterward that this was the first success of the campaign.

Not willing to tire his audience, he preached a very short sermon; but it was his manifesto, and all the better for being short. He took his text from Nehemiah, Chapter II., verses 19 and 20—" *But when Sanballat the Horonite, and Tobiah the servant, the Ammonite, and Geshem the Arabian, heard it, they laughed us to scorn, and despised us, and said: 'What is this thing that ye do? Will ye rebel against the King?'*

"*Then answered I them and said unto them, 'The God of Heaven, He will prosper us; therefore, we His servants will arise and build.'* "

"Fellow-parishioners," he said, "you see the state of this church. Concerning the cause of it I require none of you to judge. I enter no plea against any man. Another will judge, who said, '*Destroy this temple and in three days I will rear it up.*' But He spake of the temple of His body; which was destroyed and is raised up; and its living and irrevocable triumph I, or some other servant of God, will celebrate at this altar, Sunday by Sunday, that whosoever will may see, yes, and taste it. The state of this poor shell is but a little matter to a God whose majesty once inhabited a stable; yet the honour of this, too, shall be restored. You wonder how, perhaps. *It may be the Lord will work for us; for there is no restraint to the Lord to save by many or by few.* Go to your homes now and ponder this; and having pondered, if you will, pray for us."

As the Raymonds left the church they found Squire Moyle waiting by the porch. Honoria stood just behind him. The rest of the congregation had drawn off a little distance to watch. The Squire lifted his hat to Humility, and turned to Mr. Raymond with a sour frown.

"That means war?"

"It means that I stay," said the Vicar. "The war, if it comes, comes from your side."

"I don't think the worse of 'ee for fighting. You're not going to law then?"

Mr. Raymond smiled. "I don't doubt you've put yourself within the reach of it. But if it eases your mind to know, I am not going to law."

The Squire grunted, raised his hat again and strode off, gripping Honoria by the hand.

She had not glanced towards Taffy. Clearly she was not allowed to speak to him.

The meaning of the Vicar's sermon became plain next morning, when he walked down to the village and called on Joel Hugh, the carpenter.

"I knows what thee'rt come after," began Joel, "but 'tis no use, parson dear. Th' old fellow owns the roofs over us, and if I do a day's work for 'ee, out I goes, neck and crop."

Mr. Raymond had expected this. "It's not for work I'm come," said he; "but to hire a few tools, if you're minded to spare them."

Joel scratched his head. "Might manage that, now. But, Lord bless 'ee! thee'll never make no hand of it." He chose out saw, hammer, plane and auger, and packed them up in a carpenter's frail, with a few other tools. "Don't 'ee talk about payment, now; naybors must be nayborly. Only, you see, a man must look after his own."

Mr. Raymond climbed the hill toward the towans with the carpenter's frail slung over his shoulder. As luck would have it, near the top he met Squire Moyle descending on horseback. The Vicar nodded "Good-morning" in passing, but had not gone a dozen steps when the old man reined up and called after him.

"Hi!"

The Vicar halted.

"Whose basket is that you're carrying?" Then, getting no answer, "Wait till next Saturday night, when Joel Hugh comes to thank you. I suppose you know he rents his cottage by the week?"

"No harm shall come to him through me," said the Vicar, and retraced his steps down the hill. The Squire followed at a foot-pace, grinning as he went.

That night Mr. Raymond went back to his beloved books, but not to read; and early next morning was ready at the cross-roads for the van which plied twice a week between Innis village and Truro. He had three boxes with him—heavy boxes, as Calvin the van-driver remarked when it came to lifting them on board.

"Thee'rt not leaving us, surely?" said he.

"No."

"But however didst get these lumping boxes up the hill?"

"My son helped me."

He had modestly calculated on averaging a shilling a volume for his books; but discovered on leaving the shop at Truro that it worked out at one-and-threepence. He returned to Nannizabuloe that night with one box only—but it was packed full of tools—and a copy of Fuller's "Holy State," which at the last moment had proved too precious to be parted with—at least, just yet.

The woodwork of the old pews—painted deal for

the most part, but mixed with a few boards of good red pine and one or two of teak, relics of some forgotten shipwreck—lay stacked in the belfry and around the font under the west gallery. Mr. Raymond and Taffy spent an hour in overhauling it, chose out the boards for their first pew, and fell to work.

At the end of another hour the pair broke off and looked at each other. Taffy could not help laughing. His own knowledge of carpentry had been picked up by watching Joel Hugh at work, and just sufficed to tell him that his father was possibly the worst carpenter in the world.

"I think my fingers must be all thumbs," declared Mr. Raymond.

The puckers in his face set Taffy laughing afresh. They both laughed and fell to work again, the boy explained his notions of the difficult art of mortising. They were rudimentary, but sound as far as they went, and his father recognised this. Moreover, when the boy had a tool to handle he did it with a natural deftness, in spite of his ignorance. He was Humility's child, born with the skill-of-hand of generations of lace-workers. He did a dozen things wrongly, but he neither fumbled, nor hammered his fingers, nor wounded them with the chisel—which was Humility's husband's way.

At the end of four days of strenuous effort, they had their first pew built. It was a recognisable pew, though it leaned to one side, and the door (for it had a door) fell to with a bang if not cautiously treated. The triumph was, the seat could be sat upon without risk. Mr. Raymond and Taffy tested it with their combined weight on the Saturday evening, and went home full of its praises.

"But look at your clothes," said Humility; and they looked.

"This is serious," said Mr. Raymond. "Dear, you must make us a couple of working suits of corduroy or some such stuff: otherwise this pew-making won't pay."

Humility stood out against this for a day or two. That *her* husband and child should go dressed like common workmen! But there was no help for it, and on the Monday week Taffy went forth to work in moleskin breeches, blue guernsey, and loose white smock. As for Mr. Raymond, the only badge of his calling was his round clerical hat; and as all the miners in the neighbourhood wore hats of the same soft felt and only a trifle higher in the crown, this hardly amounted to a distinction.

Humility's eyes were full of tears as she watched them from the door that morning. But Taffy felt as proud as Punch. A little before noon he carried out a board that required sawing, and rested it on a flat tombstone where, with his knee upon it, he could get a good purchase. He was sawing away when he heard a dog barking, and looked up to see Honoria coming along the path with George's terrier frisking at her heels.

She halted outside the lych-gate, and Taffy, vain of his new clothes, drew himself up and nodded.

"Good-morning," said Honoria. "I'm not allowed to speak to you and I'm not going to, after this." She swooped on the puppy and held him.

"See what George brought home from Plymouth for me. Isn't he a beauty?"

Held so, by the scruff of his neck, he was not a beauty. Taffy had it on the tip of his tongue to tell her about the collar. He wished he had brought it.

"I wonder," she went on pensively, "your mother had the heart to dress you out in that style. But I suppose now you'll be growing up into quite a common boy."

Taffy decided to say nothing about the collar. "I like the clothes," he declared defiantly.

"Then you can't have the common instincts of a gentleman. Well, good-bye! Grandfather has salvation all right this time; he said he'd put the stick about me if I dared to speak to you."

"He won't know."

"Won't know? Why I shall tell him, of course, when I get back."

"But—but he *mustn't* beat you!"

She eyed him for a moment or two in silence. "Mustn't he? I advise you to go and tell him." She walked away slowly, whistling; but by-and-by broke into a run and was gone, the puppy scampering behind her.

As the days grew longer and the weather milder, Taffy and his father worked late into the evenings; sometimes, if the job needed to be finished, by the light of a couple of candles.

One evening, about nine o'clock, the boy as he planed a bench paused suddenly. "What's that?"

They listened. The door stood open, and after a second or two they heard the sound of feet tiptoeing away up the path outside.

"Spies, perhaps," said his father. "If so, let them go in peace."

But he was not altogether easy. There had been strange doings up at the Bryanite Chapel of late. He still visited a few of his parishioners regularly—hill farmers and their wives for the most part, who did not happen to be tenants of Squire Moyle, and on whom his visits therefore could bring no harm; and one or two had hinted of strange doings, now that the Bryanites had hold of the old Squire. They themselves had been up—just to look; they confessed it shamefacedly, much in the style of men who have been drinking overnight. Without pressing them and showing himself curious, the Vicar could get at no particulars. But as the summer grew he felt a moral sultriness, as it were, growing with it. The people were off their balance, restless; and behind their behaviour he had a sense, now of something electric, menacing, now of a hand holding it in check. Slowly in those days the conviction deepened in him that he was an alien on this coast, that between him and the hearts of the race he ministered to there stretched an impalpable, impenetrable veil. And all this while the faces he passed on the road, though shy, were kindlier than they had been in the days before his self-confidence left him—it seemed not so long ago.

On a Saturday night early in May, the footsteps were heard again, and this time in the porch itself. While Mr. Raymond and Taffy listened the big latch went up with a creak, and a dark figure slipped into the church.

" Who is there ? " challenged Mr. Raymond from the chancel where he stood peering out of the small circle of light.

" A friend. Pass, friend, and all's well ! " answered a squeaky voice. " Bless you, I've sarved in the militia before now."

It was Jacky Pascoe, with his coat-collar turned up high about his ears.

" What do you want ? " Mr. Raymond demanded sharply.

" A job."

" We can pay for no work here."

" Wait till thee'rt asked, Parson, dear. I've been spying in upon 'ee these nights past. Pretty carpenters you be ! T'other night, as I was a-peeping, the Lord said to me, ' Arise, go, and for goodness' sake show them chaps how to do it fitty.' ' Dear Lord,' I said, ' Thou knowest I be a Bryanite.' The Lord said to me, ' None of your back answers ! Go and do as I tell 'ee.' So here I be."

Mr. Raymond hesitated. " Squire Moyle is your friend, I hear, and the friend of your chapel. What will he say if he discovers that you are helping us ? "

Jacky scratched his head. " I reckon the Lord must have thought o' that, too. Suppose you put me to work in the vestry ? There's only one window looks in on the vestry : you can block that up with a curtain, and there I'll be like a weevil in a biscuit."

When this screen was fixed, the little Bryanite looked round and rubbed his hands. " Now I'll tell 'ee a prabble," he said—" a prabble about this candle

I'm holding. When God Almighty said '*Let there be light,*' He gave every man a candle—to some folks, same as you, long sixes perhaps and best wax; to others, a farthing dip. But they all helps to light up; and the beauty of it is, Parson"—he laid a hand on Mr. Raymond's cuff—"there isn't one of 'em burns a ha'porth the worse for every candle that's lit from en. Now sit down, you and the boy, and I'll larn 'ee how to join a board."

CHAPTER XIV.

VOICES FROM THE SEA.

BEFORE winter and the long nights came around again, Taffy had become quite a clever carpenter. From the first his quickness fairly astonished the Bryanite, who at the best was but a journeyman and soon owned himself beaten.

" I doubt," said he, " if you'll ever make so good a man as your father ; but you can't help making a better workman." He added, with his eyes on the boy's face, " There's one thing in which you might copy en. He hasn't much of a gift : *but he lays it 'pon the altar.*"

By this time Taffy had resumed his lessons. Every day he carried a book or two in his satchel with his dinner, and read or translated aloud while his father worked. Two hours were allowed for this in the morning, and again two in the afternoon. Sometimes a day would be set apart during which they talked nothing but Latin. Difficulties in the text of their authors they postponed until the evening, and worked them out at home, after supper, with the help of grammar and dictionary.

The boy was not unhappy, on the whole ; though for weeks together he longed for sight of George Vyell, who seemed to have vanished into space, or into that limbo where his childhood lay like a toy in a lumber room. Taffy seldom turned the key of that room. The stories he imagined now were not about fairies or heroes, but about himself. He wanted to be a great man and astonish the world. Just how the world was to be astonished he did not clearly see; but the triumph, in whatever shape it came, was to involve a new gown for his mother, and for his father a whole library of books.

Mr. Raymond never went back to his books now, except to help Taffy. The Commentary on the Epistle to the Hebrews was laid aside. "Some day!" he told Humility. The Sunday congregation had dwindled to a very few, mostly farm people; Squire Moyle having threatened to expel any tenant of his who dared to set foot within the church.

In the autumn two things happened which set Taffy wondering.

During the first three years at Nannizabuloe, old Mrs. Venning had regularly been carried downstairs to dine with the family. The sea-air (she said) had put new life into her. But now she seldom moved from her room, and Taffy seldom saw her except at night, when—after the old childish custom—he knocked at her door to wish her pleasant dreams and pull up the weights of the tall clock which stood by her bed's head.

One night he asked carelessly, "What do you want with the clock? Lying here you don't need to know the time; and its ticking must keep you awake."

"So it does, child; but bless you, I like it."

"Like being kept awake?"

"Dear, yes! I have enough of rest and quiet up here. You mind the litany I used to say over to you?—Parson Kempthorne taught it to us girls when I was in service with him; 'twas made up, he said, by another old Devonshire parson, years and years ago—

"'When I lie within my bed
Sick in heart and sick in head,
And with doubts discomforted,
Sweet Spirit, comfort me!

When the house do sigh and weep—'

That's it. You wouldn't think how quiet it is up here all day. But at night, when you're in bed and sleeping, all the house begins to talk; little creakings of furniture, you know, and the wind in the chimney and sometimes the rain in the gutter, running—it's all talk to me. Mostly it's quite sociable, too; but sometimes, in rainy weather, the tune changes and then it's like some poor soul in bed and sobbing to itself. That's when the verse comes in:

"'When the house do sigh and weep
And the world is drowned in sleep,
Yet my eyes the watch do keep,
Sweet Spirit, comfort me!'

And then the clock's ticking is a wonderful comfort. *Tick-tack, tick-tack!* and I think of you stretched asleep and happy and growing up to be a man, and the minutes running and trickling away to my deliverance——"

"Granny!"

"My dear, I'm as well off as most; but that

isn't saying I shan't be glad to go and take the pain in my joints to a better land. Before we came here, in militia-time, I used to lie and listen for the buglers, but now I've only the clock. No more bugles for me, I reckon, till I hear them blown across Jordan."

Taffy remembered how he too had lain and listened to the bugles; and with that he saw his childhood, as it were a small round globe set within a far larger one and wrapped around with other folks' thoughts. He kissed his grandmother and went away wondering; and as he lay down that night it still seemed wonderful to him that she should have heard those bugles, and more wonderful, that night after night for years she should have been thinking of him while he slept, and he never have guessed it.

One morning, some three weeks later, he and his father were putting on their oil-skins before starting to work—for it had been blowing hard through the night and the gale was breaking up in floods of rain—when they heard a voice hallooing in the distance. Humility heard it too and turned swiftly to Taffy. "Run upstairs, dear. I expect it's someone sent from Tresedder farm; and if so, he'll want to see your father alone."

Mr. Raymond frowned. "No," he said; "the time is past for that."

A fist hammered on the door. Mr. Raymond threw it open.

"Brigantine—on the sands! Half a mile this side of the light-house!" Taffy saw across his father's shoulder a gleam of yellow oilskins and a flapping sou'-wester hat. The panting voice belonged to Sam Udy—son of old Bill Udy—a labourer at Tresedder.

"I'll go at once," said Mr. Raymond. "Run you for the coast-guard!"

The oilskins went by the window; the side gate clashed to.

"Is it a wreck?" cried Taffy. "May I go with you?"

"Yes, there may be a message to run with."

From the edge of the towans, where the ground dipped steeply to the long beach, they saw the wreck, about a mile up the coast, and as well as they could judge a hundred or a hundred and twenty yards out. She lay almost on her beam ends, with the waves sweeping high across her starboard quarter and never less than six ranks of ugly breakers between her and dry land. A score of watchers—in the distance they looked like emmets—were gathered by the edge of the surf. But the coast-guard had not arrived yet.

"The tide is ebbing, and the rocket may reach. Can you see anyone aboard?"

Taffy spied through his hands, but could see no one. His father set off running, and he followed, half-blinded by the rain, now floundering in loose sand, now tripping in a rabbit hole. They had covered three-fourths of the distance when Mr. Raymond pulled up and waved his hat as the coast-guard carriage swept into view over a ridge to the right and came plunging across the main valley of the towans. It passed them close—the horses fetlock-deep in sand, with heads down and heaving, smoking shoulders; the coast-guardsmen with keen strong faces like heroes'—and the boy longed to copy his father and send a cheer after them as they went galloping by. But something rose in his throat.

He ran after the carriage, and reached the shore just as the first rocket shot singing out towards the wreck. By this time at least a hundred miners had gathered, and between their legs he caught a glimpse of two figures stretched at length on the wet sand. He had never looked on a dead body before. The faces of these were hidden by the crowd; and he hung about the fringe of it dreading, and yet courting, a sight of them.

The first rocket was swept down to leeward of the wreck. The chief officer judged his second beautifully, and the line fell clean across the vessel and all but amidships. A figure started up from the lee of the deckhouse, and springing into the main shrouds, grasped it and made it fast. The beach being too low for them to work the cradle clear above the breakers, the coast-guardsmen carried the shore end of the line up the shelving cliff and fixed it. Within ten minutes the cradle was run out, and within twenty the first man came swinging shoreward.

Four men were brought ashore alive, the captain last. The rest of the crew of six lay on the sands with Mr. Raymond kneeling beside them. He had covered their faces, and now gave the order to lift them into the carriage. Taffy noticed that he was obeyed without demur or question. And there flashed on his memory a grey morning, not unlike this one, when he had missed his father at breakfast: "He had been called away suddenly," Humility explained, "and there would be no lessons that day," and she kept the boy indoors all the morning and busy with a netting-stitch he had been bothering her to teach him.

"Father," he asked as they followed the cart, "does this often happen?"

"Your mother hasn't thought it well for you to see these sights."

"Then it *has* happened, often?"

"I have buried seventeen," said Mr. Raymond.

That afternoon he showed Taffy their graves. "I know the names of all but two. The bodies have marks about them—tattooed, you know—and that helps. And I write to their relatives or friends and restore whatever small property may be found on them. I have often wished to put up some gravestone, or a wooden cross at least, with their names."

He went to his chest in the vestry and took out a book—a cheap account book, ruled for figures. Taffy turned over the pages.

Nov. 3rd, 187–. Brig "James and Maria": J. D., fair-haired, height 5 ft. 8 in., marked on chest with initials and cross swords, tattooed, also anchor and coil of rope on right fore-arm: large brown mole on right shoulder-blade. Striped flannel drawers: otherwise naked: no property of any kind.

Ditto. Grown man, age 40 or thereabouts: dark; iron grey beard: lovers' knot tattooed on right fore-arm, with initials R. L., E. W., in the loops: clad in flannel shirt, guernsey, trousers (blue sea-cloth), socks (heather-mixture), all unmarked. Silver chain in pocket, with Freemason's token: a half-crown, a florin, and fourpence——and so on. On the opposite page were entered the full names and details afterwards discovered, with notes of the Vicar's correspondence, and position of the grave.

"They ought to have gravestones," said Mr. Raymond. "But as it is, I can only get about thirty shillings for the funeral from the county rate. The balance has come out of my pocket—from two to three pounds for each. From the beginning the Squire refused to help to bury sailors. He took the ground that it wasn't a local claim."

"Hullo!" said Taffy, for as he turned the leaves his eye fell on this entry:—

Jan 30th, 187–. S.S. "Rifleman" (all hands). Cargo, China clay: W. P., age about eighteen, fair skin, reddish hair, short and curled, height 5 ft. 10¾ in. Initials tattooed on chest under a three-masted ship and semicircle of seven stars; clad in flannel singlet and trousers (cloth): singlet marked with same initials in red cotton: pockets empty——

"But he was in the Navy!" cried Taffy, with his finger on the entry.

"Which one? Yes, he was in the Navy. You'll see it on the opposite page. He deserted, poor boy, in Cork Harbour, and shipped on board a tramp steamer as donkey-man. She loaded at Fowey and was wrecked on the voyage back. William Pellow he was called: his mother lives but ten miles up the coast: she never heard of it until six weeks after."

"But we—I, I mean—knew him. He was one of the sailor boys on Joby's van. You remember their helping us with the luggage at *Indian Queens'?* He showed me his tattoo marks that day."

And again he saw his childhood as it were set about with an enchanted hedge, across which many voices would have called to him, and some from near, but all had hung muted and arrested.

The inquest on the two drowned sailors was held next day at the *Fifteen Balls,* down in Innis village. Later in the afternoon, the four survivors walked up to the church, headed by the Captain.

"We've been hearing," said the Captain, "of your difficulties, sir: likewise your kindness to other poor seafaring chaps. We'd have liked to make ye a small offering for your church, but sixteen shillings is all we can raise between us. So we come to say that if you can put us on to a job, why we're staying over the funeral, and a day's work or more after that won't hurt us one way or another."

Mr. Raymond led them to the chancel and pointed out a new beam, on which he and Jacky Pascoe had been working a week past, and over which they had been cudgelling their brains how to get it lifted and fixed in place.

"I can send to one of the miners and borrow a couple of ladders."

"Ladders? Lord love ye, sir, and begging your pardon, we don't want ladders. With a sling, Bill, hey?—and a couple of tackles. You leave it to we, sir."

He went off to turn over the gear salved from his vessel, and early next forenoon had the apparatus rigged up and ready. He was obliged to leave it at this point, having been summoned across to Falmouth to report to his agents. His last words, before starting were addressed to his crew. "I reckon you can fix it now, boys. There's only one thing more, and don't you forget it: Hats off; and any man that wants to spit must go outside."

That afternoon Taffy learnt for the first time what could be done with a few ropes and pulleys. The seamen seemed to spin ropes out of themselves like spiders. By three o'clock the beam was hoisted and fixed; and they broke off their work to attend their shipmates' funeral. After the funeral they fell to again, though more silently, and before nightfall the beam shone with a new coat of varnish.

They left early next morning, after a good deal of handshaking, and Taffy looked after them wistfully as they turned to wave their caps and trudged away over the rise towards the cross-roads. Away to the left in the wintry sunshine a speck of scarlet caught his eye against the blue-grey of the towans. He watched it as it came slowly towards him, and his heart leapt—yet not quite as he had expected it to leap.

For it was George Vyell. George had lately been promoted to "pink" and made a gallant figure on his strapping grey hunter. For the first time Taffy felt ashamed of his working-suit, and would have slipped back to the church. But George had seen him, and pulled up.

"Hullo!" said he.

"Hullo!" said Taffy; and, absurdly enough, could find no more to say.

"How are you getting on?"

" Oh, I'm all right." There was another pause. " How's Honoria ? "

" Oh, she's all right. I'm riding over there now : they meet at Tredinnis to-day." He tapped his boot with his hunting crop.

" Don't you have any lessons now ? " asked Taffy, after a while.

" Dear me, yes ; I've got a tutor. He's no good at it. But what made you ask ? "

Really Taffy could not tell. He had asked merely for the sake of saying something. George pulled out a gold watch.

" I must be getting on. Well, good-bye ! "

" Good-bye ! "

And that was all.

CHAPTER XV.

TAFFY'S APPRENTICESHIP.

THEY could manage the carpentering now. And Jacky Pascoe, who, in addition to his other trades, was something of a glazier, had taken the damaged east window in hand. For six months it had remained boarded up, darkening the chancel. Mr. Raymond removed the boards and fixed them up again on the outside, and the Bryanite worked behind them night after night. He could only be spied upon through two lancet windows at the west end of the church, and these they curtained.

But what continually bothered them was their ignorance of iron-work. Staples, rivets, hinges were for ever wanted. At length, one evening, toward the end of March, the Bryanite laid down his tools.

"Tell 'ee what 'tis, Parson. You must send the boy to someone that'll teach en smithy-work. There's no sense in this cold hammering."

"Wheelwright Hocken holds his shop and cottage from the Squire."

"Why not put the boy to Mendarva the Smith, over to Benny Beneath? He's a first-rate workman."

"That is more than six miles away."

"No matter for that. There's Joll's Farm close

by ; Farmer Joll would board and lodge en for nine shillings a week, and glad of the chance ; and he could come home for Sundays."

Mr. Raymond, as soon as he reached home, sat down and wrote a letter to Mendarva the Smith and another to Farmer Joll. Within a week the bargains were struck, and it was settled that Taffy should go at once.

" I may be calling before long, to look you up," said the Bryanite, " but mind you do no more than nod when you see me."

Joll's Farm lay somewhere near Carwithiel, across the moor where Taffy had gone fishing with George and Honoria. On the Monday morning when he stepped through the white front gate, with his bag on his shoulder, and paused for a good look at the building, it seemed to him a very comfortable farm-stead, and vastly superior to the tumble-down farms around Nannizabuloe. The flagged path, which led up to the front door between great bunches of purple honesty, was swept as clean as a dairy.

A dark-haired maid opened the door and led him to the great kitchen at the back. Hams wrapped in paper hung from the rafters, and strings of onions. The pans over the fire-place were bright as mirrors, and through the open window he heard the voices of children at play as well as the clacking of poultry in the town-place.

" I'll go and tell the mistress," said the maid ; but she paused at the door. " I suppose you don't remember me, now ? "

" No," said Taffy truthfully.

" My name's Lizzie Pezzack. You was with the

young lady, that day, when she bought my doll. I mind you quite well. But I put my hair up last Easter, and that makes a difference."

"Why, you were only a child!"

"I was seventeen last week. And—I say, do you know the Bryanite, over to St. Ann's—Preacher Jackey Pascoe?"

He nodded, remembering the caution given him.

"I got salvation off him. Master and mis'ess they've got salvation too; but they take it very quiet. They're very fond of one another; if you please one, you'll please 'em both. They let me walk over to prayer-meetin' once a week. But I don't go by Mendarva's shop—that's where you work—though 'tis the shortest way; because there's a woman buried in the road there, with a stake through her, and I'm a terrible coward for ghosts."

She paused as if expecting him to say something; but Taffy was staring at a "neck" of corn, elaborately plaited, which hung above the mantel-shelf. And just then Mrs. Joll entered the kitchen.

Taffy—without any reason—had expected to see a middle-aged housewife. But Mrs. Joll was hardly over thirty; a shapely woman, with a plain, pleasant face and auburn hair, the wealth of which she concealed by wearing it drawn straight back from the forehead and plaited in the severest coil behind. She shook hands.

"You'll like a drink of milk before I show you your room?"

Taffy was grateful for the milk. While he drank it, the voices of the children outside rose suddenly to shouts of laughter.

"That will be their father come home," said Mrs. Joll, and going to the side door called to him. "John, put the children down! Mr. Raymond's son is here."

Mr. Joll, who had been galloping round the farm-yard with a small girl of three on his back, and a boy of six tugging at his coat-tails, pulled up, and wiped his good-natured face.

"Kindly welcome," said he, coming forward and shaking hands, while the two children stared at Taffy.

After a minute the boy said, "My name's Bob. Come and play horses, too."

Farmer Joll looked at Taffy with a shyness that was comic. "Shall we?"

"Mr. Raymond will be tired enough already," his wife suggested.

"Not a bit," declared Taffy; and hoisting Bob on his back, he set off furiously prancing after the farmer.

By dinner-time he and the family were fast friends, and after dinner the farmer took him off to be introduced to Mendarva the Smith.

Mendarva's forge stood on a triangle of turf beside the high-road, where a cart-track branched off to descend to Joll's Farm in the valley. And Mendarva was a dark giant of a man with a beard like those you see on the statues of Nineveh. On Sundays he parted his beard carefully and tied the ends with little bows of scarlet ribbon; but on week days it curled at will over his mighty chest. He had one assistant whom he called "the Dane"; a red-haired youth as tall as himself and straighter from the waist down.

Mendarva's knees had come together with years of poising and swinging his great hammer.

"He's little, but he'll grow," said he, after eyeing Taffy up and down. "Dane, come fore and tell me if we'll make a workman of en."

The Dane stepped forward and passed his hands over the boy's shoulders and down his ribs. "He's slight, but he'll fill out. Good pair o' shoulders. Give's hold o' your hand, my son."

Taffy obeyed ; not very well liking to be handled thus like a prize bullock.

"Hand like a lady's. Tidy wrist, though. He'll do, master."

So Taffy was passed, given a leathern apron, and set to his first task of keeping the forge-fire raked and the bellows going, while the hammers took up the music he was to listen to for a year to come.

This music kept the day merry ; and beyond the window along the bright high-road there was usually something worth seeing—farm-carts, jowters' carts, the doctor and his gig, pedlars and Johnny-fortnights, the miller's waggons from the valley-bottom below Joll's Farm, and on Tuesdays and Fridays the market-van going and returning. Mendarva knew or speculated upon everybody, and with half the passers-by broke off work and gave the time of day, leaning on his hammer. But down at the farm all was strangely quiet, in spite of the children's voices ; and at night the quietness positively kept him awake, listening to the pur-r of the pigeons in their cote against the house-wall, thinking of his grandmother awake at home and harkening to the *tick-tack* of her tall clock. Often when he awoke to the early summer daybreak and saw through his attic-window the grey shadows of the sheep still and long on the slope above the farmstead, his ear was wanting something, asking for something ; for the murmur of the sea never reached this inland valley. And he would lie and long for the chirruping of the two children in the next room and the drawing of bolts and clatter of milk-pails below stairs.

He had plenty to eat, and that plenty simple and good, and clean linen to sleep between. The kitchen was his except on Saturday nights, when Mrs. Joll and Lizzie tubbed the children there, and then he would carry his books off to the best parlour or stroll around the farm with Mr. Joll and discuss the stock. There were no loose rails in Mr. Joll's gates, no farm implements lying out in the weather to rust. Mr. Joll worked early and late, and his shoulders had a tell-tale stoop—for he was a man in the prime of life, perhaps some five years older than his wife.

One Saturday evening he unburdened his heart to Taffy. It happened at the end of the hay-harvest, and the two were leaning over a gate discussing the yet unthatched rick.

" What I say is," declared the farmer quite inconsequently, " a man must be able to lay his troubles 'pon the Lord. I don't mean his work, but his troubles ; and go home and shut the door and be happy with his wife and children. Now, I tell you that for months—iss, years—after Bob was born I kept plaguing myself in the fields, thinking that some harm might have happened to the child. Why, I used to make an excuse and creep home, and then if I see'd a blind pulled down you wouldn't think how my heart'd go thump; and I'd stand wi' my head on the door-hapse an' say, 'If so be the Lord have took'n, I must go and comfort Susan—not my will, but Thine, Lord—but, Lord, don't 'ee be cruel this time!' And then find the cheeld right as ninepence and the blind only pulled down to keep the sun off the carpet. After a while my wife guessed what was wrong—I used to make up such poor twiddling pretences. She said, 'Look here, the Lord and me'll see after Bob; and if you can't keep to your own work without poking your nose into ours, then I married for worse and not for better.' Then it came upon me that by leaving the Lord to look after my job I'd been treating Him like a farm-labourer. It's the things you can't help He looks after—not the work."

A few evenings later there came a knock at the door, and Lizzie, who went to open it, returned with the Bryanite skipping behind her.

"Blessings be upon this here house!" he cried, cutting a sort of double shuffle on the threshold. He shook hands with the farmer and his wife, and nodded toward Taffy. "So you've got Parson Raymond's boy here!"

"Yes," said Mrs. Joll; and turned to Taffy. "He've come to pray a bit: perhaps you would rather be in the parlour?"

Taffy asked to be allowed to stay; and presently Mr. Pascoe had them all down on their knees. He began by invoking God's protection on the household; but his prayer soon ceased to be a prayer. It broke into ejaculations of praise—"Friends, I be too happy to ask for anything—Glory, glory! The blood! The precious blood! O deliverance! O streams of redemption running!" The farmer and his wife began to chime in—"Hallelujah!" "Glory!" and Lizzie Pezzack to sob. Taffy, kneeling before a kitchen chair, peeped between his palms, and saw her shoulders heaving.

The Bryanite sprang to his feet, overturning the settle with a crash. "Tid'n no use. I must skip! Who'll dance wi' me?"

He held out his hands to Mrs. Joll. She took them, and skipped once shamefacedly. Lizzie, with flaming cheeks, pushed her aside. "Leave me try, mis'ess; I shall die if I don't." She caught the preacher's hands, and the two leapt about the kitchen. "I can dance higher than mis'ess!" Farmer Joll looked on with a dazed face. "Hallelujah!" "Amen!" he said at intervals, quite mechanically. The pair stood under the bacon rack and began to whirl like dervishes—hands clasped, toes together, bodies leaning back and almost rigid. They whirled until Taffy's brain whirled with them.

With a louder sob Lizzie let go her hold and tottered back into a chair, laughing hysterically. The Bryanite leaned against the table, panting.

There was a long pause. Mrs. Joll took a napkin from the dresser and fell to fanning the girl's face, then to slapping it briskly. "Get up and lay the table," she commanded; "the preacher'll stay to supper."

"Thank 'ee, ma'am, I don't care if I do," said he; and ten minutes later they were all seated at supper and discussing the fall in wheat in the most matter-of-fact voices. Only their faces twitched now and again.

"I hear you had the preacher down to Joll's last night," said Mendarva the Smith. "What'st think of en?"

"I can't make him out," was Taffy's colourless but truthful answer.

"He's a bellows of a man. I do hear he's heating up th' old Squire Moyle's soul to knack an angel out of en. He'll find that a job and a half. You mark my words, there'll be Dover over in your parish one o' these days."

During work-hours Mendarva bestowed most of his talk on Taffy. The Dane seldom opened his lips except to join in the anvil chorus—

"Here goes one—
Sing, sing, Johnny!
Here goes two—
Sing, Johnny, sing!
Whack'n till he's red,
Whack'n till he's dead,
And whop! goes the widow with
A brand new ring!"

and when the boy took a hammer and joined in he fell silent. Taffy soon observed that a singular friendship knit these two men, who were both unmarried. Mendarva had been a famous wrestler in his day, and his great ambition now was to train the other to win the County belt. Often after work the pair would try a hitch together on the triangle of turf, with Taffy for stickler, Mendarva illustrating and explaining, the Dane nodding seriously whenever he understood, but never answering a word. Afterwards the boy recalled these bouts very vividly —the clear evening sky, the shoulders of the two big men shining against the level sun as they gripped and swayed, their long shadows on the grass under which (as he remembered) the poor self-murdered woman lay buried.

He thought of her at night, sometimes, as he worked alone at the forge; for Mendarva allowed him the keys and use of the smithy overtime, in consideration of a small payment for coal. And then he blew his fire and hammered, with a couple of candles on the bench and a Homer between them; and beat the long hexameters into his memory. The incongruity of it never struck him. He was going to be a great man, and somehow this was going to be the way. These scraps of iron—these tools of his forging—were to grow into the arms and shield of Achilles. In its own time would come the magic moment, the shield find its true circumference and swing to the balance of his arm, proof and complete.

ἐν δ᾽ ἐτἴθει ποταμοῖο μέγα σθένος Ὠκεανοῖο
ἄντυγα πὰδ πυμάτην σάκεος πύκα ποιητοῖ . . .

CHAPTER XVI.

LIZZIE AND HONORIA.

His apprenticeship lasted a year and six months, and all this while he lived with the Jolls, walking home every Sunday morning and returning every Sunday night, rain or shine. He carried his deftness of hand into his new trade, and it was Mendarva who begged and obtained an extension of the time agreed on. " Rather than lose the boy I'll tache en for love." So Taffy stayed on for another six months.

He was now in his seventeenth year—a boy no longer. One evening, as he blew up his smithy fire, the glow of it fell on the form of a woman standing just outside the window and watching him. He had no silly fears of ghosts: but the thought of the buried woman flashed across his mind and he dropped his pincers with a clatter.

" 'Tis only me," said the woman. " You needn't to be afeard." And he saw it was the girl Lizzie.

She stepped inside the forge and seated herself on the Dane's anvil.

" I was walking back from prayer-meeting," she said. " 'Tis nigher this way, but I don't ever dare to come. Might, I dessay, if I'd somebody to see me home."

" Ghosts ? " asked Taffy, picking up the pincers and thrusting the bar back into the hot cinders.

"I dunno: I gets frightened o' the very shadows on the road sometimes. I suppose, now, you never walks out that way?"

"Which way?"

"Why, towards where your home is. That's the way I comes."

"No, I don't." Taffy blew at the cinders until they glowed again. "It's only on Sundays I go over there."

"That's a pity," said Lizzie candidly. "I'm kept in, Sunday evenings, to look after the children while farmer and mis'ess goes to Chapel. That's the agreement I came 'pon."

Taffy nodded.

"It would be nice now, wouldn't it——" She broke off, clasping her knees and staring at the blaze.

"What would be nice?"

Lizzie laughed confusedly. "Aw, you make me say 't. I can't abear any of the young men up to the Chapel. If me and you——"

Taffy ceased blowing. The fire died down, and in the darkness he could hear her breathing hard.

"They're so rough," she went on, "and t'other night I met young Squire Vyell riding along the road, and he stopped me and wanted to kiss me."

"George Vyell? Surely he didn't?" Taffy blew up the fire again.

"Iss he did. I don't see why not, neither."

"Why he shouldn't kiss you?"

"Why he shouldn't want to."

Taffy frowned, carried the white hot bar to his anvil, and began to hammer. He despised girls, as a rule, and their ways. Decidedly Lizzie annoyed him; and yet as he worked he could not help glancing at her now and then, as she sat and watched him. By-and-by he saw that her eyes were full of tears.

"What's the matter?" he asked abruptly.

"I—I can't walk home alone. I'm afeard!"

He tossed his hammer aside, raked out the fire, and reached his coat off its peg. As he swung round in the darkness to put it on, he blundered against Lizzie or Lizzie blundered against him. She clutched at him nervously.

"Clumsy! can't you see the doorway?"

She passed out, and he followed and locked the door. As they crossed the turf to the high-road, she slipped her arm into his. "I feel safe, that way. Let it stay, co!" After a few paces, she added, "You're different from the others—that's why I like you."

"How?"

"I dunno; but you *be* diff'rent. You don't think about girls, for one thing."

Taffy did not answer. He felt angry, ashamed, uncomfortable. He did not turn once to look at her face, dimly visible by the light of the young moon—the hunter's moon—now sinking over the slope of the hill. Thick dust—too thick for the heavy dew to lay—covered the cart-track down to the farm, muffling their footsteps. Lizzie paused by the gate.

"Best go in separate," she said; paused again and whispered, "You may if you like."

"May do what?"

"What—what young Squire Vyell wanted."

They were face to face now. She held up her lips, and as she did so they parted in an amorous little laugh. The moonlight was on her face. Taffy bent swiftly and kissed her.

"Oh, you hurt!" With another little laugh she slipped up the garden path and into the house.

Ten minutes later Taffy followed, hating himself.

For the next fortnight he avoided her; and then, late one evening she came again. He was prepared for this, and had locked the door of the smithy and let down the shutter while he worked. She tapped upon the outside of the shutter with her knuckles.

"Let me in!"

"Can't you leave me alone?" he answered pettishly. "I want to work, and you interrupt."

"I don't want no love-making—I don't indeed. I'll sit quiet as a mouse. But I'm afeard, out here."

"Nonsense!"

"I'm afeard o' the ghost. There's something comin'—let me in, co-o!"

Taffy unlocked the door and held it half opened while he listened.

"Yes, there's somebody coming, on horseback. Now, look here—it's no ghost, and I can't have you about here with people passing. I—I don't want you here at all; so make haste and slip away home, that's a good girl."

Lizzie glided like a shadow into the dark lane as the trample of hoofs drew close, and the rider pulled up beside the door.

"You're working late, I see. Is it too late to make a shoe for Aide-de-camp here?"

It was Honoria. She dismounted and stood at the doorway, holding her horse's bridle.

"No," said Taffy: "that is, if you don't mind the waiting."

With his leathern apron he wiped the Dane's anvil for a seat, while she hitched up Aide-de-camp and stepped into the glow of the forge-fire.

"The hounds took us three miles beyond Carwithiel: and there, just as they lost, Aide-de-camp cast his off-hind shoe. I didn't find it out at first, and now I've had to walk him all the way back. Are you alone here?"

"Yes."

"Who was that I saw leaving as I came up?"

"You saw someone?"

"Yes." She nodded, looking him straight in the face. "It looked like a woman. Who was she?"

"That was Lizzie Pezzack, the girl who sold you her doll, once. She's a servant down at the farm where I lodge."

Honoria said no more for the moment, but seated herself on the Dane's anvil, while Taffy chose a bar of iron and stepped out to examine Aide-de-camp's hoof. He returned and in silence began to blow up the fire.

"I dare say you were astonished to see me," she remarked at length.

"Yes."

"I'm still forbidden to speak to you. The last time I did it, grandfather beat me."

"The old brute!" Taffy nipped the hot iron savagely in his pincers.

"I wonder if he'll do it again. Somehow I don't think he will."

Taffy looked at her. She had drawn herself up, and was smiling. In her close-fitting habit she seemed very slight, yet tall, and a woman grown. He took the bar to the anvil and began to beat it flat. His teeth were shut, and with every blow he said to himself "Brute!"

"That's beautiful," Honoria went on. "I stopped Mendarva the other day, and he told me wonders about you. He says he tried you with a hard-boiled egg, and you swung the hammer and chipped the shell all round without bruising the white a bit. Is that true?"

Taffy nodded.

"And your learning—the Latin and Greek, I mean; do you still go on with it?"

He nodded again, towards a volume of Euripides that lay open on the workbench.

"And the stories you used to tell George and me; do you go on telling them to yourself?"

He was obliged to confess that he never did. She sat for a while watching the sparks as they flew. Then she said, "I should like to hear you tell one again. That one about Aslog and Orm, who ran away by night across the ice-fields and took a boat and came to an island with a house on it, and found a table spread and the fire lit, but no inhabitants anywhere—You remember? It began 'Once upon a time, not far from the city of Drontheim, there lived a rich man——'"

Taffy considered a moment and began "Once upon a time, not far from the city of Drontheim——"

He paused, eyed the horse-shoe cooling between the pincers, and shook his head. It was no use. Apollo had been too long in service with Admetus, and the tale would not come.

"At any rate," Honoria persisted, "you can tell me something out of your books: something you have just been reading."

So he began to tell her the story of Ion, and managed well enough in describing the boy and how he ministered before the shrine at Delphi, sweeping the temple and scaring the birds away from the precincts: but when he came to the plot of the play and, looking up, caught Honoria's eyes, it suddenly occurred to him that all the rest of the story was a sensual one, and he could not tell it to her. He blushed, faltered, and finally broke down.

"But it was beautiful," said she, "so far as it went: and it's just what I wanted. I shall remember that boy Ion now, whenever I think of you helping your father in the church at home. If the rest of the story is not nice, I don't want to hear it."

How had she guessed? It was delicious, at any rate, to know that she thought of him; and Taffy felt how delicious it was, while he fitted and hammered the shoe on Aide-de-camp's hoof, she standing by with a candle in either hand, the flame scarcely quivering in the windless night.

When all was done, she raised a foot for him to give her a mount. "Good-night!" she called, shaking the reins. Half a minute later Taffy stood by the door of the forge, listening to the echoes of Aide-de-camp's canter, and the palm of his hand tingled where her foot had rested.

CHAPTER XVII.

THE SQUIRE'S WEIRD.

HE took leave of Mendarva and the Jolls just before Christmas. The smith was unaffectedly sorry to lose him. "But," said he, "the Dane will be entered for the championship next summer, so I s'pose I must look forward to that."

Every one in the Joll household gave him a small present on his leaving. Lizzie's was a New Testament, with her name on the flyleaf, and under it, "Converted April 19, 187—." Taffy did not want the gift, but took it rather than hurt her feelings.

Farmer Joll said, "Well, wish 'ee well! Been pretty comfiable, I hope. Now you'm goin', I don't mind telling 'ee I didn't like your coming a bit. But now 'tis wunnerful to me you've been wi' us less than two year'; we've made such friends."

At home Taffy bought a small forge and set it up in the church at the west end of the north aisle. Mr. Raymond, under his direction, had been purchasing the necessary tools for some months past, and now the main expense was the cost of coal, which pinched them a little. But they managed to keep the fire alight, and the work went forward briskly. Save that he still forbade the parish to lend them the least help, the old Squire had ceased to interfere.

Mr. Raymond's hair was greyer, and Taffy might have observed—but did not—how readily towards the close of a day's laborious carpentry he would drop work and turn to Dindorf's *Poetæ Scenici Græci*, through which they were reading their way. On Sundays the congregation rarely numbered a dozen. It seemed that, as the end of the Vicar's task drew nearer, so the prospect of filling the church receded and became more shadowy. And if his was a queer plight, Jacky Pascoe's was queerer. The Bryanite continued to come by night and help, but at rarer intervals. He was discomforted in mind, as anyone could see, and at length he took Mr. Raymond aside and made confession.

"I must go away; that's what 'tis. My burden is too great for me to bear."

"Why," said Mr. Raymond, who had grown surprisingly tolerant during the last twelve months, "what cause have you, of all men, to feel dejected? You can set the folk here on fire like flax." He sighed.

"That's azactly the reason—I can set 'em afire with a breath, but I can't hold 'em under. I make 'em too strong for me—*and I'm afeard.* Parson, dear, it's the gospel truth; for two years I've a been strivin' agen myself, wrastlin' upon my knees, and all to hold this parish in." He mopped his face. "'Tis like fightin' with beasts at Ephesus," he said.

"Do you want to hold them in?"

"I do, and I don't. I've got to try, anyway. Sometimes I tell mysel' 'tis putting a hand to the plough and turning back; and then I reckon I'll go on. But when the time comes I can't. I'm afeard, I tell 'ee." He paused. "I've laid it before the Lord, but He don't seem to help. There's two voices inside o' me. 'Tis a terrible responsibility."

"But the people: what are you afraid of their doing?"

"I don't know. You don't know what a runaway hoss will do, but you're afeared all the same." He sank his voice. "There's wantonness, for one thing—six love-children born in the parish this year, and more coming. They do say that Vashti Clemow destroyed her child. And Old Man Johns—him they found dead on the rocks under the Island—he didn't go there by accident. 'Twas a calm day, too."

As often as not Taffy worked late and blew his forge-fire alone in the church, the tap of his hammer making hollow music in the desolate aisles. He was working thus one windy night in February, when the door rattled open and in walked a totally unexpected visitor—Sir Harry Vyell.

"Good evening! I was riding by and saw your light in the windows dancing up and down. I thought I would hitch up the mare and drop in for a chat. But go on with your work."

Taffy wondered what had brought him so far from his home at that time of night, but asked no questions. And Sir Harry placed a hassock on one of the belfry steps, and taking his seat, watched for a while in silence. He wore his long riding-boots and an overcoat with the collar turned up about a neckcloth less nattily folded than usual.

"I wish," he said at length, "that my boy George

was clever like you. You were great friends once—you remember Plymouth, hey? But I dare say you've not seen much of each other lately."

Taffy shook his head.

"George is a bit wild. Oxford might have done something for him; made a man of him, I mean. But he wouldn't go. I believe in wild oats to a certain extent. I have told him from the first he must look after himself and decide for himself. That's my theory. It makes a youngster self-reliant. He goes and comes as he likes. If he comes home late from hunting I ask no questions; I don't wait dinner. Don't you agree with me?"

"I don't know," Taffy answered, wondering why he should be consulted.

"Self-reliance is what a man wants."

"Couldn't he have learnt that at school?"

Sir Harry fidgeted with the riding-crop in his hands. "Well, you see, he's an only son——I dare say it was selfish of me. You don't mind my talking about George?"

Taffy laughed. "I like it. But——"

Sir Harry laughed too, in an embarrassed way. "But you don't suppose I rode over from Carwithiel for that? Well, well! The fact is—one gets foolish as one grows old—George went out hunting this morning, and didn't turn up for dinner. I kept to my rule and dined alone. Nine o'clock came; half-past; no George. At ten Hoskins locked up as usual, and off I went to bed. But I couldn't sleep. After a while it struck me that he might be sleeping here over at Tredinnis; that is, if no accident had happened. No sleep for me until I made sure; so

I jumped out, dressed, slipped down to the stables, saddled the mare and rode over. I left the mare by Tredinnis great gates and crept down to Moyle's stables like a housebreaker, looked in through the window, and sure enough there was George's grey in the loose box to the right. So George is sleeping there, and I'm easy in my mind. No doubt you think me an old fool ?"

But Taffy was not thinking anything of the sort.

"I couldn't wish better than that. You understand ?"

"Not quite."

"He lost his mother early. He wants a woman to look after him, and for him to think about. If he and Honoria would only make up a match. . . . And Carwithiel would be quite a different house."

Taffy hesitated, with a hand on the forge-bellows.

"I dare say it's news to you, what I'm telling. But it has been in my mind this long while. Why don't you blow up the fire ? I bet Miss Honoria has thought of it too : girls are deep. She has a head on her shoulders. I'll warrant she sends half a dozen of my servants packing within a week. As it is, they rob me to a stair. I know it, and I haven't the pluck to interfere."

"What does the old Squire say ?" Taffy managed to ask.

"It has never come to *saying* anything. But I believe he thinks of it, too, when he happens to think of anything but his soul. He'll be pleased ; everyone will be pleased. The properties touch, you see."

"I see."

"To tell you the truth, he's failing fast. This

religion of his is a symptom: all of his family have taken to it in the end. If he hadn't the constitution of a horse, he'd have been converted ten years before this. What puzzles me is, he's so quiet. You mark my words"—Sir Harry rose, buttoned his coat and shook his riding-crop prophetically—"he's brewing up for something. There'll be the devil of a flare-up before he has done."

It came with the Midsummer bonfires. At nine o'clock on St. John's Eve, Mr. Raymond read prayers in the church. It was his rule to celebrate thus the vigils of all saints in the English calendar and some few Cornish saints besides; and he regularly announced these services on the preceding Sundays: but no parishioner dreamed of attending them.

To-night, as usual, he and Taffy had prayed alone: and the lad was standing after service at the church door, with his surplice on his arm (for he always wore a surplice and read the lessons on these vigils), when the flame of the first bonfire shot up from the headland over Innis village.

Almost on the moment, a flame answered it from the point where the lighthouse stood; and, within ten minutes, the horizon of the towans was cressetted with these beacon-fires: surely (thought Taffy) with many more than usual. And he remembered that Jacky Pascoe had thrown out a hint of a great revival to be held on Baal-fire Night (as he called it).

The night was sultry and all but windless. For once the tormented sands had rest. The flame of the bonfires shone yellow — orange-yellow — and steady. He could see the dark figures of men and women, passing between him and the nearest, on the high wastrel in front of Tredinnis great gates. Their voices reached him in a confused murmur, broken now and then by a child's scream of delight. And yet a hush seemed to hang over sea and land: an expectant hush. For weeks the sky had not rained. Day after day, a dull indigo blue possessed it, deepening with night into duller purple, as if the whole heavens were gathering into one big thunder-cloud, which menaced but never broke. And in the hush of those nights a listener could almost fancy he heard, between whiles, the rabbits stirring uneasily in their burrows.

By-and-by the bonfire on the wastrel appeared to be giving out sparks of light which blazed independently; yet without decreasing its own volume of flame. The sparks came dancing, nearer and larger: the voices grew more distinct. The revellers had kindled torches and were advancing in procession to visit other bonfires. The torches, too, were supposed to bless the fields they passed across. Small blessing had they ever brought to the barren towans.

The procession rose and sank as it came over the uneven ridges like a fiery snake; topped the nearest ridge and came pouring down past the churchyard wall. At its head danced Lizzie Pezzack, shrieking like a creature possessed, her hair loose and streaming while she whirled her torch. Taffy knew these torches; bundles of canvas steeped in tar and fastened in the middle to a stout stick or piece of chain. Lizzie's was fastened to a chain; and as he watched her uplifted arm swinging the blazing mass he found time to wonder how she escaped setting her hair on fire. Other torch-bearers tossed their arms and shouted as they passed. The smoke was suffocating, and across the patch of quiet graveyard the heat smote on Taffy's face. But in the crowd he saw two figures clearly—Jacky Pascoe and Squire Moyle; and the Bryanite's face was agitated and white in the infernal glare. He had given an arm to the Squire, who was clearly the centre of the procession and tottered forward with jaws working and cavernous eyes.

"He's saved!" a voice shouted.

Others took up the cry. "Saved!" "The Squire's saved!" "Saved to-night—saved to glory!"

The Squire paused, still leaning on the Bryanite's arm. While the procession swayed around him, he gazed across the gate as a man who had lost his bearings. No glint of torchlight reached his cavernous eyes; but the sight of Mr. Raymond's surpliced figure standing behind Taff's shoulder in the full glare seemed to rouse him. He lifted a fist and shook it slowly.

"Com'st along, sir!" urged the Bryanite.

But the Squire stood irresolute, muttering to himself.

"Com'st along, sir!"

"Lev' me be, I tell 'ee!" He laid both hands on the gate and spoke across it to Mr. Raymond, his head nodding while his voice rose.

"D'ee hear what they say? I'm saved. I'm the Squire of this parish, and I'm goin' to Heaven. I make no account of you and your church. Old Satan's the fellow I'm after, and I'm going to have him out o' this parish to-night or my name's not Squire Moyle."

"That's of it, Squire!" "Hunt 'en!" "Out with 'en!"

He turned on the crowd.

"Hunt 'en? Iss fay I will! Come along, boys—back to Tredinnis! No, no"—this to the Bryanite—"we'll go back. I'll show 'ee sport—we'll hunt th' old Divvle by scent and view to-night. I'm Squire Moyle, ain't I? And I've a pack o' hounds, ha'n't I? Back, boys—back, I tell 'ee!"

Lizzie Pezzack swung her torch. "Back—back to Tredinnis!" The crowd took up the cry, "Back to Tredinnis!" The old man shook off the Bryanite's hand, and as the procession wheeled and re-formed itself confusedly, rushed to the head of it, waving his hat—

"Back!—Back to Tredinnis!"

"God help them!" said Mr. Raymond; and taking Taffy by the arm, drew him back into the church.

The shouting died away up the road. For three-quarters of an hour father and son worked in silence. The reddened sky shed its glow gently through the clear glass windows, suffusing the shadows beneath the arched roof. And in the silence the lad wondered what was happening up at Tredinnis.

Jim the Whip took oath afterward that it was no fault of his. He had suspected three of the hounds for a day or two—Chorister, White Boy, and Bellman—and had separated them from the pack. That very evening he had done the same with Rifler, who was chewing at the straw in a queer fashion and seemed quarrelsome. He had said nothing to the Squire, whose temper had been ugly for a week past. He had hoped it was a false alarm—had thought it better to wait, and so on.

The Squire went down to the kennels with a lantern, Jim shivering behind him. They had their horses saddled outside and ready, and the crowd was waiting along the drive and up by the great gates. The Squire saw at a glance that two couples were missing, and in two seconds had their names on his tongue. He was like a madman. He shouted to Jim to open the doors. "Better not, maister!" pleaded Jim. The old man cursed, smote him across the neck with the butt-end of his whip, and unlocked the doors himself. Jim, though half stunned, staggered forward to prevent him, and took another blow, which felled him. He dropped across the threshold of Chorister's kennel; the doors of all opened outwards, and the weight of his body kept this one shut. But he saw the other three hounds run out, saw the Squire turn with a ghastly face, drop the lantern, and run for it as White Boy snapped at his boot. Jim heard the crash of the lantern and the snap of teeth, and with that he fainted off in the darkness. He had cut his forehead against the bars of the big kennel, and when he came to himself one of the hounds was licking his face through the grating.

Men told for years after how the old Squire came galloping up the drive that night, hoof to belly, his chin almost on mare Nonsuch's neck, his face like a man's who hears hell cracking behind him, and of the three dusky hounds which followed (the tale said) with clapping jaws and eyes like coach-lamps.

Down in the quiet church Taffy heard the outcry, and, laying down his plane, looked up and saw that his father had heard it too. Mr. Raymond's mild eyes, shining through his spectacles, asked as plainly as words: "What was *that?*"

"Listen!"

For a minute—two minutes—they heard nothing more. Then out of the silence broke a rapid, muffled beat of hoofs, and Mr. Raymond clutched Taffy's arm as a yell—a cry not human, or if human, insane—ripped the night as you might rip linen, and fetched them to their feet. Taffy gained the porch first; and just at that moment a black shadow heaved itself on the churchyard wall and came hurling over with a thud——a clatter of dropping stones——then a groan.

Before they could grasp what was happening the old Squire had extricated himself from the fallen mare, and came staggering across the graves.

"Hide me!——"

He came with both arms outstretched, his face turned sideways. Behind him, from the far side of the wall, came sounds—horrible shuffling sounds—and in the dusk they saw the head of one of the hounds above the coping and his forepaws clinging as he strained to heave himself over.

"Off! Keep 'en off!"

They caught him by both hands, dragged him within, and slammed the door.

"Hide me! Hi——!"

The word ended with a thud as he pitched headlong on the slate pavement. Through the barred door the scream of the mare Nonesuch answered it.

CHAPTER XVIII.

THE BARRIERS FALL.

THERE were marks of teeth on his right boot, but no marks at all on his body. Fright—or fright following on that evening's frenzy—had killed him.

He was buried three days later, and Mr. Raymond read the service. No rain had fallen, and the blood of the three hounds still stained the gravel dividing the grave from the porch, where the crowd had shot them down.

For a while his death made small difference to the family at the Parsonage. They had fought his enmity and proved it not formidable for brave hearts. But they had scarcely realised their success, and wondered why his death did not affect them more.

About this time Taffy began to carry out a scheme which he and his father had often discussed, but hitherto had found no leisure for—the setting up of wooden crosses on the graves of the drowned sailormen. They had wished for slate, but good slate was expensive and hard to come by, and Taffy had no skill in stone-cutting. Since wood it must be, he resolved to put his best work into it. The names, etc., should be engraved, not painted merely.

Some of the pew-fronts in the church had panels elaborately carved in flat and shallow relief—fine Jacobean designs, all of them. He took careful rubbings of their traceries, and set to work to copy them on the face of his crosses.

One afternoon, some three weeks after the Squire's funeral, he happened to return to the house for a tracing which he had forgotten, and found Honoria seated in the kitchen and talking with his father and mother. She was dressed in black, of course, and either this or the solemnity of her visit gave her quite a grown-up look. But, to be sure, she was mistress of Tredinnis now, and a child no longer.

Taffy guessed the meaning of her visit at once. And no doubt this act of formal reconciliation between Tredinnis House and the Parsonage had cost her some nervousness. As Taffy entered his parents stood up and seemed just as awkward as their visitor. "Another time, perhaps," he heard his father say. Honoria rose almost at once, and would not stay to drink tea, though Humility pressed her.

"I suppose," said Taffy next day, looking up from his Virgil, "I suppose Miss Honoria wants to make friends now and help on the restoration?"

Mr. Raymond, who was on his knees fastening a loose hinge in a pew-door, took a screw from between his lips.

"Yes, she proposed that."

"It must be splendid for you, dad!"

"I don't quite see," answered Mr. Raymond, with his head well inside the pew.

Taffy stood up, put his hands in his pockets, and took a turn up and down the aisle.

"Why," said he, coming to a halt, "it means that you have won. It's victory, dad, and *I* call it glorious!" His lip trembled. He wanted to put a hand on his father's shoulder; but his abominable shyness stood between.

"We won long ago, my boy." And Mr. Raymond wheeled round on his knees, pushed up his spectacles, and quoted the famous lines, very solemnly and slowly:

> "'And not by eastern windows only,
> When daylight comes, comes in the light;
> In front the sun climbs slow, how slowly!
> But westward, look, the land is bright!'"

"I see," Taffy nodded. "And—I say, that's jolly. Who wrote it?"

"A man I used to see in the streets of Oxford and always turned to stare after: a man with big ugly shaped feet and the face of a god—a young tormented god. Those were days when young men's thoughts tormented them. Taffy," he asked abruptly, "should you like to go to Oxford?"

"Don't, father!" The boy bit his lip to keep back the tears. "Talk of something else—something cheerful. It has been a splendid fight, just splendid! And now it's over I'm almost sorry."

"What is over?"

"Well, I suppose—now that Honoria wants to help—we can hire workmen and have the whole job finished in a month, or two at farthest: and you——"

Mr. Raymond stood up, and leaning against a bench-end, examined the thread of the screw between his fingers.

"That is one way of looking at it, no doubt," he said slowly; "and I hope God will forgive me if I have put my own pride before His service. But a man desires to leave some completed work behind him—something to which people may point and say, '*he* did it.' There was my book, now: for years I thought that was to be my work. But God thought otherwise and (to correct my pride, perhaps) chose this task instead. To set a small forsaken country church in order and make it worthy of His presence —that is not the mission I should have chosen. But so be it: I have accepted it. Only, to let others step in at the last and finish even this—I say He must forgive me, but I cannot."

"Your book—you can go back to it and finish it."

"I have burnt it."

"Dad!"

"I burned it. I had to. It was a temptation to me, and until I lifted it from the grate and the flakes crumbled in my hands the surrender was not complete."

Taffy felt a sudden gush of pity. And as he pitied suddenly he understood his father.

"It had to be complete?"

"Either the book or the surrender. My boy" —and in his voice there echoed the aspiration and the despair of the true scholar, who abhors imperfection and incompleteness in a world where nothing is either perfect or complete; "it is different with you. I borrowed you, so to say, for the time. Without you I must have failed; but this was never your work. For myself, I have learnt my lessons; but, please God, you shall be my Solomon and be granted a temple to build."

Taffy had lost his shyness now. He laid a hand on his father's sleeve.

"We will go on then."

"Yes, we will go on."

"And Jacky? Where has he been? I haven't seen him since the Squire died."

Mr. Raymond searched in his coat-pocket and handed over a crumpled letter. It ran:—

"DEAR FRIEND,—this is to say that you will not see me no more. The dear Lord tells me that I have made a cauch of it. He don't say how, all He says is go and do better somewheres else.

"Seems to me a terrable thing to think *Religion* can be bad for any man. It have done me such powars of good. The late Moyle esq he was like a dirty pan all the milk turned sour no matter what. Dear friend I pored Praise into him and it come out Prayer and all for him self. But the dear Lord says I was to blame as much as Moyle esq so must do better next time but feel terrable timid.

"My respects to Mas^r Taffy. Dear friend I done my best I come like *Nicodemus* by night. Seeming to me when Christians fall out tis over what they pray for. When they *praise God* forget diff^nses and I cant think where the quaraling comes in and so no more at present from

"Yours resp^ffly

"J. PASCOE."

After supper that night, in the Parsonage kitchen

Humility kept rising from her chair, and laying her needlework aside to re-arrange the pans and kettles on the hearth. This restlessness was so unusual that Taffy, seated in the ingle with a book on his knee, had half raised his head to twit her when he felt a hand laid softly on his hair, and looked up into his mother's eyes.

"Taffy, should you like to go to Oxford?"

"Don't, mother!"

"But you can." The tears in her eyes answered his at once. She turned to his father. "Tell him!"

"Yes, my boy, you can go," said Mr. Raymond; "that is, if you can win a scholarship. Your mother and I have been talking it over."

"But——" Taffy began, and could get no further.

"We have money enough—with care," said Mr. Raymond.

But the boy's eyes were on his mother. Her cheeks, usually so pale, were flushed; but she turned her face away and walked slowly back to her chair. "The lace-work," he heard her say: "I have been saving—from the beginning——"

"For this?" He followed and took her hand. With the other she covered her eyes; but nodded.

"O mother—mother!" He knelt and let his brow drop on her lap. She ceased to weep; her palms rested on his bowed head, but now and then her body shook. And but for the ticking of the tall clock there was silence in the room.

It was wonderful; and the wonder of it grew when they recovered themselves and fell to discussing their plans. In spite of his idolatry, Mr. Raymond could not help remembering certain slights which he, a poor miller's son, had undergone at Christ Church. He had chosen Magdalen, which Taffy knew to be the most beautiful of all the colleges; and the news that his name had been entered on the college books for years past gave him a delicious shock. It was now July. He would matriculate in the October term, and in January enter for a demyship. But (the marvels followed so fast on each other's heels) there would be an examination held in ten days' time—actually in ten days' time—a "certificate" examination, Mr. Raymond called it—which would excuse the boy not only the ordinary Matriculation test, but Responsions too. And, in short, Taffy was to pack his box and go.

"But the subjects?"

"You have been reading them and the prescribed books for four months past. And I have had sets of the old papers by me for a guide. Your mathematics are shaky—but I think you should do well enough."

It was now Humility's turn, and the discussion plunged among shirts and collars. Never had evening been so happy; and whether they talked of mathematics or of collars, Taffy could not help observing how from time to time his father's and mother's eyes would meet and say, as plainly as words, "We have done rightly." "Yes, we have done rightly."

And the wonder of it remained next morning, when he awoke to a changed world and took down his books with a new purpose. Already his box had been carried into old Mrs. Venning's room, and his mother and grandmother were busy, the one packing and repacking, the other making a new and important suggestion every minute.

He was to go up alone, and to lodge in Trinity College, where an old friend of Mr. Raymond's, a resident fellow just then abroad and spending his Long Vacation in the Tyrol, had placed his own room at the boy's service.

To see Oxford—to be lodging in college! He had to hug his mother in the midst of her packing.

"You will be going by the Great Western," she said. "You won't be seeing Honiton on your way."

When the great morning came, Mr. Raymond travelled with him in the van to Truro, to see him off. Humility went upstairs to her mother's room, and the two women prayed together—

"They also serve who only stand and wait."

CHAPTER XIX.

OXFORD.

" Know you her secret none can utter ?
    Hers of the Book, the tripled Crown ? "

" EIGHT o'clock, sir ! "

Taffy heard the voice speaking above a noise which his dreams confused with the rattle of yesterday's journey. He was still in the train, rushing through the rich levels of Somersetshire. He saw the broad horizon, the cattle at pasture, the bridges and flagged pools flying past the window—and sat up rubbing his eyes. Blenkiron, the scout, stood between him and the morning sunshine emptying a can of water into the tub beside his bed.

Blenkiron wore a white waistcoat and a tie of orange and blue, the colours of the College Servants' Cricket Club. These were signs of the Long Vacation. For the rest his presence would have become an archdeacon ; and he guided Taffy's choice of a breakfast with an air which suggested the hand of iron beneath the glove of velvet.

" And begging your pardon, sir, but will you be lunching in ? "

Taffy would consult Mr. Blenkiron's convenience.

" The fact is, sir, we've arranged to play Teddy

'All this afternoon at Cowley, and the drag starts at one-thirty sharp."

"Then I'll get my lunch out of college," said Taffy, wondering who Teddy Hall might be.

"I thank you, sir. I had, indeed, took the liberty of telling the manciple that you was not a gentleman to give more trouble than you could 'elp. Fried sole, pot of tea, toast, pot of blackberry jam, commons of bread——" Mr. Blenkiron disappeared.

Taffy sprang out of bed and ran to the open window in the next room. The gardens lay below him—smooth turf flanked with a border of gay flowers, flanked on the other side with yews, and beyond the yews with an avenue of limes, and beyond these with tall elms. A straight gravelled walk divided the turf. At the end of it two yews of magnificent spread guarded a great iron gate. Beyond these the chimneys and battlements of Wadham College stood grey against the pale eastern sky, and over them the larks were singing.

So this was Oxford; more beautiful than all his dreams! And since his examination would not begin until to-morrow, he had a whole long day to make acquaintance with her. Half a dozen times he had to interrupt his dressing to run and gaze out of the window, skipping back when he heard Blenkiron's tread on the staircase. And at breakfast again he must jump up and examine the door. Yes, there was a second door outside—a heavy *oak*—just as his father had described. What stories had he heard about these oaks! He was handling this one almost idolatrously when Blenkiron appeared suddenly at the head of the stairs. Blenkiron was good enough to explain at some length how the door worked, while Taffy, who did not need his instruction in the least, blushed to the roots of his hair.

For, indeed, it was like first love, this adoration of Oxford; shamefast, shy of its own raptures; so shy, indeed, that when he put on his hat and walked out into the streets he could not pluck up courage to ask his way. Some of the colleges he recognised from his father's description; of one or two he discovered the names by peeping through their gateways and reading the notices pinned up by the porters' lodges, for it never occurred to him that he was free to step inside and ramble through the quadrangles. He wondered where the river lay, and where Magdalen, and where Christ Church. He passed along the Turl and down Brasenose Lane; and at the foot of it, beyond the great chestnut-tree leaning over Exeter wall, the vision of noble square, the dome of the Radcliffe, and St. Mary's spire caught his breath and held him gasping. His feet took him by the gate of Brasenose and across the High. On the farther pavement he halted, round-eyed, held at gaze by the beauty of the Virgin's porch, with the creeper drooping like a veil over its twisted pillars.

High up, white pigeons wheeled round the spire or fluttered from niche to niche, and a queer fancy took him that they were the souls of the carved saints up there, talking to one another above the city's traffic. At length he withdrew his eyes, and reading the name "Oriel Street" on an angle of the wall above him, passed down a narrow by-lane in search of further wonders.

The clocks were striking three when, after regaining the High and lunching at a pastrycook's, Taffy turned down into St. Aldates and recognised Tom Tower ahead of him. The great gates were closed. Through the open wicket he had a glimpse of green turf and an idle fountain; and while he peered in, a jolly-looking porter stepped out of the lodge for a breath of air and nodded in the friendliest manner.

"You can walk through if you want to. Were you looking for anyone?"

"No," said Taffy, and explained proudly, "My father used to be at Christ Church."

The porter seemed interested. "What name?" he asked.

"Raymond."

"That must have been before my time. I suppose you'll be wanting to see the Cathedral. That's the door—right opposite."

Taffy thanked him and walked across the great empty quadrangle. Within the Cathedral the organ was sounding and pausing, and from time to time a boy's voice broke in upon the music like a flute, the pure treble rising to the roof as though it were the very voice of the building, and every pillar sustained its petition, "*Lord have mercy upon us, and incline our hearts to keep this law!*" Neither organist nor chorister was visible, and Taffy tiptoed along the aisles in dread of disturbing them. For the moment this voice adoring in the noble building expressed to him the completest, the most perfect thing in life. All his own boyish handiwork, remember, under his father's eye had been guided toward the worship of God.

" . . . *and incline our hearts to keep this law.*" The music ceased. He heard the organist speaking, up in the loft; criticising, no doubt: and it reminded him somehow of the small sounds of home and his mother moving about her housework in the hush between breakfast and noon.

He stepped out into the sunlight again, and wandering through archway and cloister found himself at length beyond the college walls and at the junction of two avenues of elms, between the trunks of which shone the acres of a noble meadow, level and green. The avenues ran at a right angle, east and south; the one old, with trees of magnificent girth, the other new and interset with poplars.

Taffy stood irresolute. One of these avenues, he felt sure, must lead to the river; but which?

Two old gentlemen stepped out from the wicket of the Meadow Buildings, and passed him, talking together. The taller—a lean man, with a stoop—was clearly a clergyman. The other wore cap and gown, and Taffy remarked, as he went by, that his cap was of velvet; and also that he walked with his arms crossed just above the wrists, his right hand clutching his left cuff, and his left hand his right cuff, his elbows hugged close to his sides.

After a few paces the clergyman paused, said something to his companion, and the two turned back towards the boy.

"Were you wanting to know your way?"

"I was looking for the river," Taffy answered.

He was thinking that he had never in his life seen a face so full of goodness.

"Then this is your first visit to Oxford? Suppose, now, you come with us? and we will take you by the river and tell you the names of the barges. There is not much else to see, I'm afraid, in Vacation time."

He glanced at his companion in the velvet cap, who drew down an extraordinary bushy pair of eyebrows (yet he, too, had a beautiful face) and seemed to come out of a dream.

"So much the better, boy, if you come up to Oxford to worship false gods."

Taffy was taken aback.

"Eight false gods in little blue caps, seated in a trough and tugging at eight poles; and all to discover if they can get from Putney to Mortlake sooner than eight others in little blue caps of a lighter shade. What do they *do* at Mortlake when they get there in such a hurry? Eh, boy?"

"I—I'm sure I don't know," stammered Taffy.

The clergyman broke out laughing, and turned to him. "Are you going to tell us your name?"

"Raymond, sir. My father used to be at Christ Church."

"What? Are you Sam Raymond's son?"

"You knew my father?"

"A very little. I was his senior by a year or two. But I know something about him." He turned to the other. "Let me introduce the son of a man after your own heart—of a man fighting for God in the wilds, and building an altar there with his own hands and by the lamp of sacrifice."

"But how do you know all this?" cried Taffy.

"Oh," the old clergyman smiled, "we are not so ignorant up here as you suppose."

They walked by the river bank, and there Taffy saw the college barges and was told the name of each. Also he saw a racing eight go by: it belonged to the Vacation Rowing Club. From the barges they turned aside and followed the windings of the Cherwell. The clergyman did most of the talking; but now and then the old gentleman in the velvet cap interposed a question about the church at home, its architecture, the materials it was built of, and so forth; or about Taffy's own work, his carpentry, his apprenticeship with Mendarva the Smith. And to all these questions the boy found himself replying with an ease which astonished him.

Suddenly the old clergyman said, "There is your College!"

And unperceived by Taffy a pair of kindly eyes watched his own as they met the first vision of that lovely tower rising above the trees and (so like a thing of life it seemed) lifting its pinnacles exultantly into the blue heaven.

"Well?"

All three had come to a halt. The boy turned, blushing furiously.

"This is the best of all, sir."

"Boy," said old Velvet-cap, "do you know the meaning of 'edification'? There stands your lesson for four years to come, if you can learn it in that time. Do you think it easy? Come and see how it has been learnt by men who have spent their lives face to face with it."

They crossed the street by Magdalen bridge, and passed under Pugin's gateway, by the Chapel door and into the famous cloisters. All was quiet here; so quiet that even the voices of the sparrows chattering in the ivy seemed but a part of the silence. The shadow of the great tower fell across the grass.

"This is how one generation read the lesson. Come and see how another, and a later, read it."

A narrow passage led them out of gloom into sudden sunlight; and the sunlight spread itself on fair grass-plots and gravelled walks, flower-beds and the pale yellow façade of a block of buildings in the classical style, stately and elegant, with a colonnade which only needed a few promenading figures in laced coats and tie-wigs to complete the agreeable picture.

"What do you make of that?"

As a matter of fact Taffy's thoughts had run back to the theatre at Plymouth with its sudden changes of scenery. And he stood for a moment while he collected them.

"It's different: I mean," he added, feeling that this was intolerably lame, "it means something different; I cannot tell what."

"It means the difference between godly fear and civil ease, between a house of prayer and one of no prayer. It spells the moral change which came over this University when religion, the spring and source of collegiate life, was discarded. The cloisters behind you were built for men who walked with God."

"But why," objected Taffy, plucking up courage, "couldn't they do that in the sunlight?"

Velvet-cap opened his mouth. The boy felt he

was going to be denounced; when a merry laugh from the old clergyman averted the storm.

"Be content," he said to his companion; "we are Gothic enough in Oxford nowadays. And the lad is right too. There was hope even for eighteenth-century Magdalen while its buildings looked on sunlight and on that tower. You and the rest of us lay too much stress on prayer. The lesson of that tower (with all deference to your amazing discernment and equally amazing whims) is not prayer, but praise. And when all men unite to worship God, it'll be praise, not prayer, that brings them together.

> "'Praise is devotion fit for noble minds,
> The differing world's agreeing sacrifice.'"

"Oh, if you're going to fling quotations from a tapster's son at my head. . . . Let me see . . . how does it go on? . . . Where—something or other—different faiths—

> "'Where Heaven divided faiths united finds. . .'"

And in a moment the pair were in hot pursuit after the quotation, tripping each other up like two schoolboys at a game. Taffy never forgot the final stanza, the last line of which they recovered exactly in the middle of the street, Velvet-cap standing between two tram-lines, right in the path of an advancing car, while he declaimed—

> "'By penitence when we ourselves forsake,
> 'Tis but in wise design on piteous Heaven;
> In praise—'"

(The gesture was magnificent)

"'In praise we nobly give what God may take,
And are without a beggar's blush forgiven.'

—Confound these trams!"

The old clergyman shook hands with Taffy in some haste. "And when you reach home give my respects to your father. Stay, you don't know my name. Here is my card, or you'll forget it."

"Mine, too," said Velvet-cap.

Taffy stood staring after them as they walked off down the lane which skirts the Botanical Gardens. The names on the two cards were famous ones, as even he knew. He walked back toward Trinity a proud and happy boy. Half-way up Queen's Lane, finding himself between blank walls, with nobody in sight, he even skipped.

CHAPTER XX.

TAFFY GIVES A PROMISE.

THE postman halted by the foot-bridge and blew his horn. The sound sent the rabbits scampering into their burrows; and just as they began to pop out again, Taffy came charging across the slope. Whereupon they drew back their noses in disgust, and to avoid the sand scattered by his toes.

The postman held up a blue envelope and waved it. " Here, 'tis come, at last ! "

" It may not be good news," said Taffy, clutching it, and then turning it over in his hand.

" Well, that's true. And till you open it, it won't be any news at all."

" I wanted mother to be first to know."

" Oh, very well—only, as you say, it mightn't be good news."

" If it's bad news, I want to be alone. But why should they trouble to write ? "

" True again. I s'pose now you're sure it *is* from them ? "

" I can tell by the seal."

" Take it home, then," said the postman. " Only if you think 'tis for the sake of a twiddling sixteen shilling a week that I traipse all these miles every day——"

Taffy fingered the seal. "If you would really like to know——"

"Don't 'ee mention it. Not on any account." He waved his hand magnanimously and trudged off toward Tredinnis.

Taffy waited until he disappeared behind the first sand-hill, and broke the seal. A slip of parchment lay inside the envelope.

"*This is to certify*——"

He had passed! He pulled off his cap and waved it round his head. And once more the rabbits popped back into their burrows.

Toot—toot—toot!—It was that diabolical postman. He had fetched a circuit round the sand-hill, and was peeping round the north side of it and grinning as he blew his horn.

Taffy set off running, and never stopped until he reached the Parsonage and burst into the kitchen.

"Mother—It's all right! I've passed!"

* * * * * *

Somebody was knocking at the door. Taffy jumped up from his knees, and Humility made the lap of her apron smooth.

"May I come in?" asked Honoria, and pushed the door open. She stepped into the middle of the kitchen and dropped Taffy an elaborate courtesy. "A thousand congratulations, sir!"

"Why, how did you know?"

"Well, I met the postman; and I looked in through the window before knocking."

Taffy bit his lip. "People seem to be taking a deal of interest in us all of a sudden," he said to his mother.

Humility looked distressed, uncomfortable. Honoria ignored the snub. "I am starting for Carwithiel to-day," she said, "for a week's visit, and thought I would look in—after hearing what the postman told me—and pay my compliments."

She talked for a minute or two on matters of no importance, asked after old Mrs. Venning's health, and left, turning at the door and giving Humility a cheerful little nod.

"Taffy, you ought not to have spoken so." Humility's eyes were tearful.

Taffy's conscience was already accusing him. He snatched up his cap and ran out.

"Miss Honoria!"

She did not turn.

"Miss Honoria—I am sorry!" He overtook her, but she turned her face away. "Forgive me!"

She halted, and after a moment looked him in the eyes. He saw then that she had been crying.

"The first time I came to see you he whipped me," she said slowly.

"I am sorry; indeed I am."

"Taffy——"

"Miss Honoria."

"I said—Taffy."

"Honoria, then."

"Do you know what it is to feel lonely here?"

Taffy remembered the afternoons when he had roamed the sand-hills longing for George's company. "Why, yes," said he; "it used to be always lonely."

"I think we have been the loneliest children in the whole world—you and I and George—only George didn't feel it the same way. And now it's coming to an end with you. You are going up to Oxford, and soon you will have heaps of friends. Can you not understand? Suppose there were two prisoners, alone in the same prison, but shut in different cells, and one heard that the other's release had come. He would feel—would he not?—that now he was going to be lonelier than ever. And yet he might be glad of the other's liberty, and if the chance were given, might be the happier for shaking hands with the other and wishing him joy."

Taffy had never heard her speak at all like this.

"But you are going to Carwithiel, and George is famous company."

"I am going over to Carwithiel because I hate Tredinnis. I hate every stone of it, and will sell the place as soon as ever I come of age. And George is the best fellow in the world. Some day I shall marry him (oh, it is all arranged!), and we shall live at Carwithiel and be quite happy; for I like him, and he likes people to be happy. And we shall talk of you. Being out of the world ourselves, we shall talk of you, and the great things you are going to do, and the great things you are doing. We shall say to each other, 'It's all very well for the world to be proud of him, but we have the best right, for we grew up with him and know the stories he used to tell us; and when the time came for his going, it was we who waved from the door——"

"Honoria——"

"But there is one thing you haven't told, and you shall now, if you care to—about your examination and what you did at Oxford."

So he sat down beside her on a sand-hill and told her: about the long low-ceiled room in the quadrangle of the Bodleian, the old marbles which lined the walls, the examiner at the blue baize table, and the little deal tables (all scribbled over with names and dates and verses and ribald remarks) at which the candidates wrote; also of the *viva voce* examination in the antechamber of the Convocation House. He told it all as if it were the great event he honestly felt it to be.

"And the others," said she, "those who were writing around you, and the examiner—how did you feel towards them?"

Taffy stared at her. "I don't know that I thought much about them."

"Didn't you feel as if it was a battle and you wanted to beat them all?"

He broke out laughing. "Why, the examiner was an old man, as dry as a stick! And I hardly remember what the others were like—except one, a white-headed boy with a pimply face. I couldn't help noticing him, because whenever I looked up there he was at the next table, staring at me and chewing a quill."

"I can't understand," she confessed. "Often and often I have tried to think myself a man—a man with ambition. And to me that has always meant fighting. I see myself a man, and the people between me and the prize have all to be knocked down or pushed out of the way. But you don't even see them—all you see is a pimply-faced boy sucking a quill. Taffy——"

"Yes?"

"I wish you would write to me when you get to Oxford. Write regularly. Tell me all you do."

"You will like to hear?"

"Of course I shall. So will George. But it's not only that. You have such an easy way of going forward; you take it for granted you're going to be a great man——"

"I don't."

"Yes, you do. You think it just lies with yourself, and it is nobody's business to interfere with you. You don't even notice those who are on the same path. Now a woman would notice every one, and find out all about them."

"Who said I wanted to be a great man?"

"Don't be silly, that's a good boy! There's your father coming out of the church porch, and you haven't told him yet. Run to him, but promise first."

"What?"

"That you will write."

"I promise."

CHAPTER XXI.

HONORIA'S LETTERS.

I.

"CARWITHIEL, *Oct.* 25, 18—

"MY DEAR TAFFY,—Your letter was full of news, and I read it over twice: once to myself, and again after dinner to George and Sir Harry. We pictured you dining in the college hall. Thanks to your description, it was not very difficult: the long tables, the silver tankards, the dark panels and the dark pictures above, and the dons on the daïs, aloof and very sedate. It reminded me of Ivanhoe—I don't know why; and no doubt if ever I see Magdalen, it will not be like my fancy in the least. But that's how I see it; and you at a table near the bottom of the hall, like the youthful squire in the story-books—the one, you know, who sits at the feast below the salt until he is recognised and forced to step up and take his seat with honour at the high table. I began to explain all this to George, but found that he had dropped asleep in his chair. He was tired out after a long day with the pheasants.

"I shall stay here for a week or two yet, perhaps. You know how I hate Tredinnis. On my way over, I called at the Parsonage and saw your mother. She was writing that very day, she said, and promised to send my remembrances, which I hope duly reached you. The Vicar was away at the church, of course. There is great talk of the Bishop coming in February, when all will be ready. George sends his love; I saw him for a few minutes at breakfast this morning, before he started for another day with the pheasants.

"Your friend,

"HONORIA."

2.

"CARWITHIEL, *Nov.* 19, 18—.

"MY DEAR TAFFY,—Still here, you see! I am slipping this into a parcel containing a fire-screen which I have worked with my very own hands; and I trust you will be able to recognise the shield upon it and the Magdalen lilies. I send it, first, as a birthday present; and I chose the shield—well, I dare say that going in for a demy-ship is a matter-of-fact affair to you, who have grown so exceedingly matter-of-fact; but to me it seems a tremendous adventure; and so I chose a shield—for I suppose the dons would frown if you wore a cockade in your college cap. I return to Tredinnis to-morrow; so your news, whatever it is, must be addressed to me there. But it is safe to be good news.

"Your friend,

"HONORIA."

3.

"TREDINNIS, *Nov.* 27, 18—.

"MOST HONOURED SCHOLAR,—Behold me, an hour ago, a great lady, seated in lonely grandeur at the head of my own ancestral table. This is the first time I have used the dining-room ; usually I take all my meals in the morning-room, at a small table beside the fire. But to-night I had the great table spread and the plate spread out, and wore my best gown, and solemnly took my grandfather's chair and glowered at the ghost of a small girl shivering at the far end of the long white cloth. When I had enough of this (which was pretty soon) I ordered up some champagne and drank to the health of Theophilus John Raymond, Demy of Magdalen College, Oxford. I graciously poured out a second glass for the small ghost at the other end of the table ; and it gave her the courage to confess that she, too, in a timid way, had taken an interest in you for years, and hoped you were going to be a great man. Having thus discovered a bond between us, we grew very friendly ; and we talked a great deal about you afterwards in the drawing-room, where I lost her for a few minutes and found her hiding in the great mirror over the fire-place—a habit of hers.

"It is time for me to practise ceremony, for it seems that George and I are to be married some time in the spring. For my part I think my lord would be content to wait longer ; for so long as he is happy and sees others cheerful he is not one to hurry or worry. But Sir Harry is the impatient one : and has begun to talk of his decease. He doesn't believe in it a bit, and at times when he composes his features and attempts to be lugubrious I have to take up a book and hide my smiles. But he is clever enough to see that it worries George.

"I saw both your father and mother this morning.

Mr. Raymond has been kept to the house by a chill; nothing serious: but he is fretting to be out again and at work in that draughty church. He will accept no help; and the mistress of Tredinnis has no right to press it on him. I shall never understand men and how they fight. I supposed that the war lay between him and my grandfather. But it seems he was fighting an idea all the while; for here is my grandfather beaten and dead and gone; and still the Vicar will give no quarter. If you had not assured me that your demy-ship means eighty pounds a year, I could believe that men fight for shadows only. Your mother and grandmother are both well. . . ."

* * * * * *

It was a raw December afternoon—within a week of the end of term—and Taffy had returned from skating in Christ Church meadow, when he found a telegram lying on his table. There was just time to see the Dean, to pack, and to snatch a meal in hall, before rattling off to his train. At Didcot he had the best part of an hour to wait for the night-mail westward.

"*Your father dangerously ill. Come at once.*"

There was no signature. Yet Taffy knew who had ridden to the office with that telegram. The flying dark held visions of her, and the express throbbed westward to the beat of Aide-de-camp's gallop. Nor was he surprised at all to find her on the platform at Truro Station. The Tredinnis phaeton was waiting outside.

He seemed to her but a boy after all, as he stepped

out of the train in the chill dawn : a wan-faced boy, and sorely in need of comfort.

"You must be brave," said she, gathering up the reins as he climbed to the seat beside her.

Surely yes ; he had been telling himself this very thing all night. The groom hoisted in his portmanteau, and with a slam of the door they were off. The cold air sang past Taffy's ears. It put vigour into him, and his courage rose as he faced his shattered prospects, shattered dreams. He must be strong now for his mother's sake ; a man to work and be leant upon.

And so it was that whereas Honoria had found him a boy, Humility found him a man. As her arms went about him in her grief, she felt his body, that it was taller, broader ; and knew in the midst of her tears that this was not the child she had parted from seven short weeks ago, but a man to act and give orders and be relied upon.

"He called for you . . . many times," was all she could say.

For Taffy had come too late. Mr. Raymond was dead. He had aggravated a slight chill by going back to his work too soon, and the bitter draughts of the church had cut him down within sight of his goal. A year before he might have been less impatient. The chill struck into his lungs. On December 1st he had taken to his bed, and he never rallied.

"He called for me ?"

"Many times."

They went up the stairs together and stood beside the bed. The thought uppermost in Taffy's mind was—" He called for me. He wanted me. He was my father and I never knew him."

But Humility in her sorrow groped amid such questions as these, " What has happened? Who am I? Am I she who yesterday had a husband and a child? To-day my husband is gone and my child is no longer the same child."

In her room old Mrs. Venning remembered the first days of her own widowhood, and life seemed to her a very short affair, after all.

Honoria saw Taffy beside the grave. It was no season for out-of-door flowers, and she had rifled her hothouses for a wreath. The exotics shivered in the north-westerly wind; they looked meaningless, impertinent, in the gusty churchyard. Humility, before the coffin left the house, had brought the dead man's old blue working-blouse, and spread it for a pall. No flowers grew in the Parsonage garden; but pressed in her Bible lay a very little bunch, gathered, years ago, in the meadows by Honiton. This she divided and, unseen by anyone, pinned the half upon the breast of the patched garment.

On the evening after the funeral and for the next day or two she was strangely quiet, and seemed to be waiting for Taffy to make some sign. Dearly as mother and son loved one another, they had to find their new positions, each toward each. Now Taffy had known nothing of his parents' income. He assumed that it was little enough. and that he must now leave Oxford and work to support the household. He knew some Latin and Greek; but without a degree he had little chance of teaching what he knew.

He was a fair carpenter, and a more than passable smith. . . . He revolved many schemes, but chiefly found himself wondering what it would cost to enter an architect's office.

"I suppose," said he, "father left no will?"

"Oh yes, he did," said Humility, and produced it: a single sheet of foolscap signed on her wedding day. It gave her all her husband's property absolutely—whatever it might be.

"Well," said Taffy, "I'm glad. I suppose there's enough for you to rent a small cottage, while I look about for work?"

"Who talks about your finding work? You will go back to Oxford, of course."

"Oh, shall I?" said Taffy, taken aback.

"Certainly; it was your father's wish."

"But the money?"

"With your scholarship there's enough to keep you there for the four years. After that, no doubt, you will be earning a good income."

"But——" He remembered what had been said about the lace-money, and could not help wondering.

"Taffy," said his mother, touching his hand, "leave all this to me until your degree is taken. You have a race to run and must not start unprepared. If you could have seen *his* joy when the news came of the demy-ship!"

Taffy kissed her and went up to his room. He found his books laid out on the little table there.

* * * * * *

4.

"TREDINNIS, *February* 13, 18—.

"MY DEAR TAFFY,—I have a valentine for you, if you care to accept it; but I don't suppose you will, and indeed I hope in my heart that you will not. But I must offer it. Your father's living is vacant, and my trustees (that is to say, Sir Harry; for the other, a second cousin of mine who lives in London, never interferes) can put in someone as a stop-gap, thus allowing me to present you to it when the time comes, if you have any thought of Holy Orders. You will understand exactly why I offer it; and also, I hope, you will know that I think it wholly unworthy of you. But turn it over in your mind and give me your answer.

"George and I are to be married at the end of April. May is an unlucky month. It shall be a week—even a fortnight—earlier, if that fits in with your vacation, and you care to come. See how obliging I am! I yield to you what I have refused to Sir Harry. We shall try to persuade the Bishop to come and open the church on the same day.

"Always your friend,

"HONORIA."

5.

"TREDINNIS, *February* 21.

"MY DEAR TAFFY,—No, I am not offended in the least; but very glad. I do not think you are fitted for the priesthood; but my doubts have nothing to do with your doubts, which I don't understand, though you tried to explain them so carefully.

You will come through *them*, I expect. I don't know that I have any reasons that could be put on paper: only, somehow, I cannot *see* you in a black coat and clerical hat.

"You complain that I never write about George. You don't deserve to hear, since you refuse to come to our wedding. But would *you* talk, if you happened to be in love? There, I have told you more than ever I told George, whose conceit has to be kept down. Let this console you.

"Our new parson, when he comes, is to lodge down in Innis Village. Your mother—but no doubt she has told you—stays in the Parsonage while she pleases. She and your grandmother are both well. I see her every day: I have so much to learn, and she is so wise. Her beautiful eyes—but oh, Taffy, it must be terrible to be a widow! She smiles and is always cheerful; but the *look* in them! How can I describe it? When I find her alone with her lace-work, or sometimes (but it is not often) with her hands in her lap, she seems to come out of her silence with an effort, as others withdraw themselves from talk. I wonder if she does talk in those silences of hers. Another thing, it is only a few weeks now since she put on a widow's cap, and yet I cannot remember her—can scarcely picture her—without it. I am sure that if I happened to call one day when she had laid it aside, I should begin to talk quite as if we were strangers.

"Believe me, yours sincerely,

"HONORIA."

But the wedding, after all, did not take place until

the beginning of October, a week before the close of the Long Vacation; and Taffy, after all, was present. The postponement had been enforced by many delays in building and furnishing the new wing at Carwithiel; for Sir Harry insisted that the young couple must live under one roof with him, and Honoria (as we know) hated the very stones of Tredinnis.

The Bishop came to spend a week in the neighbourhood; the first three days as Honoria's guest. On the Saturday he consecrated the work of restoration in the church, and in the afternoon held a confirmation service. Taffy and Honoria knelt together to receive his blessing. It was the girl's wish. The shadow of her responsibility to God and man lay heavy on her during the few months before her marriage: and Taffy, already weary and dispirited with his early doubtings, suffered her mood of exaltation to overcome him like a wave and sweep him back to rest for a while on the still waters of faith. Together they listened while the Bishop discoursed on the dead Vicar's labours with fluency and feeling; with so much feeling, indeed, that Taffy could not help wondering why his father had been left to fight the battle alone.

On the Sunday and Monday two near parishes claimed the Bishop. On the Tuesday he sent his luggage over to Carwithiel, whither he was to follow after the wedding service, to spend a day or two with Sir Harry. It had been Honoria's wish that George should choose Taffy for his best man; but George had already invited one of his sporting friends, a young Squire Philpotts from the eastern side of the Duchy; and as the date fell at the beginning of the hunting season, he insisted on a "pink" wedding. Honoria consulted the Bishop by letter. "Did he approve of a 'pink' wedding so soon after the bride's confirmation?" The Bishop saw no harm in it.

So a "pink" wedding it was, and the scarlet coats made a lively patch of colour in the gray churchyard: but it gave Taffy a feeling that he was left out in the cold. He escorted his mother to the church, and left her for a few minutes in the Vicarage pew. The bridegroom and his friends were gathered in a showy cluster by the chancel step, but the bride had not arrived, and he stepped out to help in marshalling the crowd of miners and mine-girls, fishermen, and mothers with unruly children—a hundred or so in all, lining the path or straggling among the graves.

Close by the gate he came on a girl who stood alone.

"Hullo, Lizzie—you here?"

"Why not?" she asked, looking at him sullenly.

"Oh, no reason at all."

"There might ha' been a reason," said she, speaking low and hurriedly. "You might ha' saved me from this, Mr. Raymond; and her too; one time, you might."

"Why, what on earth is the matter?" He looked up. The Tredinnis carriage and pair of grays came over the knoll at a smart trot, and drew up before the gate.

"Matter?" Lizzie echoed with a short laugh. "Oh, nuthin'. I'm goin' to lay the curse on her, that's all."

"You shall not!" There was no time to lose.

Honoria's trustee—the second cousin from London, a tall, clean-shaven man with a shiny bald head, and a shiny hat in his hand—had stepped out and was helping the bride to alight. What Lizzie meant Taffy could not tell; but there must be no scene. He caught her hand. " Mind—I say you shall not! " he whispered.

" Lemme go—you're creamin' my fingers."

" Be quiet then."

At that moment Honoria passed up the path. Her wedding gown almost brushed him as he stood wringing Lizzie's hand. She did not appear to see him; but he saw her face beneath the bridal veil, and it was hard and white.

" The proud toad! " said Lizzie. " I'm no better'n dirt, I suppose, though from the start she wasn' above robbin' me. Aw, she's sly . . . Mr. Raymond, I'll curse her as she comes out, see if I don't! "

" And I swear you shall not," said Taffy. The scent of Honoria's orange-blossom seemed to cling about them as they stood.

Lizzie looked at him vindictively. " You wanted her yourself, *I* know. You weren't good enough, neither. Let go my fingers! "

" Go home, now. See, the people have all gone in."

" Go'st way in too, then, and leave me here to wait for her."

Taffy shut his teeth, let go her hand, and taking her by the shoulders, swung her round face toward the gate.

" March! " he commanded, and she moved off

whimpering. Once she looked back. "March!" he repeated, and followed her down the road as one follows and threatens a mutinous dog.

* * * * * *

The scene by the church gate had puzzled Honoria, and in her first letter (written from Italy) she came straight to the point, as her custom was. "I hope there is nothing between you and that girl who used to be at Joll's. I say nothing about our hopes for you, but you have your own career to look to; and as I know you are too honourable to flatter an ignorant girl when you mean nothing, so I trust you are too wise to be caught by a foolish fancy. Forgive a staid matron (of one week's standing) for writing so plainly, but what I saw made me uneasy—without cause, no doubt. Your future, remember, is not yours only. And now I shall trust you, and never come back to this subject."

"We are like children abroad," she went on. "George's French is wonderful, but not so wonderful as his Italian. When he goes to take a ticket he first of all shouts the name of the station he wishes to arrive at (for some reason he believes all foreigners to be deaf), then he begins counting down francs one by one, very slowly, watching the clerk's face. When the clerk's face tells him he has doled out enough, he shouts 'Hold hard!' and clutches the ticket. It takes time; but all the people here are friends with him at once—especially the children, whom he punches in the ribs and tells to 'buck up.' Their mothers nod and smile and openly admire him; and I—well, I am happy and want everyone else to be happy."

CHAPTER XXII.

MEN AS TOWERS.

It was May morning, and Taffy made one of the group gathered on the roof of Magdalen Tower. In the groves below and across the river meadows all the birds were singing together. Beyond the glimmering suburbs, St. Clement's and Cowley St. John, over the dark rise by Bullingdon Green, the waning moon seemed to stand still and wait, poised on her nether horn. Below her the morning sky waited, clean and virginal, letting her veil of mist slip lower and lower until it rested in folds upon Shotover. While it dropped a shaft of light tore through it and smote flashing on the vane high above Taffy's head, turning the dark side of the turrets to purple and casting lilac shadows on the surplices of the choir. For a moment the whole dewy shadow of the tower trembled on the western sky, and melted and was gone as a flood of gold broke on the eastward-turned faces. The clock below struck five and ceased. There was a sudden baring of heads ; a hush ; and gently, borne aloft on boys' voices, clear and strong, rose the first notes of the hymn—

> " Te Deum Patrem colimus,
> Te laudibus prosequimur,
> Qui corpus cibo reficis,
> Coelesti mentem gratia."

In the pauses Taffy heard, faint and far below, the noise of cowhorns blown by the street boys gathered at the foot of the tower and beyond the bridge. Close beside him a small urchin of a chorister was singing away with the face of an ecstatic seraph; whence that ecstasy arose the urchin would have been puzzled to tell. There flashed into Taffy's brain the vision of the whole earth lauding and adoring—sun-worshippers and Christians, priests and small children; nation after nation prostrating itself and arising to join the chant—"the differing world's agreeing sacrifice." Yes, it was Praise that made men brothers; Praise, the creature's first and last act of homage to his Creator; Praise that made him kin with the angels. Praise had lifted this tower; had expressed itself in its soaring pinnacles; and he for the moment was incorporate with the tower and part of its builder's purpose. "Lord, make men as towers!"—he remembered his father's prayer in the field by Tewkesbury, and at last he understood. "All towers carry a lamp of some kind"—why, of course they did. He looked about him. The small chorister's face was glowing—

"Triune Deus, hominum
Salutis auctor optime,
Immensum hoc mysterium
Ovante lingua canimus!"

Silence—and then with a shout the tunable bells broke forth, rocking the tower. Someone seized Taffy's college cap and sent it spinning over the battlements. Caps? For a second or two they darkened the sky like a flock of birds. A few gowns followed, expanding as they dropped, like clumsy parachutes. The company—all but a few severe dons and their friends—tumbled laughing down the ladder, down the winding stair, and out into sunshine. The world was pagan after all.

* * * * * *

At breakfast Taffy found a letter on his table, addressed in his mother's hand. As a rule she wrote twice a week, and this was not one of the usual days for hearing from her. But nothing was too good to happen that morning. He snatched up the letter and broke the seal.

" My dearest boy," it ran, " I want you home at once to consult with me. Something has happened (forgive me, dear, for not preparing you ; but the blow fell on me yesterday so suddenly)—something which makes it doubtful, and more than doubtful, that you can continue at Oxford. And something else *they say* has happened which I will never believe in unless I hear it from my boy's lips. I have this comfort, at any rate, that he will never tell me a falsehood. This is a matter which cannot be explained by letter, and cannot wait until the end of term. Come home quickly, dear ; for until you are here I can have no peace of mind."

So once again Taffy travelled homewards by the night mail.

* * * * * *

" Mother, it's a lie ! "

Taffy's face was hot, but he looked straight into his mother's eyes. She too was rosy-red : being ever a shamefast woman. And to speak of these things to her own boy——

"Thank God!" she murmured, and her fingers gripped the arms of her chair.

"It's a lie! Where is the girl?"

"She is in the workhouse, I believe. I don't know who spread it, or how many have heard. But Honoria believes it."

"Honoria! She cannot——" He came to a sudden halt. "But, mother, even supposing Honoria believes it, I don't see——"

He was looking straight at her. Her eyes sank. Light began to break in on him.

"Mother!"

Humility did not look up.

"Mother! Don't tell me that she—that Honoria——"

"She made us promise—your father and me. . . . God knows it did no more than repay what your father had suffered. . . . Your future was everything to us. . . ."

"And I have been maintained at Oxford by her money," he said, pausing in his bitterness on every word.

"Not by that only, Taffy! There was your scholarship . . . and it was true about my savings on the lace-work. . . ."

But he brushed her feeble explanations away with a little gesture of impatience. "Oh why, mother?—Oh why?"

She heard him groan and stretched out her arms.

"Taffy, forgive me—forgive us! We did wrongly, I see—I see it as plain now as you. But we did it for your sake."

" You should have told me. I was not a child. Yes, yes, you should have told me."

Yes ; there lay the truth. They had treated him as a child when he was no longer a child. They had swathed him round with love, forgetting that boys grow and demand to see with their own eyes and walk on their own feet. To every mother of sons there comes sooner or later the sharp lesson which came to Humility that morning ; and few can find any defence but that which Humility stammered, sitting in her chair and gazing piteously up at the tall youth confronting her : " I did it for your sake." Be pitiful, oh accusing sons, in that hour ! For, terrible as your case may be against them, your mothers are speaking the simple truth.

Taffy took her hand. " The money must be paid back, every penny of it."

" Yes, dear."

" How much ? "

Humility kept a small account-book in the work-box beside her. She opened the pages, but, seeing his outstretched hand, gave it obediently to Taffy, who took it to the window.

" Almost two hundred pounds." He knit his brows and began to drum with his fingers on the window-pane. " And we must put the interest at five per cent. . . . With my first in Moderations I might find some post as an usher in a small school. . . . There's an agency which puts you in the way of such things : I must look up the address. . . . We will leave this house, of course."

" Must we ? "

" Why of course we must. We are living here by

her favour. A cottage will do—only it must have four rooms, because of grandmother. . . . I will step over and talk with Mendarva. He may be able to give me a job. It will keep me going, at any rate, until I hear from the agency."

" You forget that I have over forty pounds a year —or, rather, mother has. The capital came from the sale of her farm, years ago."

" Did it ? " said Taffy grimly. " You forget that I have never been told. Well, that's good, so far as it goes. But now I'll step over and see Mendarva. If only I could catch this cowardly lie somewhere on my way ! "

He kissed his mother, caught up his cap, and flung out of the house. The sea breeze came humming across the sandhills. He opened his lungs to it, and it was wine to his blood ; he felt strong enough to slay dragons. " But who could the liar be ? Not Lizzie herself, surely ! Not——"

He pulled up short in a hollow of the towans.

" Not—George ? "

Treachery is a hideous thing ; and to youth so incomprehensibly hideous that it darkens the sun. Yet every trusting man must be betrayed. That was one of the lessons of Christ's life on earth. It is the last and severest test ; it kills many, morally, and no man who has once met and looked it in the face departs the same man, though he may be a stronger one.

" *Not George ?* "

Taffy stood there so still that the rabbits crept out and, catching sight of him, paused in the mouths of their burrows. When at length he moved on it was to take, not the path which wound inland to Mendarva's, but the one which led straight over the higher moors to Carwithiel.

It was between one and two o'clock when he reached the house and asked to see Mr. and Mrs. George Vyell. They were not at home, the footman said; had left for Falmouth the evening before to join some friends on a yachting cruise. Sir Harry was at home; was, indeed, lunching at that moment; but would no doubt be pleased to see Mr. Raymond.

Sir Harry had finished his lunch, and sat sipping his claret and tossing scraps of biscuits to the dogs.

"Hullo, Raymond!—thought you were in Oxford. Sit down, my boy; delighted to see you. Thomas, a knife and fork for Mr. Raymond. The cutlets are cold, I'm afraid; but I can recommend the cold saddle, and the ham—it's a York ham. Go to the sideboard and forage for yourself. I wanted company. My boy and Honoria are at Falmouth yachting, and have left me alone. What, you won't eat? A glass of claret, then, at any rate."

"To tell the truth, Sir Harry," Taffy began awkwardly. "I've come on a disagreeable business."

Sir Harry's face fell. He hated disagreeable business. He flipped a piece of biscuit at his spaniel's nose and sat back, crossing his legs.

"Won't it keep?"

"To me it's important."

"Oh, fire away then: only help yourself to the claret first."

"A girl—Lizzie Pezzack, living over at Langona—has had a child born——"

"Stop a moment. Do I know her?—Ah, to be sure—daughter of old Pezzack, the light-keeper—a brown-coloured girl with her hair over her eyes. Well, I'm not surprised. Wants money, I suppose? Who's the father?"

"I don't know."

"Well, but—damn it all!—somebody knows." Sir Harry reached for the bottle and refilled his glass.

"The one thing I know is that Honoria—Mrs. George, I mean—has heard about it, and suspects me."

Sir Harry lifted his glass and glanced at him over the rim. "That's the devil. Does she, now?" He sipped. "She hasn't been herself for a day or two—this explains it. I thought it was change of air she wanted. She's in the deuce of a rage, you bet."

"She is," said Taffy grimly.

"There's no prude like your young married woman. But it'll blow over, my boy. My advice to you is to keep out of the way for a while."

"But—but it's a lie!" broke in the indignant Taffy. "As far as I am concerned there's not a grain of truth in it!"

"Oh—I beg your pardon, I'm sure." Here Honoria's terrier (the one which George had bought for her at Plymouth) interrupted by begging for a biscuit, and Sir Harry balanced one carefully on its nose. "On trust—good dog! What does the girl say herself?"

"I don't know. I've not seen her."

"Then, my dear fellow—it's awkward, I admit—but I'm dashed if I see what you expect me to do."

The baronet pulled out a handkerchief and began flicking the crumbs off his knees.

Taffy watched him for a minute in silence. He was asking himself why he had come. Well, he had come in a hot fit of indignation, meaning to face Honoria and force her to take back the insult of her suspicion. But after all—suppose George were at the bottom of it ? Clearly Sir Henry knew nothing, and in any case could not be asked to expose his own son. And Honoria ? Let be that she would never believe—that he had no proof, no evidence even—this were a pretty way of beginning to discharge his debt to her ! The terrier thrust a cold muzzle against his hand. The room was very still. Sir Harry poured out another glassful and held out the decanter. " Come, you must drink ; I insist ! "

Taffy looked up. " Thank you, I will."

He could now and with a clear conscience. In those quiet moments he had taken the great resolution. The debt should be paid back, and with interest ; not at five per cent., but at a rate beyond the creditor's power of reckoning. For the interest to be guarded for her should be her continued belief in the man she loved. Yes, *but if George were innocent ?* Why, then the sacrifice would be idle ; that was all.

He swallowed the wine, and stood up.

" Must you be going ? I wanted a chat with you about Oxford," grumbled Sir Harry ; but noting the lad's face, how white and drawn it was, he relented, and put a hand on his shoulder. " Don't take it too seriously, my boy. It'll blow over—it'll blow over. Honoria likes you, I know. We'll see what the trollop says: and if I get a chance of putting in a good word, you may depend on me."

He walked with Taffy to the door—good, easy man—and waved a hand from the porch. On the whole, he was rather glad than not to see his young friend's back.

* * * * * *

From his smithy window Mendarva spied Taffy coming along the road, and stepped out on the green to shake hands with him.

"Pleased to see your face, my son! You'll excuse my not asking 'ee inside; but the fact is"—he jerked his thumb towards the smithy—"we've a-got our troubles in there."

It came on our youth with something of a shock that the world had room for any trouble beside his own.

"'Tis the Dane. He went over to Truro yesterday to the wrastlin', an' got thrawed. I tell'n there's no call to be shamed. 'Twas Luke the Wendron fella did it—in the treble play—inside lock backward, and as pretty a chip as ever I see." Mendarva began to illustrate it with foot and ankle, but checked himself, and glanced nervously over his shoulder. "Isn' lookin', I hope? He's in a terrible pore about it. Won't trust hissel' to spake, and don't want to see nobody. But, as I tell'n, there's no call to be shamed; the fella took the belt in the las' round, and turned his man over like a tab. He's a proper angletwitch, that Wendron fella. Stank 'pon en both ends, and he'll rise up in the middle and look at 'ee. There was no one a patch on en but the Dane; and I'll back the Dane next time they clinch.

'Tis a nuisance, though, to have'n like this—with a big job coming on, too, over to the light-house."

Taffy looked steadily at the smith. "What's doing at the light-house ? "

"Ha'n't 'ee heerd ? " Mendarva began a long tale, the sum of which was that the light-house had begun of late to show signs of age, to rock at times in an ominous manner. The Trinity House surveyor had been down and reported, and Mendarva had the contract for some immediate repairs. "But 'tis patching an old kettle, my son. The foundations be clamped down to the rock, and the clamps have worked loose. The whole thing'll have to come down in the end ; you mark my words."

"But, these repairs ? " Taffy interrupted: "You'll be wanting hands."

"Why, o' course."

"And a foreman—a clerk of the works——"

* * * * * *

While Mendarva was telling his tale, over a hill two miles to the westward a small donkey-cart crawled for a minute against the sky-line and disappeared beyond the ridge which hid the towans. An old man trudged at the donkey's head ; and a young woman sat in the cart with a bundle in her arms.

The old man trudged along so deep in thought that when the donkey without rhyme or reason came to a halt, half-way down the hill, he too halted, and stood pulling a wisp of grey side-whiskers.

"Look here," he said. "You ent goin' to tell ? That's your las' word, is it ? "

The young woman looked down on the bundle and nodded her head.

"There, that'll do. If you weant, you weant; I've tek'n 'ee back, an' us must fit and make the best o't. The cheeld'll never be good for much—born lame like that. But 'twas to be, I s'pose."

Lizzie sat dumb, but hugged the bundle closer.

"'Tis like a judgment. If your mother'd been spared, 'twudn' have happened. But 'twas to be, I s'pose. The Lord's ways be past findin' out."

He woke up and struck the donkey across the rump.

"Gwan you! Gee up! What d'ee mean by stoppin' like that?"

CHAPTER XXIII.

THE SERVICE OF THE LAMP.

THE Chief Engineer of the Trinity House was a man of few words. He and Taffy had spent the afternoon clambering about the rocks below the light-house, peering into its foundations. Here and there, where weed coated the rocks and made foothold slippery, he took the hand which Taffy held out. Now and then he paused for a pinch of snuff. The round of inspection finished, he took an extraordinarily long pinch.

"What's *your* opinion?" he asked, cocking his head on one side and examining the young man much as he had examined the light-house. "You have one, I suppose?"

"Yes, sir; but of course it doesn't count for much."

"I asked for it."

"Well, then, I think, sir, we have wasted a year's work; and if we go on tinkering we shall waste more."

"Pull it down and rebuild, you say?"

"Yes, sir; but not on the same rock."

"Why?"

"This rock was ill-chosen. You see, sir, just here

a ridge of elvan crops up through the slate; the rock, out yonder, is good elvan, and that is why the sea has made an island of it, wearing away the softer stuff inshore. The mischief here lies in the rock, not in the light-house."

"The sea has weakened our base?"

"Partly: but the light-house has done more. In a strong gale the foundations begin to work, and in the chafing the rock gets the worst of it."

"What about concrete?"

"You might fill up the sockets with concrete; but I doubt, sir, if the case would hold for any time. The rock is a mere shell in places, especially on the north-western side."

"H'm. You were at Oxford for a time, were you not?"

"Yes, sir," Taffy answered, wondering.

"I've heard about you. Where do you live?"

Taffy pointed to the last of a line of three white-washed cottages behind the light-house.

"Alone?"

"No, sir; with my mother and my grandmother. She is an invalid."

"I wonder if your mother would be kind enough to offer me a cup of tea?"

In the small kitchen, on the walls of which, and even on the dresser, Taffy's books fought for room with Humility's plates and tin-ware, the Chief Engineer proved to be a most courteous old gentleman. Towards Humility he bore himself with an antique politeness which flattered her considerably. And when he praised her tea she almost forgave him for his detestable habit of snuff-taking.

He had heard something (it appeared) from the President of Taffy's college, and also from—— (he named Taffy's old friend in the velvet college-cap). In later days Taffy maintained not only that every man must try to stand alone, but that he ought to try the harder because of its impossibility; for in fact it was impossible to escape from men's helpfulness. And though his work was done in lonely places where in the end fame came out to seek him, he remained the same boy who, waking in the dark, had heard the bugles speaking comfort.

As a matter of fact his college had generously offered him a chance which would have cost him nothing or next to nothing, of continuing to read for his degree. But he had chosen his line, and against Humility's entreaties he stuck to it. The Chief Engineer took a ceremonious leave. He had to drive back to his hotel, and Taffy escorted him to his carriage.

"I shall run over again to-morrow," he said at parting; "and we'll have a look at that island rock." He was driven off, secretly a little puzzled.

Well, it puzzled Taffy at times why he should be working here with Mendarva's men for twenty shillings a week (it had been eighteen, to begin with) when he might be reading for his degree and a fellowship. Yet in his heart he knew the reason. *That* would be building, after all, on the foundations which Honoria had laid.

Pride had helped chance to bring him here, to the very spot where Lizzie Pezzack lived. He met her daily, and several times a day. She, and his mother and grandmother, were all the women-folk in the hamlet—if three cottages deserve that name. In the first cottage Lizzie lived with her father, who was chief light-houseman, and her crippled child; two under-keepers, unmarried men, managed together in the second; and this accident allowed Taffy to rent the third from the Brethren of the Trinity House and live close to his daily work. Unless brought by business, no one visited that windy peninsula; no one passed within sight of it; no tree grew upon it or could be seen from it. At daybreak Taffy's workmen came trudging along the track where the short turf and gentians grew between the wheel-ruts; and in the evening went trudging back, the level sun flashing on their empty dinner-cans. The eight souls left behind had one common gospel—Cleanliness. Very little dust found its way thither; but the salt, spray-laden air kept them constantly polishing window-panes and brass-work. To wash, to scour, to polish, grew into the one absorbing business of life. They had no gossip; even in their own dwellings they spoke but little; their speech shrank and dwindled away in the continuous roar of the sea. But from morning to night, mechanically, they washed and scoured and polished. Paper was not whiter than the deal table and dresser which Humility scrubbed daily with soap and water, and once a week with lemon-juice as well. Never was cleaner linen to sight and smell than that which she pegged out by the furze-brake on the ridge. All the life of the small colony, though lonely, grew wholesome as it was simple of purpose in cottages thus sweetened and kept sweet by limewash and the salt wind.

And through it moved the forlorn figure of Lizzie Pezzack's child. Somehow Lizzie had taught the boy to walk, with the help of a crutch, as early as most children; but the wind made cruel sport with his first efforts in the open, knocking the crutch from under him at every third step, and laying him flat. The child had pluck, however; and when autumn came round again, could face a fairly stiff breeze.

It was about this time that word came of the Trinity Board's intention to replace the old lighthouse with one upon the outer rock. For the Chief Engineer had visited it and decided that Taffy was right. To be sure no mention was made of Taffy in his report; but the great man took the first opportunity to offer him the post of foreman of the works, so there was certainly nothing to be grumbled at. The work did not actually start until the following spring; for the rock, to receive the foundations, had to be bored some feet below high-water level, and this could only be attempted on calm days or when a southerly wind blew from the high land well over the workmen's heads, leaving the inshore water smooth. On such days Taffy, looking up from his work, would catch sight of a small figure on the cliff-top leaning aslant to the wind and watching.

For the child was adventurous and took no account of his lameness. Perhaps if he thought of it at all, having no chance to compare himself with other children, he accepted his lameness as a condition of childhood—something he would grow out of. His mother could not keep him indoors; he fidgeted continually. But he would sit or stand quiet by the hour on the cliff-top watching the men as they drilled and fixed the dynamite, and waiting for the bang of it. Best of all, however, were the days when his grandfather allowed him inside the light-house, to clamber about the staircase and ladders, to watch the oiling and trimming of the great lantern, and the ships moving slowly on the horizon. He asked a thousand questions about them.

"I think," said he one day before he was three years old, "that my father is in one of those ships."

"Bless the child!" exclaimed old Pezzack. "Who says you have a father?"

"*Everybody* has a father. Dicky Tregenza has one; they both work down at the rock. I asked Dicky, and he told me."

"Told 'ee what?"

"That everybody has a father. I asked him if mine was out in one of those ships, and he said very likely. I asked mother, too, but she was washing-up and wouldn't listen."

Old Pezzack regarded the child grimly. "'Twas to be, I s'pose," he muttered.

Lizzie Pezzack had never set foot inside the Raymonds' cottage. Humility, gentle soul as she was, could on some points be as unchristian as other women. As time went on it seemed that not a soul beside herself and Taffy knew of Honoria's suspicion. She even doubted, and Taffy doubted too, if Lizzie herself knew such an accusation had been made. Certainly never by word or look had Lizzie hinted at it. Yet Humility could not find it in her heart to forgive her. "She may be innocent," was the thought; "but through her came the injury to my son." Taffy by this time had no doubt at all. It was George who poisoned Honoria's ear; George's shame and Honoria's pride would explain why the whisper had never gone further; and nothing else would explain.

Did his mother guess this? He believed so at times, but they never spoke of it.

The lame child was often in the Raymonds' kitchen. Lizzie did not forbid or resent this. And he liked Humility, and would talk to her at length while he nibbled one of her dripping-cakes. "People don't tell the truth," he observed sagely on one of these occasions. (He pronounced it "troof," by the way.) "*I* know why we live here. It's because we're near the sea. My father's on the sea somewhere looking for us, and grandfather lights the lamp every night to tell him where we are. One night he'll see it and bring his ship in and take us all off together."

"Who told you all this?"

"Nobody. People won't tell me nothing (nofing). I has to make it out in my head."

At times, when his small limbs grew weary (though he never acknowledged this) he would stretch himself on the short turf of the headland and lie staring up at the white gulls. No one ever came near enough to surprise the look which then crept over the child's face. But Taffy, passing him at a distance, remembered another small boy, and shivered to remember and compare—

> "A boy's will is the wind's will,
> And the thoughts of youth are long, long thoughts."

—but how when the boy is a cripple?

One afternoon he was stooping to inspect an obstinate piece of boring when the man at his elbow said:

"Hullo! edn' that young Joey Pezzack in diffities up there? Blest if the cheeld won't break his neck wan of these days!"

Taffy caught up a coil of rope, sprang into a boat, and pushed across to land. "Don't move!" he shouted. At the foot of the cliff he picked up Joey's crutch and ran at full speed up the path worn by the workmen. This led him round to the verge ten feet above the ledge where the child clung white and silent. He looped the rope in a running noose and lowered it.

"Slip this under your arms. Can you manage, or shall I come down? I'll come if you're hurt."

"I've twisted my foot. It's all right, now you're come," said the little man bravely; and slid the rope round himself in the most business-like way.

"The grass was slipper——" he began, as soon as his feet touched firm earth: and with that he broke down and fell to sobbing in Taffy's arms.

Taffy carried him—a featherweight—to the cottage where Lizzie stood by her table washing up. She saw them at the gate and came running out.

"It's all right. He slipped—out on the cliff. Nothing more than a scratch or two, and perhaps a sprained ankle."

He watched while she set Joey in a chair and began to pull off his stockings. He had never seen the child's foot naked. She turned suddenly, caught him looking, and pulled the stocking back over the deformity.

" Have you heard ? " she asked.

" What ? "

" *She* has a boy! Ah ! " she laughed harshly, " I thought that would hurt you. Well, you *have* been a silly ! "

" I don't think I understand."

" You don't think you understand ! " she mimicked. " And you're not fond of her, eh ? Never were fond of her, eh ? You silly—to let him take her, and never tell ! "

" Tell ? "

She faced him, hardening her gaze. " Yes, tell——" She nodded slowly; while Joey, unobserved by either, looked up with wide, round eyes.

" Men don't fight like that." The words were out before it struck him that one man had, almost certainly, fought like that. Her face, however, told him nothing. She could not know. " *You* have never told," he added.

" Because——" she began, but could not tell him the whole truth. And yet what he said was true. " Because you would not let me," she muttered.

" In the churchyard, you mean—on her wedding day ? "

" Before that."

" But before that I never guessed."

" All the same I knew what you were. You wouldn' have let me. It came to the same thing. And if I had told—— Oh, you make it hard for me ! " she wailed.

He stared at her, understanding this only—that somehow he could control her will.

" I will never let you tell," he said gravely.

"I hate her!"

"You shall not tell."

"Listen"—she drew close and touched his arm. "He never cared for her; it's not his way to care. She cares for him now, I dessay—not as she might have cared for *you*—but she's his wife, and some women are like that. There's her pride, any way. Suppose—suppose he came back to me?"

"If I caught him——" Taffy began: but the poor child, who for two minutes had been twisting his face heroically, interrupted with a wail:

"Oh, mother! my foot—it hurts so!"

CHAPTER XXIV.

FACE TO FACE.

THE first winter had interrupted all work upon the rock; but Taffy and his men had used the calm days of the following spring and summer to such purpose that before the end of July the foundations began to show above high-water neaps, and in September he was able to report that the building could be pushed forward in any ordinary weather. The workmen were carried to and from the mainland by a wire hawser and cradle, and the rising breastwork of masonry protected them from the beat of the sea. Progress was slow, for each separate stone had to be dovetailed above, below, and on all sides with the blocks adjoining it, besides being cemented; and care to be taken that no salt mingled with the fresh water, or found its way into the joints of the building. Taffy studied the barometer hour by hour, and kept a constant look-out to windward against sudden gales.

On November 16th the men had finished their dinner, and sat smoking under the lee of the wall, when Taffy, with his pocket-aneroid in his hand, gave the order to snug down and man the cradle for shore. They stared. The morning had been a halcyon one; and the northerly breeze, which had sprung up with the turn of the tide and was freshening, carried no cloud across the sky. Two vessels, a brigantine and a three-masted schooner, were merrily reaching down-channel before it, the brigantine leading; at two miles' distance they could see distinctly the white foam running from her bluff bows, and her forward deck from bulwark to bulwark as she heeled to it.

One or two grumbled. Half a day's work meant half a day's pay to them. It was all very well for the Cap'n, who drew his by the week.

"Come, look alive!" Taffy called sharply. He pinned his faith to the barometer, and as he shut it in its case he glanced at the brigantine and saw that her crew were busy with the braces, flattening the forward canvas. "See there, boys. There'll be a gale from the west'ard before night."

For a minute the brigantine seemed to have run into a calm. The schooner, half a mile behind her, came reaching along steadily.

"That there two-master's got a fool for a skipper," grumbled a voice. But almost at the moment the wind took her right aback—or would have done so had the crew not been preparing for it. Her stern swung slowly around into view, and within two minutes she was fetching away from them on the port tack, her sails hauled closer and closer as she went. Already the schooner was preparing to follow suit.

"Snug down, boys! We must be out of this in half an hour."

And sure enough, by the time Taffy gained the cliff by the old light-house, the sky had darkened, and a stiff breeze from the north-west, crossing the tide, was beginning to work up a nasty sea around the rock and lop it from time to time over the masonry and the platforms where half an hour before his men had been standing. The two vessels had disappeared in the weather ; and as Taffy stared in their driection a spit of rain—the first—took him viciously in the face.

He turned his back to it and hurried homeward. As he passed the light-house door old Pezzack called out to him :

" Hi ! wait a bit ! Would 'ee mind seein' Joey home ? I dunno what his mother sent him over here for, not I. He'll get hisself leakin'."

Joey came hobbling out, and put his right hand in Taffy's with the fist doubled.

" What's that in your hand ? "

Joey looked up shyly. " You won't tell ? "

" Not if it's a secret."

The child opened his palm and disclosed a bright half-crown piece.

" Where on earth did you get that ? "

" The soldier gave it to me."

" The soldier ? nonsense ! What tale are you making up ? "

" Well, he had a red coat, so he *must* be a soldier. He gave it to me, and told me to be a good boy and run off and play."

Taffy came to a halt. " Is he here—up at the cottages ? "

" How funnily you say that ! No, he's just rode

away. I watched him from the light-house windows. He can't be gone far yet."

"Look here, Joey—can you run?"

"Yes, if you hold my hand; only you mustn't go too fast. Oh, you're hurting!"

Taffy took the child in his arms, and with the wind at his back went up the hill with long stride. "There he is!" cried Joey as they gained the ridge; and he pointed; and Taffy, looking along the ridge, saw a speck of scarlet moving against the lead-coloured moors—half a mile away perhaps, or a little more. He sat the child down, for the cottages were close by. "Run home, sonny. I'm going to have a look at the soldier, too."

The first bad squall broke on the headland just as Taffy started to run. It was as if a bag of water had burst right overhead, and within a quarter of a minute he was drenched to the skin. So fiercely it went howling inland along the ridge that he half expected to see the horse urged into a gallop before it. But the rider, now standing high for a moment against the sky-line, went plodding on. For a while horse and man disappeared over the rise; but Taffy guessed that on hitting the cross-path beyond it they would strike away to the left and descend toward Langona Creek; and he began to slant his course to the left in anticipation. The tide, he knew, would be running in strong; and with this wind behind it he hoped—and caught himself praying—that it would be high enough to cover the wooden foot-bridge and make the ford impassable; and if so, the horseman would be delayed and forced to head back and fetch a circuit farther up the valley.

By this time the squalls were coming fast on each other's heels, and the strength of them flung him forward at each stride. He had lost his hat, and the rain poured down his back and squished in his boots. But all he felt was the hate in his heart. It had gathered there little by little for three years and a half, pent up, fed by his silent thoughts as a reservoir by small mountain streams; and with so tranquil a surface that at times—poor youth!—he had honestly believed it reflected God's calm, had been proud of his magnanimity, and said "forgive us our trespasses, as we forgive them that trespass against us." Now as he ran he prayed to the same God to delay the traitor at the ford.

Dusk was falling when George, yet unaware of pursuit, turned down the sunken lane which ended beside the ford. And by the shore, when the small waves lapped against his mare's fore-feet, he heard Taffy's shout for the first time and turned in his saddle. Even so it was a second or two before he recognised the figure which came plunging down the low cliff on his left, avoiding a fall only by wild clutches at the swaying elder boughs.

"Hello!" he shouted cheerfully. "Looks nasty, doesn't it?"

Taffy came down the beach, near enough to see that the mare's legs were plastered with mud, and to look up into his enemy's face.

"Get down," he panted.

"Hey?"

"Get down, I tell you. Come off your horse and put up your fists!"

"What the devil is the matter? Hello! . . . Keep off, I tell you! Are you mad?"

"Come off and fight."

"By God, I'll break your head in if you don't let go. . . . You idiot!"—as the mare plunged and tore the stirrup-leather from Taffy's grip—"She'll brain you, if you fool round her heels like that!"

"Come off, then."

"Very well." George backed a little, swung himself out of the saddle and faced him on the beach. "Now perhaps you'll explain."

"You've come from the headland?"

"Well?"

"From Lizzie Pezzack's."

"Well, and what then?"

"Only this, that so sure as you've a wife at home, if you come to the headland again I'll kill you; and if you're a man, you'll put up your fists now."

"Oh, that's it? May I ask what you have to do with my wife, or with Lizzie Pezzack?"

"Whose child is Lizzie's?"

"Not yours, is it?"

"You said so once; you told your wife so; liar that you were."

"Very good, my gentleman. You shall have what you want. Woa, mare!" He led her up the beach and sought for a branch to tie his reins to. The mare hung back, terrified by the swishing of the whipped boughs and the roar of the gale overhead: her hoofs, as George dragged her forward, scuffled with the loose-lying stones on the beach. After a minute he desisted and turned on Taffy again.

"Look here; before we have this out there's one

thing I'd like to know. When you were at Oxford, was Honoria maintaining you there ?"

"If you must know—yes."

"And when—when this happened, she stopped the supplies ?"

"Yes."

"Well, then, I didn't know it. She never told me."

"She never told *me*."

"You don't say——"

"I do. I never knew it until too late."

"Well, now, I'm going to fight you. I don't swallow being called a liar. But I tell you this first, that I'm damned sorry. I never guessed that it injured your prospects."

At another time, in another mood, Taffy might have remembered that George was George, and heir to Sir Harry's nature. As it was, the apology threw oil on the flame.

"You cur! Do you think it was *that?* And *you* are Honoria's husband!" He advanced with an ugly laugh. "For the last time, put up your fists."

They had been standing within two yards of each other; and even so, shouted at the pitch of their voices to make themselves heard above the gale. As Taffy took a step forward George lifted his whip. His left hand held the bridle on which the reluctant mare was dragging, and the action was merely instinctive, to guard against sudden attack.

But as he did so his face and uplifted arm were suddenly painted clear against the darkness. The mare plunged more wildly than ever. Taffy dropped his hands and swung round. Behind him, the black contour of the hill, the whole sky welled up a pale blue light which gathered brightness while he stared. The very stones on the beach at his feet shone separate and distinct.

"What is it?" George gasped.

"A ship on the rocks! Quick, man! Will the mare reach to Innis?"

"She'll have to." George wheeled her round. She was fagged out with two long gallops after hounds that day, but for the moment sheer terror made her lively enough.

"Ride, then! Call up the coast-guard. By the flare she must be somewhere off the creek here. Ride!"

A clatter of hoofs answered him as the mare pounded up the lane.

CHAPTER XXV.

THE WRECK OF THE "SAMARITAN."

TAFFY stood for a moment listening. He judged the wreck to be somewhere on the near side of the light-house, between it and the mouth of the creek; that was, if she had already struck. If not, the gale and the set of the tide together would be sweeping her eastward, perhaps right across the mouth of the creek. And if he could discover this his course would be to run back, intercept the coast-guard, and send him around by the upper bridge.

He waited for a second signal to guide him—a flare or a rocket: but none came. The beach lay in the lew of the weather, deep in the hills' hollow and trebly land-locked by the windings of the creek, but above him the sky kept its screaming as though the bare ridges of the headland were being shelled by artillery.

He resolved to keep along the lower slopes and search his way down to the creek's mouth, when he would have sight of any signal shown along the coast for a mile or two to the east and north-east. The night was now as black as a wolf's throat, but he knew every path and fence. So he scrambled up the low cliff and began to run, following the line of stunted oaks and tamarisks which fenced it, and on the ridges—where the blown hail took him in the face—crouching and scuttling like a crab sideways, moving his legs only from the knees down.

In this way he had covered half a mile and more when his right foot plunged in a rabbit hole and he was pitched headlong into the tamarisks below. Their boughs bent under his weight, but they were tough, and he caught at them, and just saved himself from rolling over into the black water. He picked himself up and began to rub his twisted ankle. And at that instant, in a lull between two gusts, his ear caught the sound of splashing, yet a sound so unlike the lapping of the driven tide that he peered over and down between the tamarisk boughs.

"Hullo there!"

"Hullo!" a voice answered. "Is that someone alive? Here, mate—for Christ's sake!"

"Hold on! Whereabouts are you?"

"Down in this here cruel water." The words ended in a shuddering cough.

"Right—hold on for a moment!" Taffy's ankle pained him, but the wrench was not serious. The cliff shelved easily. He slid down, clutching at the tamarisk boughs which whipped his face. "Where are you? I can't see."

"Here!" The voice was not a dozen yards away.

"Swimming?"

"No—I've got a water-breaker—can't hold on much longer."

"I believe you can touch bottom there."

"Hey? I can't hear."

"Try to touch bottom. It's firm sand hereabouts."

"So I can." The splashing and coughing came nearer, came close. Taffy stretched out a hand. A hand, icy-cold, fumbled and gripped it in the darkness.

"Christ! Where's a place to lie down?"

"Here, on this rock." They peered at each other, but could not see. The man's teeth chattered close to Taffy's ear.

"Warm my hands, mate—there's a good chap." He lay on the rock and panted. Taffy took his hands and began to rub them briskly.

"Where's the ship?"

"Where's the ship?" He seemed to turn over the question in his mind, and then stretched himself with a sigh. "How the hell should I know?"

"What's her name?" Taffy had to ask the question twice.

"The *Samaritan*, of Newport, brigantine. Coals she carried. Ha'n't you such a thing as a match? It seems funny to me, talkin' here like this, and me not knowin' you from Adam."

He panted between the words, and when he had finished lay back and panted again.

"Hurt?" asked Taffy after a while.

The man sat up and began to feel his limbs, quite as though they belonged to some other body. "No, I reckon not."

"Then we'd best be starting. The tide's rising. My house is just above here."

He led the way along the slippery foreshore until he found what he sought, a foot-track slanting up the cliff. Here he gave the sailor a hand and they mounted together. On the grass slope above they met the gale and were forced to drop on their hands and knees and crawl, Taffy leading and shouting instructions, the sailor answering each with "Ay, ay, mate!" to show that he understood.

But about half-way up these answers ceased, and Taffy, looking round and calling, found himself alone. He groped his way back for twenty yards, and found the man stretched on his face and moaning.

"I can't . . . I can't! My poor brother! I can't!"

Taffy knelt beside him on the soaking turf. "Your brother? Had you a brother on board?"

The man bowed his face again upon the turf. Taffy, upright on both knees, heard him sobbing like a child in the roaring darkness.

"Come," he coaxed, and putting out a hand, touched his wet hair. "Come." They crept forward again, but still as he followed the sailor cried for his drowned brother, up the long slope to the ridge of the headland, where, with the light-house and warm cottage windows in view, all speech and hearing were drowned by stinging hail and the blown grit of the causeway.

Humility opened the door to them.

"Taffy! Where have you been?"

"There has been a wreck."

"Yes, yes—the coast-guard is down by the light-house. The men there saw her before she struck. They kept signalling till it fell dark. They had sent off before that."

She drew back, shrinking against the dresser as the lamplight fell on the stranger. Taffy turned and stared too. The man's face was running with blood;

and looking at his own hands he saw that they also were scarlet.

He helped the poor wretch to a chair.

"Bandages: can you manage?" She nodded, and stepped to a cupboard. The sailor began to wail again like an infant.

"See—above the temple here: the cut isn't serious." Taffy took down a lantern and lit it. The candle shone red through the smears his fingers left on the horn panes. "I must go and help, if you can manage."

"I can manage," she answered quietly.

He strode out, and closing the door behind him with an effort, faced the gale again. Down in the lee of the light-house the lamps of the coast-guard carriage gleamed foggily through the rain. The men were there discussing, George among them. He had just galloped up.

The Chief Officer went off to question the survivor, while the rest began their search. They searched all that night; they burned flares and shouted; their torches dotted the cliffs. After an hour the Chief Officer returned. He could make nothing of the sailor, who had fallen silly from exhaustion or the blow on his head; but he divided his men into three parties, and they began to hunt more systematically. Taffy was told off to help the westernmost gang and search the rocks below the light-house. Once or twice he and his comrades paused in their work, hearing, as they thought, a cry for help. But when they listened, it was only one of the other parties hailing.

The gale began to abate soon after midnight, and

before dawn had blown itself out. Day came, filtered slowly through the wrack of it to the south-east; and soon they heard a whistle blown, and there on the cliff above them was George Vyell on horseback, in his red coat, with an arm thrown out and pointing eastward. He turned and galloped off in that direction.

They scrambled up and followed. To their astonishment, after following the cliffs for a few hundred yards, he headed inland, down and across the very slope up which Taffy had crawled with the sailor.

They lost sight of his red coat among the ridges. Two or three—Taffy amongst them—ran along the upper ground for a better view.

"Well, this beats all!" panted the foremost.

Below them George came into view again, heading now at full gallop for a group of men gathered by the shore of the creek, a good half-mile from its mouth. And beyond—midway across the sandy bed where the river wound—lay the hull of a vessel, high and dry; her deck, naked of wheelhouse and hatches, canted toward them as if to cover from the morning the long wounds ripped by her uprooted masts.

The men beside him shouted and ran on, but Taffy stood still. It was monstrous—a thing inconceivable—that the seas should have lifted a vessel of three hundred tons and carried her half a mile up that shallow creek. Yet there she lay. A horrible thought seized him. Could she have been there last night when he had drawn the sailor ashore? And had he left four or five others to drown close by, in the darkness? No, the tide at that hour had scarcely passed half-flood. He thanked God for that.

Well, there she lay, high and dry, with plenty to attend to her. It was time for him to discover the damage done to the light-house plant and machinery, perhaps to the building itself. In half an hour the workmen would be arriving.

He walked slowly back to the house, and found Humility preparing breakfast.

"Where is he?" Taffy asked, meaning the sailor. "In bed?"

"Didn't you meet him? He went out five minutes ago—I couldn't keep him—to look for his brother, he said."

Taffy drank a cupful of tea, took up a crust, and made for the door.

"Go to bed, dear," his mother pleaded. "You must be worn out."

"I must see how the works have stood it."

On the whole, they had stood it well. The gale, indeed, had torn away the wire table and cage, and thus cut off for the time all access to the outer rock; for while the sea ran at its present height the scramble out along the ridge could not be attempted even at low water. But from the cliff he could see the worst. The waves had washed over the building, tearing off the temporary covers, and churning all within. Planks, scaffolding—everything floatable—had gone, and strewed the rock with matchwood; and—a marvel to see—one of his two heaviest winches had been lifted from inside, hurled clean over the wall, and lay collapsed in the wreckage of its cast-iron frame. But, so far as he could see, the dove-tailed masonry stood intact. A voice hailed him.

"What a night! What a night!"

It was old Pezzack, aloft on the gallery of the light-house in his yellow oilers, already polishing the lantern panes.

Taffy's workmen came straggling and gathered about him. They discussed the damage together but without addressing Taffy; until a little pock-marked fellow, the wag of the gang, nudged a mate slily and said aloud—

"By God, Bill, we *can* build a bit—you and me and the boss!"

All the men laughed; and Taffy laughed too, blushing. Yes; this had been in his mind. He had measured his work against the sea in its fury, and the sea had not beaten him.

A cry broke in upon their laughter. It came from the base of the cliff to the right: a cry so insistent that they ran toward it in a body.

Far below them, on the edge of a great boulder which rose from the broken water and seemed to overhang it, stood the rescued sailor. He was pointing.

Taffy was the first to reach him!

"It's my brother! It's my brother Sam!"

Taffy flung himself full length on the rock and peered over. A tangle of ore-weed awash rose and fell about its base; and from under this, as the frothy waves drew back, he saw a man's ankle protruding, and a foot still wearing a shoe.

"It's my brother!" wailed the sailor again. "I can swear to the shoe of en!"

CHAPTER XXVI.

SALVAGE.

ONE of the masons lowered himself into the pool, and thrusting an arm beneath the ore-weed, began to grope.

"He's pinned here. The rock's right on top of him."

Taffy examined the rock. It weighed fifteen tons if an ounce; but there were fresh and deep scratches upon it. He pointed these out to the men, who looked and felt them with their hands and stared at the subsiding waves, trying to bring their minds to the measure of the spent gale.

"Here, I must get out of this!" said the man in the pool, as a small wave dashed in and sent its spray over his bowed shoulders.

"You ban't going to leave en?" wailed the sailor. "You ban't going to leave my brother Sam?"

He was a small, fussy man, with red whiskers; and even his sorrow gave him little dignity. The men were tender with him.

"Nothing to be done till the tide goes back."

"But you won't leave en? Say you won't leave en! He've a wife and three children. He was a saved man, sir, a very religious man; not like me, sir. He was highly respected in the neighbourhood of St. Austell. I shouldn't wonder if the newspapers had a word about en . . ." The tears were running down his face.

"We must wait for the tide," said Taffy gently, and tried to lead him away, but he would not go. So they left him to watch and wait while they returned to their work.

Before noon they recovered and fixed the broken wire cable. The iron cradle had disappeared, but to rig up a sling and carry out an endless line was no difficult job, and when this was done Taffy crossed over to the island rock and began to inspect damages. His working gear had suffered heavily, two of his windlasses were disabled, scaffolding, platforms, hods, and loose planks had vanished; a few small tools only remained, mixed together in a mash of puddled lime. But the masonry stood unhurt, all except a few feet of the upper course on the seaward side, where the gale, giving the cement no time to set, had shaken the dove-tailed stones in their sockets—a matter easily repaired.

Shortly before three a shout recalled them to the mainland. The tide was drawing towards low water, and three of the men set to work at once to open a channel and drain off the pool about the base of the big rock. While this was doing, half a dozen splashed in with iron bars and pickaxes; the rest rigged two stout ropes with tackles, and hauled. The stone did not budge. For more than an hour they prised and levered and strained. And all the while the sailor ran to and fro, snatching up now a pick and now a crowbar, now lending a hand to haul, and again breaking off to lament aloud.

The tide turned, the winter dark came down, and at half-past four Taffy gave the word to desist. They had to hold back the sailor, or he would have jumped in and drowned beside his brother.

Taffy slept little that night, though he needed sleep. The salving of this body had become almost a personal dispute between the sea and him. The gale had shattered two of his windlasses; but two remained, and by one o'clock next day he had both slung over to the mainland and fixed beside the rock. The news spreading inland fetched two or three score onlookers before ebb of tide—miners for the most part, whose help could be counted on. The men of the coast-guard had left the wreck, to bear a hand if needed. George had come too. And happening to glance upwards while he directed his men, Taffy saw a carriage with two horses drawn up on the grassy edge of the cliff: a groom at the horses' heads and in the carriage a figure seated, silhouetted there high against the clear blue heaven. Well he recognised, even at that distance, the poise of her head, though for almost four years he had never set eyes on her,—nor had wished to.

He knew that her eyes were on him now. He felt like a general on the eve of an engagement. By the almanac the tide would not turn until 4.35. At four, perhaps, they could begin; but even at four the winter twilight would be on them, and he had taken care to provide torches and distribute them among the crowd. His own men were making the most of the daylight left, drilling holes for dear life in the upper surface of the boulder, and fixing the Lewis-wedges and rings. They looked to him for every order, and he gave it in a clear, ringing voice which he knew must carry to the cliff top. He did not look at George.

He felt sure in his own mind that the wedges and rings would hold ; but to make doubly sure he gave orders to loop an extra chain under the jutting base of the boulder. The mason who fixed it, standing waist-high in water as the tide ebbed, called for a rope and hitched it round the ankle of the dead man. The dead man's brother jumped down beside him and grasped the slack of it.

At a signal from Taffy the crowd began to light their torches. He looked at his watch, at the tide, and gave the word to man the windlasses. Then with a glance towards the cliff he started the working chant—" *Ayee-ho, Ayee-ho !* " The two gangs —twenty men to each windlass—took it up with one voice, and to the deep intoned chant the chains tautened, shuddered for a moment, and began to lift.

" *Ayee-ho !* "

Silently, irresistibly, the chain drew the rock from its bed. To Taffy it seemed an endless time, to the crowd but a few moments before the brute mass swung clear. A few thrust their torches down towards the pit where the sailor knelt. Taffy did not look, but gave the word to pass down the coffin which had been brought in readiness. A clergyman —his father's successor, but a stranger to him— climbed down after it : and he stood in the quiet crowd watching the light-house above and the lamps which the groom had lit in Honoria's carriage, and listening to the bated voices of the few at their dreadful task below.

It was five o'clock and past before the word came up to lower the tackle and draw the coffin up. The Vicar clambered out to wait it, and when it came, borrowed a lantern and headed the bearers. The crowd fell in behind.

"I am the resurrection and the life. . . ."

They began to shuffle forwards and up the difficult track; but presently came to a halt with one accord, the Vicar ceasing in the middle of a sentence.

Out of the night, over the hidden sea, came the sound of men's voices lifted, thrilling the darkness thrice: the sound of three British cheers.

Whose were the voices? They never knew. A few had noticed as twilight fell a brig in the offing, standing inshore as she tacked down channel. She, no doubt, as they worked in their circle of torch-light, had sailed in close before going about, her crews gathered forward, her master perhaps watching through his night-glass had guessed the act, saluted it, and passed on her way unknown to her own destiny.

They strained their eyes. A man beside Taffy declared he could see something—the faint glow of a binnacle lamp as she stood away. Taffy could see nothing. The voice ahead began to speak again. The Vicar, pausing now and again to make sure of his path, was reading from a page which he held close to his lantern.

"*Thine eyes shall see the King in His beauty: they shall behold the land that is very far off.*

"*Thou shalt not see a fierce people, a people of a deeper speech than thou canst perceive; of a stammering tongue that thou canst not understand.*

"*But there the glorious Lord will be unto us a place of broad rivers and streams; wherein shall go no galley with oars, neither shall gallant ship pass thereby.*

"*For the Lord is our judge, the Lord is our lawgiver, the Lord is our king; he will save us.*

"*Thy tacklings are loosed; they could not well strengthen their mast, they could not spread the sail; then is the prey of a great spoil divided; the lame take the prey.*"

Here the Vicar turned back a page, and his voice rang higher:

"*Behold a king shall reign in righteousness, and princes shall rule in judgment.*

"*And a man shall be as an hiding place from the wind, and a covert from the tempest; as rivers of water in a dry place, as the shadow of a great rock in a weary land.*

"*And the eyes of them that see shall not be dim, and the ears of them that hear shall hearken.*"

Now Taffy walked behind, thinking his own thoughts; for the cheers of those invisible sailors had done more than thrill his heart. A finger, as it were, had come out of the night and touched his brain, unsealing the wells and letting in light upon things undreamt of. Through the bright confusion of this sudden vision the Vicar's sentences sounded and fell on his ears unheeded. And yet while they faded that happened which froze and bit each separate word into his memory, to lose distinctness only when death should interfere, stop the active brain, and wipe the slate.

For while the procession halted and broke up its

formation for a moment on the brow of the cliff, a woman came running into the torchlight.

"Is my Joey there? Where's he *to*, anybody? Hev anyone seen my Joey?"

It was Lizzie Pezzack, panting and bareheaded, with a scared face.

"He's lame—you'd know en. Have 'ee got en there? He's wandered off!"

"Hush up, woman," said a bearer. "Don't keep such a pore!"

"The cheeld's right enough somewheres," said another. "'Tis a man's body we've got. Stand out of the way, for shame!"

But Lizzie, who as a rule shrank away from men and kept herself hidden, pressed nearer, turning her tragical face upon each in turn. Her eyes met George's, but she appealed to him as to the others.

"He's wandered off. Oh, say you've seen en, somebody!"

Catching sight of Taffy, she ran and gripped him by the arm.

"*You'll* help! It's my Joey. Help me find en!"

He turned half about, and almost before he knew what he sought his eyes met George's. George stepped quietly to his side.

"Let me get my mare," said George, and walked away toward the light-house railing where he had tethered her.

"We'll find the child. Our work's done here. Mr. Saul!" Taffy turned to the Chief Officer. "Spare us a man or two and some flares."

"I'll come myself," said the Chief Officer. "Go you back, my dear, and we'll fetch home your cheeld as right as ninepence. Hi, Rawlings, take a couple of men and scatter along the cliffs there to the right. Lame, you say? He can't have gone far."

Taffy, with the Chief Officer and a couple of volunteers, moved off to the left, and in less than a minute George caught them up, on horseback.

"I say," he asked, walking his mare close alongside of Taffy, "you don't think this serious, eh?"

"I don't know. Joey wasn't in the crowd, or I should have noticed him. He's daring beyond his strength." He pulled a whistle from his pocket, blew it twice, and listened. This had been his signal when firing a charge; he had often blown it to warn the child to creep away into shelter.

There was no answer.

"Mr. Vyell had best trot along the upper slope," the Chief Officer suggested, "while we search down by the creek."

"Wait a moment," Taffy answered. "Let's try the wreck first."

"But the tide's running. He'd never go there."

"He's a queer child. I know him better than you."

They ran downhill toward the creek, calling as they went, but getting no answer.

"But the wreck!" exclaimed the Chief Officer. "It's out of reason!"

"Hi! What was that?"

"Oh, my good Lord," groaned one of the volunteers, "it's the crake, master! It's Langona crake calling the drowned!"

"Hush, you fool! Listen—I thought as much! Light a flare, Mr. Saul—he's out there calling!"

The first match spluttered and went out. They drew close around the Chief Officer while he struck the second to keep off the wind, and in those few moments the child's wail reached them distinctly across the darkness.

The flame leaped up and shone, and they drew back a pace, shading their eyes from it and peering into the steel-blue landscape which sprang on them out of the night. They had halted a few yards only from the cliff, and the flare cast the shadow of its breast-high fence of tamarisks forward and almost half-way across the creek, and there on the sands, a little beyond the edge of this shadow, stood the child.

They could even see his white face. He stood on an island of sand around which the tide swirled in silence, cutting him off from the shore, cutting him off from the wreck behind.

He did not cry any more, but stood with his crutch planted by the edge of the widening stream, and looked toward them.

And Taffy looked at George.

"I know," said George quietly, and gathered up his reins. "Stand aside, please."

As they drew aside, not understanding, he called to his mare. One living creature, at any rate, could still trust all to George Vyell. She hurtled past them and rose at the tamarisk-hedge blindly. Followed silence—a long silence; then a thud on the beach below and a scuffle of stones; silence again, and then the cracking of twigs as Taffy plunged after, through the tamarisks, and slithered down the cliff.

The light died down as his feet touched the flat

slippery stones; died down, and was renewed again and showed up horse and rider scarce twenty yards ahead, labouring forward, the mare sinking fetlock deep at every plunge.

At his fourth stride Taffy's feet, too, began to sink, but at every stride he gained something. The riding may be superb, but thirteen stone is thirteen stone. Taffy weighed less than eleven.

He caught up with George on the very edge of the water. "Make her swim it!" he panted. "Her feet mustn't touch here." George grunted. A moment later all three were in the water, the tide swirling them sideways, sweeping Taffy against the mare. His right hand touched her flank at every stroke.

The tide swept them upwards—upwards for fifteen yards at least, though the channel measured less than eight feet. The child, who had been standing opposite the point where they took the water, hobbled wildly along shore. The light on the cliff behind sank and rose again.

"The crutch," Taffy gasped. The child obeyed, laying it flat on the brink and pushing it toward them. Taffy gripped it with his left hand, and with his right found the mare's bridle. George was bending forward.

"No—not that way! You can't get back! The wreck, man!—it's firmer——"

But George reached out his hand and dragged the child towards him and on to his saddle-bow. "Mine," he said quietly, and twitched the rein. The brave mare snorted, jerked the bridle from Taffy's hand, and headed back for the shore she had left.

Rider, horse, and child seemed to fall away from him into the night. He scrambled out, and snatching the crutch ran along the brink, staring at their black shadows. By-and-by the shadows came to a standstill. He heard the mare panting, the creaking of saddle-leather came across the nine or ten feet of dark water.

"It's no go," said George's voice; then to the mare, "Sally, my dear, it's no go." A moment later he asked more sharply:

"How far can you reach?"

Taffy stepped in until the waves ran by his knees. The sand held his feet, but beyond this he could not stand against the current. He reached forward holding the crutch at arm's length.

"Can you catch hold?"

"All right." Both knew that swimming would be useless now; they were too near the upper apex of the sand-bank.

"The child first. Here, Joey, my son! reach out and catch hold for your life."

Taffy felt the child's grip on the crutch-head, and drawing it steadily toward him hauled the poor child through. The light from the cliff sank and rose behind his scared face.

"Got him?"

"Yes." The sand was closing around Taffy's legs, but he managed to shift his footing a little.

"Quick, then; the bank's breaking up."

George was sinking, knee-deep and deeper. But his outstretched fingers managed to reach and hook themselves around the crutch-head.

"Steady, now . . . must work you loose first.

Get hold of the shaft if you can: the head isn't firm. Work your legs . . . that's it."

George wrenched his left foot loose and planted it against the mare's flank. Hitherto she had trusted her master. The thrust of his heel drove home her sentence, and with scream after scream—the sand holding her past hope—she plunged and fought for her life. Still as she screamed, George, silent and panting, thrust against her, thrust savagely against the quivering body, once his pride for beauty and fleetness.

"Pull!" he gasped, freeing his other foot with a wrench which left its heavy riding-boot deep in the sucking mud; and catching a new grip on the crutch-head, flung himself forward.

Taffy felt the sudden weight and pulled—and while he pulled felt in a moment no grip, no weight at all. Between two hateful screams a face slid by him, out of reach, silent, with parted lips; and as it slipped away he fell back staggering, grasping the useless, headless crutch.

The mare went on screaming. He turned his back on her, and catching Joey by the hand dragged him away across the melting island. At the sixth step the child, hauled off his crippled foot, swung blundering across his legs. He paused, lifted him in his arms and plunged forward again.

The flares on the cliff were growing in number. They cast long shadows before him. On the far side of the island the tide flowed swift and steady—a stream about fourteen yards wide—cutting him from the farther sand-bank on which, not fifty yards above, lay the wreck. He whispered to Joey, and plunged into it straight, turning as the water swept him off his legs, and giving his back to it, his hands slipped under the child's armpits, his feet thrusting against the tide in slow, rhythmical strokes.

The child after the first gasp lay still, his head obediently thrown back on Taffy's breast. The mare had ceased to scream. The water rippled in the ears as each leg-thrust drove them little by little across the current.

If George had but listened! It was so easy, after all. The sand-bank still slid past them, but less rapidly. They were close to it now, and had only to lie still and be drifted against the leaning stanchions of the wreck. Taffy flung an arm about one and checked his way quietly, as a man brings a boat alongside a quay. He hoisted Joey first upon the stanchion, then up the tilted deck to the gap of the main hatchway. Within this, with their feet on the steps and their chests leaning on the side panel of the companion, they rested and took breath.

"Cold, sonny?"

The child burst into tears.

Taffy dragged off his own coat and wrapped him in it. The small body crept close, sobbing, against his side.

Across, on the shore, voices were calling, blue eyes moving. A pair of yellow lights came towards these, travelling swiftly upon the hillside. Taffy guessed what they were.

The yellow lights moved more slowly. They joined the blue ones, and halted. Taffy listened. But the voices were still now; he heard nothing but the hiss of the black water, across which those two lamps sought and questioned him like eyes.

"God help her!"

He bowed his face on his arms. A little while, and the sands would be covered, the boats would put off; a little while. . . . Crouching from those eyes he prayed God to lengthen it.

CHAPTER XXVII.

HONORIA.

SHE was sitting there rigid, cold as a statue, when the rescuers brought them ashore and helped them up the slope. A small crowd surrounded the carriage. In the rays of their moving lanterns her face altered nothing to all their furtive glances of sympathy opposing the same white mask. Some one said, "There's only two, then!" Another, with a nudge and a nod at the carriage, told him to hold his peace. She heard. Her lips hardened.

Lizzie Pezzack had rushed down to the shore to meet the boat. She was bringing her child along with a fond, wild babble of tender names and sobs and cries of thankfulness. In pauses, choked and overcome, she caught him to her, felt his limbs, pressed his wet face against her neck and bosom. Taffy, supported by strong arms and hurried in her wake, had a hideous sense of being paraded in her triumph. The men around him who had raised a faint cheer sank their voices as they neared the carriage; but the woman went forward, jubilant and ruthless, flaunting her joy as it were a flag blown in her eyes and blindfolding them to the grief she insulted.

"Stay!"

It was Honoria's voice, cold, incisive, not to be disobeyed. He had prayed in vain. The procession halted; Lizzie checked her babble and stood staring, with an arm about Joey's neck.

"Let me see the child."

Lizzie stared, broke into a silly, triumphant laugh, and thrust the child forward against the carriage step. The poor waif, drenched, dazed, tottering without his crutch, caught at the plated handle for support. Honoria gazed down on him with eyes which took slow and pitiless account of the deformed little body, the shrunken, puny limbs.

"Thank you. So—this—is what my husband died for. Drive on, please."

Her eyes, as she lifted them to give the order, rested for a moment on Taffy—with how much scorn he cared not, could he have leapt and intercepted Lizzie's retort.

"And why not? A son's a son—curse you!—though he was your man!"

It seemed she did not hear; or hearing, did not understand. Her eyes hardened their fire on Taffy, and he, lapped in their scorn, thanked God she had not understood.

"Drive on, please."

The coachman lowered his whip. The horses moved forward at a slow walk; the carriage rolled silently away into the darkness. She had not understood. Taffy glanced at the faces about him.

"Ah, poor lady!" said someone. But no one had understood.

* * * * * *

They found George's body next morning on the

sands a little below the foot-bridge. He lay there in the morning sunshine as though asleep, with an arm flung above his head and on his face the easy smile for which men and women had liked him throughout his careless life.

The inquest was held next day, in the library at Carwithiel. Sir Harry insisted on being present, and sat beside the coroner. During Taffy's examination his lips were pursed up as though whistling a silent tune. Once or twice he nodded his head.

Taffy gave his evidence discreetly. The child had been lost; had been found in a perilous position. He and deceased had gone together to the rescue. On reaching the child, deceased—against advice—had attempted to return across the sands and had fallen into difficulties. In these his first thought had been for the child, whom he had passed to witness to drag out of danger. When it came to deceased's turn the crutch, on which all depended, had parted in two, and he had been swept away by the tide.

At the conclusion of the story Sir Harry took snuff and nodded twice. Taffy wondered how much he knew. The jury, under the coroner's direction, brought in a verdict of "death by misadventure," and added a word or two in praise of the dead man's gallantry. The coroner complimented Taffy warmly and promised to refer the case to the Royal Humane Society for public recognition. The jury nodded, and one or two said "Hear, hear!" Taffy hoped fervently he would do nothing of the sort.

The funeral took place on the fourth day, at nine o'clock in the morning. Such—in the day I write of—was the custom of the country. Friends who lived at a distance rose and shaved by candle-light, and daybreak found them horsed and well on their way to the house of mourning, their errand announced by the long black streamers tied about their hats. The sad business over and done with, these guests returned to the house, where until noon a mighty breakfast lasted and all were welcome. Their black habiliments and lowered voices alone marked the difference between it and a hunting-breakfast.

And indeed this morning Squire Willyams, who had taken over the hounds after Squire Moyle's death, had given secret orders to his huntsmen; and the pack was waiting at Three-barrow Turnpike, a couple of miles inland from Carwithiel. At half-past ten the mourners drained their glasses, shook the crumbs off their riding-breeches, and took leave; and after halting outside Carwithiel gates to unpin and pocket their hat-bands, headed for the meet with one accord.

A few minutes before noon Squire Willyams, seated on his grey by the edge of Three-barrow Brake, and listening to every sound within the covert, happened to glance an eye across the valley, and let out a low whistle.

"Well!" said one of a near group of horsemen catching sight of the rider pricking toward them down the farther slope, "I knew en for unbeliever; but this beats all!"

"And his awnly son not three hours under the mould! Brought up in France as a youngster he was, and this I s'pose is what comes of reading Voltaire. My lord for manners, and no more heart than a wormed nut—that's Sir Harry, and always was."

Squire Willyams slewed himself round in his saddle. He spoke quietly at fifteen yards' distance, but each word reached the group of horsemen as clear as a bell.

"Rablin," he said, "as a damned fool oblige me during the next few minutes by keeping your mouth shut."

With this he resumed his old attitude and his business of watching the covert side; removing his eyes for a moment to nod as Sir Harry rode up and passed on to join the group behind him.

He had scarcely done so when deep in the undergrowth of blackthorn a hound challenged.

"Spendigo for a fiver!—and well found, by the tune of it," cried Sir Harry. "See that patch of grey wall, Rablin—there, in a line beyond the Master's elbow? I lay you an even guinea that's where my gentleman comes over."

But honest reprobation mottled the face of Mr. Rablin, squireen; and as an honest man he spoke out. Let it go to his credit, because as a rule he was a snob and inclined to cringe.

"I did not expect"—he cleared his throat—"to see you out to-day, Sir Harry."

Sir Harry winced, and turned on them all a grey, woeful face.

"That's it," he said. "I can't bide home. I can't bide home."

* * * * * *

Honoria bided home with her child and mourned

for the dead. As a clever woman—far cleverer than her husband—she had seen his faults while he lived; yet had liked him enough to forgive without difficulty. But now these faults faded, and by degrees memory reared an altar to him as a man little short of divine. At the worst he had been amiable. A kinder husband never lived. She reproached herself bitterly with the half-heartedness of her response to his love; to his love while it dwelt beside her, unvarying in cheerful kindness. For (it was the truth, alas! and a worm that gnawed continually) passionate love she had never rendered him. She had been content; but how poor a thing was contentment! She had never divined his worth, had never given her worship. And all the while he had been a hero, and in the end had died as a hero. Ah, for one chance to redeem the wrong! for one moment to bow herself at his feet and acknowledge her blindness! Her prayer was ancient as widowhood, and Heaven, folding away the irreparable time, returned its first and last and only solace—a dream for the groping arms; waking and darkness, and an empty pillow for her tears.

From the first her child had been dear to her; dearer (so her memory accused her now) than his father; more demonstratively beloved, at any rate. But in those miserable months she grew to love him with a double strength. He bore George's name, and was (as Sir Harry proclaimed) a very miniature of George; repeated his shapeliness of limb, his firm shoulders, his long lean thighs—the thighs of a born horseman; learned to walk, and lo! within a week walked with his father's gait; had smiles for the whole of his small world, and for his mother a memory in each.

And yet—this was the strange part of it; a mystery she could not explain because she dared not even acknowledge it—though she loved him for being like his father, she regarded the likeness with a growing dread; nay, caught herself correcting him stealthily when he developed some trivial trait which she, and she alone, recognised as part of his father's legacy. It was what in the old days she would have called "contradictions," but there it was, and she could not help it; the nearer George in her memory approached to faultlessness, the more obstinately her instinct fought against her child's imitation of him; and yet, because the child was obstinately George's, she loved him with a double love.

There came a day when he told her a childish falsehood. She did not whip him, but stood him in front of her and began to reason with him and explain the wickedness of an untruth. By-and-by she broke off in the midst of a sentence, appalled by the shrillness of her own voice. From argument she had passed to furious scolding. And the little fellow quailed before her, his contrition beaten down under the storm of words that whistled about his ears without meaning, his small faculties disabled before this spectacle of wrath. Her fingers were closing and unclosing. They wanted a riding-switch; they wanted to grip this small body they had served and fondled, and to cut out—what? The lie? Honoria hated a lie. But while she paused and shook, a light flashed, and her eyes were open and saw—that it was not the lie.

She turned and ran, ran upstairs to her own room, flung herself on her knees beside the bed, dragged a locket from her bosom and fell to kissing George's portrait, passionately crying it for pardon. She was wicked, base; while he lived she had misprised him; and this was her abiding punishment, that not even repentance could purge her heart of dishonouring thoughts, that her love for him now could never be stainless though washed with daily tears. "'*He that is unjust, let him be unjust still.*' *Must* that be true, Father of all mercies? I misjudged him, and it is too late for atonement. But I repent and am afflicted. Though the dead know nothing—though it can never reach or avail him—give me back the power to be just!"

Late that afternoon Honoria passed an hour piously in turning over the dead man's wardrobe, shaking out and brushing the treasured garments and folding them, against moth and dust, in fresh tissue paper. It was a morbid task, perhaps, but it kept George's image constantly before her, and this was what her remorseful mood demanded. Her nerves were unstrung and her limbs languid after the recent tempest. By-and-by she locked the doors of the wardrobe, and passing into her own bedroom, flung herself on a couch with a bundle of papers—old bills, soiled and folded memoranda, sporting paragraphs cut from the newspapers—scraps found in his pockets months ago and religiously tied by her with a silken ribbon. They were mementoes of a sort, and George had written few letters while wooing—not half a dozen first and last.

Two or three receipted bills lay together in the

middle of the packet—one a saddler's, a second a nurseryman's for pot-plants (kept for the sake of its queer spelling), a third the reckoning for an hotel luncheon. She was running over them carelessly when the date at the head of this last one caught her eye. "August 3rd"—it fixed her attention because it happened to be the day before her birthday.

August 3rd—such and such a year—the August before his death; and the hotel a well-known one in Plymouth—the hotel, in fact, at which he had usually put up. . . . Without a prompting of suspicion she turned back and ran her eye over the bill. A steak, a pint of claret, vegetables, cheese, and attendance—never was a more innocent bill.

Suddenly her attention stiffened on the date. George was in Plymouth the day before her birthday. But no; as it happened, George had been in Truro on that day. She remembered, because he had brought her a diamond pendant, having written beforehand to the Truro jeweller to get a dozen down from London to choose from. Yes, she remembered it clearly, and how he had described his day in Truro. And the next morning—her birthday morning—he had produced the pendant, wrapped in silver paper. He had thrown away the case; it was ugly, and he would get her another. . . .

But the bill? She had stayed once or twice at this hotel with George, and recognised the handwriting. The bookkeeper, in compliment perhaps to a customer of standing, had written "George Vyell, Esq." in full on the bill-head, a formality omitted as a rule in luncheon-reckonings. And if this scrap of paper told the truth—why, *then George had lied!*

But why? Ah, if he had done this thing nothing else mattered, neither the how nor the why! If George had lied? . . . And the pendant—had that been bought in Plymouth and not (as he had asserted) in Truro? He had thrown away the case. Jewellers print their names inside such cases. The pendant was a handsome one. Perhaps his cheque-book would tell.

She arose, stepped half-way to the door, but came back and flung herself again upon the couch. No; she could not . . . this was the second time to-day . . . she could not face the torture again.

Yet . . . if George *had* lied!

She sat up; sat up with both hands pressed to her ears to shut out a sudden voice clamouring through them—

"*And why not? A son's a son—curse you!—though he was your man!*"

CHAPTER XXVIII.

À L'OUTRANCE.

LIZZIE PEZZACK had put Joey to bed and was smoothing his coverlet when she heard someone knocking. She passed out into the front room and opened to the visitor.

On the doorstep stood a lady in deep black—Honoria. Beyond the garden wall the lamps of her carriage blazed in the late twilight. The turf had muffled the sound of wheels, but now the jingle of shaken bits came loud through the open door.

"Ah!" said Lizzie, drawing her breath back through her teeth.

"I must speak to you, please. May I come in? I have a question . . ."

Lizzie turned her back, struck a match, and lit a candle. "What question?" she asked with her back turned, her eyes on the flame as it sank, warming the tallow, and grew bright again.

"It's . . . it's a question," Honoria began weakly; then shut the door behind her and advanced into the room. "Turn round and look at me. Ah, you hate me, I know!"

"Yes," Lizzie assented slowly, "I hate you."

"But you must answer me. You see, it isn't for me alone . . . it's not a question of our hating, in a way . . . it concerns others. . . ."

"Yes?"

"But it's cowardly of me to put it so, because it concerns me too. You don't know——"

"Maybe I do."

"But if you did——" Honoria broke off and then plunged forward desperately. "That child of yours—his father—alone here—by ourselves. . . . Think before you refuse!"

Lizzie set down the candle and eyed her.

"And *you*," she answered at length, dragging out each word—"*you* can come here and ask me that question?"

For a moment silence fell between them, and each could hear the other's breathing. Then Honoria drew herself up and faced her honestly, casting out both hands.

"Yes; I *had* to."

"*You!* a lady!"

"Ah, but be honest with me! Lady or not, what has that to do with it? We are two women—that's where it all started, and we're kept to that."

Lizzie bent her brows. "Yes, you are right," she admitted.

"And," Honoria pursued eagerly, "if I come here to sue you for the truth—it is you who force me."

"I?"

"By what you said that night, when George—when my husband—was drowned; when you cursed me. 'A son's a son,' you said, 'though he was your man.'"

"Did I say that?" Lizzie seemed to muse over the words. "You have suffered?" she asked.

"Yes, I have suffered."

"Ah, if I thought so! . . . But you have not. You are a hypocrite, Mrs. Vyell; and you are trying to cheat me now. You come here not to end *that* suffering, but to force a word from me that'll put joy and hope into you; that you'll go home hugging to your heart. Oh, I know you!"

"You do not."

"I do; because I know myself. From a child I've been dirt to your pride, an item to your money. For years I've lived a shamed woman. But one thing I bought with it—one little thing. Think the price high for it—I dessay it is; but I bought and paid for it—and often when I turn it over in my mind I don't count the price too dear."

"I don't understand."

"You may, if you try. What I bought was the power over you, my proud lady. While I keep tight lips I have you at the end of a chain. You come here to-night to break it; one little word and you'll be free and glad. But no, and no, and no! You may guess till you're tired—you may be sure in your heart; but it's all no good without that little word you'll never get from me."

"You *shall* speak!"

Lizzie shrugged her shoulders and picked up the candle.

"Simme," she said, "you'd best go back to your carriage and horses. My li'l boy's in the next room, tryin' to sleep; and 'tisn' fit he heard much of this."

She passed resolutely into the bedroom, leaving

her visitor to darkness. But Honoria, desperate now, pushed after her, scarcely knowing what she did or meant to do.

"You *shall* speak!"

The house-door opened and light footsteps came running through the outer room. It was little George, and he pulled at her skirts.

"Mummy, the horses are taking cold!"

But Honoria still advanced. "You *shall* speak!"

Joey, catching sight of her from the bed, screamed and hid his face. To him she was a thing of horror. From the night when, thrust beneath her eyes, he had cowered by her carriage-step, she had haunted his worst dreams. And now, black-robed and terrible of face, she had come to lay hands on him and carry him straight to hell.

"Mother! Take her away! take her away!"

His screams rang through the room. "Hush, dear!" cried Lizzie, running to him; and laid a hand on his shoulder.

But the child, far too terrified to know whose hand it was, flung himself from her with a wilder scream than any; flung himself all but free of the bed-clothes. As Lizzie caught and tried to hold him the thin night-shirt ripped in her fingers, laying bare the small back from shoulder to buttock.

They were woman to woman now; cast back into savagery and blindly groping for its primitive weapons. Honoria crossed the floor not knowing what she meant to do, or might do. Lizzie sprang to defence against she knew not what. But when her enemy advanced, towering, with a healthy boy dragging at her skirts, she did the one thing she could—turned with a swift cry back upon her own crippled child and caught at the bed-clothes to cover and hide his naked deformity.

While she crouched and shielded him, silence fell on the room. She had half expected Honoria to strike her; but no blow came, nor any sound. By-and-by she looked up. Honoria had come to a standstill, with rigid eyes. They were fastened on the bed. Then Lizzie understood.

She had covered the child's legs from sight; but not his back—nor the brown mole on it—the large brown mole, ringed like Saturn, set obliquely between the shoulder-blades.

She rose from the bed slowly. Honoria turned on little George with a gesture as if to fling off his velvet jacket. But Lizzie stamped her foot.

"No," she commanded hoarsely; "let be. Mine is a cripple."

"So it is true. . . ." Honoria desisted; but her eyes were wide and still fixed on the bed.

"Yes, it is true. You have all the luck. Mine is a cripple."

Still Honoria stared. Lizzie gulped down something in her throat; but her voice, when she found it again, was still hoarse and strained.

"And now—go! You have learnt what you came for. You have won, because you stop at nothing. But go, before I try to kill you for the joy in your heart!"

"Joy?" Honoria put out a hand toward the bed's foot, to steady herself. It was her turn to be weak.

"Yes—joy." Lizzie stepped between her and the

door, pointed a finger at her, and held it pointing. "In your heart you are glad already. Wait, and in a moment I shall see it in your eyes—glad, glad! Yes, your man was worthless, and you are glad. But oh! you bitter fool!"

"Let me go, please."

"Listen a bit; no hurry now. Plenty of time to be glad 'twas only your husband, not the man of your heart. Look at me, and answer—I don't count for much now, do I? Not much to hate in me, now you know the name of my child's father, and that 'tisn' Taffy Raymond!"

"Let me go." But seeing that Lizzie would not, she stopped and kissed her boy. "Run out to the carriage, dear, and say I'll be coming in a minute or two." Little George clung to her wistfully, but her tone meant obedience. Lizzie stepped aside to let him pass out.

"Now," said Honoria, "the next room is best, I think. Lead me there, and I will listen."

"You may go if you like."

"No; I will listen. Between us two there is—there is——"

"*That.*" Lizzie nodded towards the child huddling low in the bed.

"That, and much more. We cannot stop at the point you've reached. Besides, I have a question to ask."

Lizzie passed before her into the front room, lit two candles and drew down the blind.

"Ask it," she said.

"How did you know that I believed the other—Mr. Raymond—to be——" She came to a halt.

"I guessed."

"What? From the beginning?"

"No; it was after a long while. And then, all of a sudden, something seemed to make me clever."

"Did you know that, believing it, I had done him a great wrong—injured his life beyond repair?"

"I knew something had happened: that he'd given up being a gentleman and taken to builder's work. I thought maybe you were at the bottom of it. Who was it told you lies about en?"

"Must I answer that?"

"No; no need. George Vyell was a nice fellow; but he was a liar. Couldn't help it, I b'lieve. But a dirty trick like that—well, well!"

Honoria stared at her, confounded. "You never loved my husband?"

And Lizzie laughed—actually laughed; she was so weary. "No more than you did, my dear. Perhaps a little less. Eh, what two fools we are here, fending off the truth! Fools from the start—and now, simme, playing foolish to the end; ay, when all's said and naked atween us. Lev' us quit talkin' of George Vyell. We knawed George Vyell, you and me too; and here we be, left to rear children by en. But the man we hated over wasn' George Vyell."

"Yet if—as you say—you loved him—the other one—why, when you saw his life ruined and guessed the lie that ruined it—when a word could have righted him—if you loved him——"

"Why didn't I speak? Ladies are most dull, somehow; or else you don't try to see. Or else—— Wasn't he near me, passing my door ivery day? Oh, I'm ignorant and selfish. But hadn't I got him near? And wouldn't that word have lost him, sent him God knows where—to *you* perhaps? You—you'd had your chance, and squandered it like a fool. I never had no chance. I courted en, but he wouldn' look at me. He'd have come to your whistle—once. Nothing to hinder but your money. And from what I can see and guess, you piled up that money in his face like a hedge. Oh, I could pity you, now!—for now you'll never have en."

"God pity us both!" said Honoria, going; but she turned at the door. "And after our marriage you took no more thought of my—of George?" The question was an afterthought; she never thought to see it stab as it did. But Lizzie caught at the table edge, held to it swaying over a gulf of hysterics, and answered between a sob and a passing bitter laugh.

"At the last—just to try en. No harm done, as it happened. You needn' mind. He was worthless anyway."

Honoria stepped back, took her by the elbow as she swayed, and seated her in a chair; and so stood regarding her as a doctor might a patient. After a while she said—

"I think you will do me injustice, but you must believe as you like. I am not glad. I am very far from glad or happy. I doubt if I shall ever be happy again. But I do not hate you as I did."

She went out, closing the door softly.

CHAPTER XXIX.

THE SHIP OF STARS.

TAFFY guessed nothing of these passions in conflict, these weak agonies. He went about his daily work, a man grown, thinking his own thoughts; and these thoughts were of many things; but they held no room for the problem which meant everything in life to Honoria and Lizzie—yes, and to Humility, though it haunted her in less disturbing shape. Humility pondered it quietly with a mind withdrawn while her hands moved before her on the lace pillow; and pondering it, she resigned the solution to time. But it filled her thoughts constantly, none the less.

One noon Taffy returned from the light-house for his dinner to find a registered postal packet lying on the table. He glanced up and met his mother's gaze; but let the thing lie while he ate his meal, and having done, picked it up and carried it away with him unopened.

On the cliff-side, in a solitary place, he broke the seal. He guessed well enough what the packet contained: the silver medal procured for him by the too officious coroner. And the coroner, finding him obstinate against a public presentation, had forwarded the medal with an effusive letter. Taffy frowned over its opening sentences, and without reading farther crumpled the paper into a tight ball. He turned to examine the medal, holding it between finger and thumb; or rather, his eyes examined it while his brain ran back along the tangled procession of hopes and blunders, wrongs and trials and lessons hardly learnt, of which this mocking piece of silver symbolised the end and the reward. In that minute he saw Honoria and George, himself and Lizzie Pezzack as figures travelling on a road that stretched back to childhood; saw behind them the anxious eyes of his parents, Sir Harry's debonair smile, the sinister face of old Squire Moyle, malevolent yet terribly afraid; saw that the moving figures could not control their steps, that the watching faces were impotent to warn; saw finally beside the road other ways branching to left and right, and down these undestined and neglected avenues the ghosts of ambitions unattempted, lives not lived, all that might have been.

Well, here was the end of it, this ironical piece of silver. . . . With sudden anger he flung it from him; sent it spinning far out over the waters. And the sea, his old sworn enemy, took the votive offering. He watched it drop—drop; saw the tiny splash as it disappeared.

And with that he shut a door and turned a key. He had other thoughts to occupy him—great thoughts. The light-house was all but built. The Chief Engineer had paid a surprise visit, praised his work, and talked about another sea light soon to be raised on the North Welsh Coast; used words that indeed hinted, not obscurely, at promotion. And Taffy's blood tingled at the prospect. But, out of working hours, his thoughts were not of light-houses. He bought maps and charts. On Sundays he took far walks along the coast, starting at daybreak, returning as a rule long after dark, mired and footsore, and at supper too weary to talk with his mother, whose eyes watched him always.

* * * * * *

It was a still autumn evening when Honoria came riding to visit Humility; the close of a golden day. Its gold lingered yet along the west and fell on the whitewashed doorway where Humility sat with her lace-work. Behind, in the east, purple and dewy, climbed the domed shadow of the world. And over all lay that hush which the earth only knows when it rests in the few weeks after harvest. Out here, on barren cliffs above the sea, folks troubled little about harvest. But even out here they felt and knew the hush.

In sight of the whitewashed cottages Honoria slipped down from her saddle, removed Aide-de-camp's bridle, and turned him loose to browse. With the bridle on her arm she walked forward alone. She came noiselessly on the turf, and with the click of the gate her shadow fell at Humility's feet. Humility looked up and saw her standing against the sunset, in her dark habit. Even in that instant she saw also that Honoria's face, though shaded, was more beautiful than of old. "More dangerous" she told herself; and rose, knowing that the problem was to be solved at last.

"Good-evening!" she said, rising. "Oh yes—you must come inside, please; but you will have to forgive our untidiness."

Honoria followed, wondering as of old at the beautiful manners which dignified Humility's simplest words.

"I heard that you were to go."

"Yes; we have been packing for a week past. To North Wales it is—a forsaken spot, no better than this. But I suppose that's the sort of spot where light-houses are useful."

The sun slanted in upon the packed trunks and dismantled walls; but it blazed also upon brass window-catches, fender-knobs, door-handles—all polished and flashing like mirrors.

"I am come," said Honoria, "now at the last—to ask your pardon."

"At the last?" Humility seemed to muse, staring down at one of the trunks; then went on as if speaking to herself. "Yes, yes, it has been a long time."

"A long injury—a long mistake; you must believe it was an honest mistake."

"Yes," said Humility gravely. "I never doubted you had been misled. God forbid I should ask or seek to know how."

Honoria bowed her head.

"And," Humility pursued, "we had put ourselves in the wrong by accepting help. One sees now it is always best to be independent; though at the time it seemed a fine prospect for him. The worst was our not telling him. That was terribly unfair. As for the rest—well, after all, to know yourself guiltless is the great thing, is it not? What others think doesn't matter in comparison with that. And then of course he knew that I, his mother, never believed the falsehood—no, not for a moment."

"But it spoiled his life?"

Now Humility had spoken, and still stood, with her eyes resting on the trunk. Beneath its lid, she knew, and on top of Taffy's books and other treasures, lay a parcel wrapped in tissue paper—a dog collar with the inscription "*Honoria from Taffy.*" So, by lifting the lid of her thoughts a little—a very little—more, she might have given Honoria a glimpse of something which her actual answer, truthful as it was, concealed.

"No. I wouldn't say that. If it had spoilt his life—well, you have a child of your own and can understand. As it is, it has strengthened him, I think. He will make his mark—in a different way. Just now he is only a foreman among masons; but he has a career opening. Yes, I can forgive you at last."

And, being Humility, she had spoken the truth. But being a woman, even in the act of pardon she could not forego a small thrust, and in giving must withhold something.

And Honoria, being a woman, divined that something was withheld.

"And Taffy—your son—do you think that *he*——?"

"He never speaks, if he thinks of it. He will be here presently. You know—do you not? they are to light the great lantern on the new lighthouse to-night for the first time. The men have moved in, and he is down with them making preparations. You have seen the notices of the Trinity Board? They have been posted for months.

Taffy is as eager over it as a boy; but he promised to be back before sunset to drink tea with me in honour of the event; and afterwards I was to walk down to the cliff with him to see."

"Would you mind if I stayed?"

Humility considered before answering. "I had rather you stayed. He's like a boy over this business; but he's a man, after all."

After this they fell into quite trivial talk, while Humility prepared the tea things.

"Your mother—Mrs. Venning—how does she face the journey?"

"You must see her," said Humility, smiling, and led her into the room where the old lady reclined in bed, with a flush on each waxen cheek. She had heard their voices.

"Bless you"—she was quite cheerful—"I'm ready to go as far as they'll carry me! All I ask is that in the next place they'll give me a window where I can see the boy's lamp when he's built it."

Humility brought in the table and tea-things, and set them out by the invalid's bed. She went out into the kitchen to look to the kettle. In that pause Honoria found it difficult to meet Mrs. Venning's eyes; but the old lady was wise enough to leave grudges to others. It was enough, in the time left to her, to accept what happened and leave the responsibility to Providence.

Honoria, replying but scarcely listening to her talk, heard a footfall at the outer door—Taffy's footfall; then the click of a latch and Humility's voice saying, "There's a visitor inside; come to take tea with you."

"A visitor?" He was standing in the doorway. "*You?*" He blushed in his surprise.

Honoria rose. "If I may," she said, and wondered if she might hold out a hand.

But he held out his, quite frankly, and laughed. "Why, of course. They will be lighting up in half an hour. We must make haste."

Once or twice during tea he stole a glance from Honoria to his mother; and each time fondly believed that it passed undetected. His talk was all about the light-house and the preparations there, and he rattled on in the highest spirits. Two of the women knew, and the third guessed, that this chatter was with him unwonted.

At length he too seemed to be struck by this. "But what nonsense I'm talking!" he protested, breaking off midway in a sentence and blushing again. "I can't help it, though. I'm feeling just as big as the light-house to-night, with my head wound up and turning round like the lantern!"

"And your wit occulting," suggested Honoria, in her old light manner. "What is it?—three flashes to the minute?"

He laughed and hurried them from the tea-table. Mrs. Venning bade them a merry good-bye as they took leave of her.

"Come along, mother."

But Humility had changed her mind. "No," said she. "I'll wait in the doorway. I can just see the lantern from the garden gate, you know. You two can wait by the old light-house, and call to me when the time comes."

She watched them from the doorway as they took

the path toward the cliff, toward the last ray of sunset fading across the dusk of the sea. The evening was warm, and she sat bareheaded with her lace-work on her knee; but presently she put it down.

"I must be taking to spectacles soon," she said to herself. "My eyes are not what they used to be."

* * * * * *

Taffy and Honoria reached the old light-house and halted by its white-painted railing. Below them the new pillar stood up in full view, young and defiant. A full tide lapped its base, feeling this comely and untried adversary as a wrestler shakes hands before engaging. And from its base the column, after a gentle inward curve—enough to give it a look of lissomeness and elastic strength—sprang upright straight and firm to the lantern, ringed with a gallery and capped with a cupola of copper not yet greened by the weather; in outline as simple as a flower, in structure to the understanding eye almost as subtly organised, adapted and pieced into growth.

"So that is your ambition now?" said Honoria, after gazing long. She added, "I do not wonder."

"It does not stop there, I'm afraid." There was a pause, as though her words had thrown him into a brown study.

"Look!" she cried. "There is someone in the lantern—with a light in his hand. He is lighting up!"

Taffy ran back a pace or two toward the cottage and shouted, waving his hand. In a moment Humility appeared at the gate and waved in answer, while the strong light flashed seaward. They listened; but if she called, the waves at their feet drowned her voice.

They turned and gazed at the light, counting, timing the flashes; two short flashes with but five seconds between, then darkness for twenty seconds, and after it a long steady stare.

Abruptly he asked, "Would you care to cross over and see the lantern?"

"What, in the cradle?"

"I can work it easily. It's not dangerous in the least; a bit daunting, perhaps."

"But I'm not easily frightened, you know. Yes, I should like it greatly."

They descended the cliff to the cable. The iron cradle stood ready as Taffy had left it when he came ashore. She stepped in lightly, scarcely touching for a second the hand he put out to guide her.

"Better sit low," he advised; and she obeyed, disposing her skirts on the floor caked with dry mud from the workmen's boots. He followed her, and launched the cradle over the deep twilight.

A faint breeze—there had been none perceptible on the ridge—played off the face of the cliffs. The forward swing of the cradle, too, raised a slight draught of air. Honoria plucked off her hat and veil and let it fan her temples.

Half-way across, she said, "Isn't it like this—in mid-air over running water—that the witches take their oaths?"

Taffy ceased pulling on the rope. "The witches? Yes, I remember something of the sort."

"And a word spoken so is an oath and lasts for ever. Very well; answer me what I came to ask you to-night."

"What is that?" But he knew.

"That when—you know—when I tell you I was deceived . . . you will forgive." Her voice was scarcely audible.

"I forgive."

"Ah, but freely? It is only a word I want; but it has to last me like an oath."

"I forgive you freely. It was all a mistake."

"And you have found other ambitions! And they satisfy you?"

He laughed and pulled at the rope again. "They ought to," he answered gaily, "they're big enough. Come and see."

The seaward end of the cable was attached to a doorway thirty feet above the base of the lighthouse. One of the under-keepers met them here with a lantern. He stared when he caught sight of the second figure in the cradle, but touched his cap to the mistress of Carwithiel.

"Here's Mrs. Vyell, Trevarthen, come to do honour to our opening night."

"Proudly welcome, ma'am," said Trevarthen. "You'll excuse the litter we're in. This here's our cellar, but you'll find things more ship-shape upstairs. Mind your head, ma'am, with the archway—better let me lead the way perhaps."

The archway was indeed low, and they were forced to crouch and almost crawl up the first short flight of steps. But after this Honoria, following Trevarthen's lantern round and up the spiral way, found the roof heightening above her, and soon emerged into a gloomy chamber fitted with cupboards and water-tanks—the provision room. From this a ladder led straight up through a man-hole in the ceiling to the light-room store, set round with shining oil-tanks and stocked with paint-pots, brushes, cans, signalling flags, coils of rope, bags of cotton waste, tool-chests. . . . A second ladder brought them to the kitchen, and a third to the sleeping-room; and here the light of the lantern streamed down on their heads through the open man-hole above them. They heard, too, the roar of the ventilator, and the *ting-ting*, regular and sharp, of the small bell reporting that the machinery revolved.

Above, in the blaze of the great lenses, old Pezzack and the second under-keeper welcomed them. The pair had been watching and discussing the light with true professional pride; and Taffy drew up at the head of the ladder and stared at it, and nodded his slow approbation. The glare forced Honoria back against the glass wall, and she caught at its lattice for support.

But she pulled herself together, ashamed of her weakness, and glad that Taffy had not perceived it.

" This satisfies you ? " she whispered.

He faced round on her with a slow smile. " No," he said, " this light-house is useless."

" Useless ? "

" You remember the wreck—*that* wreck—the *Samaritan ?* She came ashore beneath here; right beneath our feet; by no fault or carelessness. A light-house on a coast like this—a coast without a harbour—is a joke set in a death-trap, to make game of dying men."

" But since the coast has no harbour——"

" I would build one. Look at this," he pulled a

pencil and paper from his pocket and rapidly sketched the outlines of the Bristol Channel. "What is that? A bag. Suppose a vessel taken in the mouth of it; a bag with death along the narrowing sides and death waiting at the end—no deep-water harbour—no chance anywhere. And the tides! You know the rhyme—

"From Padstow Point to Lundy Light
Is a watery grave by day or night."

Yes, there's Lundy"—he jotted down the position of the island—"Hit off the lee of Lundy, if you can, and drop hook, and pray God it holds!"

"But this harbour? What would it cost?"

"I dare say a million of money; perhaps more. But I work it out at less—at Porthquin, for instance, or Lundy itself, or even at St. Ives."

"A million!" she laughed. "Now I see the boy I used to know—the boy of dreams."

He turned on her gravely. She was exceedingly beautiful, standing there in her black habit, bare-headed in the glare of the lenses, standing with head thrown back, with eyes challenging the past, and a faint glow on either cheek. But he had no eyes for her beauty.

He opened his lips to speak. Yes, he could overwhelm her with statistics and figures, all worked out; of shipping and disasters to shipping; of wealth and senseless waste of wealth. He could bury her beneath evidence taken by Royal Commission and Parliamentary Committee, commissioners' reports, testimony of shipowners and captains; calculated tables of tides, sets of currents, prevailing winds; results of surveys hydrographical; all the mass of facts he had been accumulating and brooding over for eighteen long months. But the weight of it closed his lips, and when he opened them again it was to say, "Yes, that is my dream."

At once he turned his talk upon the light revolving in their faces; began to explain the lenses and their working in short, direct sentences. She heard his voice, but without following.

Pezzack and the under-keeper had drawn apart to the opposite side of the cage and were talking together. The lantern hid them, but she caught the murmur of their voices now and again. She was conscious of having let something slip—slip away from her for ever. If she could but recall him, and hold him to his dream! But this man, talking in short sentences, each one so sharp and clear, was not the Taffy she had known or could ever know.

In the blaze of the lenses suddenly she saw the truth. He and she had changed places. She who had used to be so practical—*she* was the dreamer now; had come thither following a dream, walking in a dream. He, the dreaming boy, had become the practical man, firm, clear-sighted, direct of purpose; with a dream yet in his heart, but a dream of great action, a dream he hid from her, certainly a dream in which she had neither part nor lot. And yet she had made him what he was; not willingly, not by kindness, but by injustice. What she had given he had taken; and was a stranger to her.

Muffled wings and white breasts began to beat against the glass. A low-lying haze—a passing stratum of sea-fog—had wrapped the light-house for a while, and these were the wings and breasts of sea-birds attracted by the light. To her they were the ghosts of dead thoughts—stifled thoughts—thoughts which had never come to birth—trying to force their way into the ring of light encompassing and enwrapping her; trying desperately, but foiled by the transparent screen.

Still she heard his voice, level and masterful, sure of his subject. In the middle of one of his sentences a sharp thud sounded on the pane behind her, as sudden as the crack of a pebble and only a little duller.

"Ah, what is that?" she cried, and touched his arm.

He thrust open one of the windows, stepped out upon the gallery, and returned in less than a minute with a small dead bird in his hand.

"A swallow," he said. "They have been preparing to fly for days. Summer is done, with our work here."

She shivered. "Let us go back," she said.

They descended the ladders. Trevarthen met them in the kitchen and went before them with his lantern. In a minute they were in the cradle again and swinging toward the cliff. The wisp of sea-fog had drifted past the light-house to leeward, and all was clear again. High over the cupola Cassiopeia leaned toward the pole, her breast flashing its eternal badge—the star-pointed W. Low in the north—as the country tale went—tied to follow her emotions, externally separate, eternally true to the fixed star of her gaze, the Waggoner tilted his wheels and drove them close and along and above the misty sea.

Taffy, pulling on the rope, looked down upon Honoria's upturned face and saw the glimmer of starlight in her eyes; but neither guessed her thoughts nor tried to.

It was only when they stood together on the cliff-side that she broke the silence. "Look," she said, and pointed upward. "Does that remind you of anything?"

He searched his memory. "No," he confessed: "that is, if you mean Cassiopeia up yonder."

"Think!—the Ship of Stars."

"The Ship of Stars?—Yes, I remember now. There was a young sailor—with a ship of stars tattooed on his chest. He was drowned on this very coast."

"Was that a part of the story you were to tell me?"

"What story? I don't understand."

"Don't you remember that day—the morning when we began lessons together? You explained the alphabet to me, and when we came to W— you said it was a ship—a ship of stars. There was a story about it, you said, and promised to tell me some day."

He laughed. "What queer things you remember!"

"But what was the story?"

"I wonder! If I ever knew, I've forgotten. I dare say I had something in my head. Now I think of it, I was always making up some foolish tale or other, in those days."

Yes; he had forgotten. "I have often tried to make up a story about that ship," she said gravely, "out of odds and ends of the stories you used to tell. I don't think I ever had the gift to invent anything on my own account. But at last, after a long while——"

"The story took shape? Tell it to me, please."

She hesitated, and broke into a bitter little laugh. "No," said she, "you never told me yours." Again it came to her with a pang that he and she had changed places. He had taken her forthrightness and left her, in exchange, his dreams. They were hers now, the gaily coloured childish fancies, and she must take her way among them alone. Dreams only! but just as a while back he had started to confess *his* dream and had broken down before her, so now in turn she knew that her tongue was held.

* * * * * *

Humility rose as they entered the kitchen together. A glance as Honoria held out her hand for good-bye told her all she needed to know.

"And you are leaving in a day or two?" Honoria asked.

"Thursday next is the day fixed."

"You are very brave."

Again the two women's eyes met, and this time the younger understood. *Whither thou goest, I will go; and where thou lodgest, I will lodge; thy people shall be my people, and thy God my God*—that which the Moabitess said for a woman's sake women are saying for men's sakes by thousands every day.

Still holding her hand, Humility drew Honoria close. "God deal kindly with you, my dear," she whispered, and kissed her.

At the gate Honoria blew a whistle, and after a

few seconds Aide-de-camp came obediently out of the darkness to be bridled. This done, Taffy lent his hand and swung her into the saddle.

" Good-night and good-bye ! "

Taffy was the first to turn back from the gate. The beat of Aide-de-camp's hoofs reminded him of something—some music he had once heard ; he could not remember where.

Humility lingered a moment longer, and followed to prepare her son's supper.

But Honoria, fleeing along the ridge, hugged one fierce thought in her defeat. The warm wind sang by her ears, the rhythm of Aide-de-camp's canter thudded upon her brain ; but her heart cried back on them and louder than either—

" He is mine, mine, mine ! He is mine, and always will be. He is lost to me, but I possess him. For what he is I have made him, and at my cost he is strong."

THE END.